DEPARTURES

W.A. HARBINSON

POOLBEG

Published 1996
by Poolbeg Press Ltd
123 Baldoyle Industrial Estate
Dublin 13, Ireland

© WA Harbinson 1996

The moral right of the author has been asserted.

A catalogue record for this book is available from the British Library.

ISBN 1 85371 640 5

All rights reserved. No part of this publication may be reproduced or transmitted in any form or by any means, electronic or mechanical, including photography, recording, or any information storage or retrieval system, without permission in writing from the publisher. The book is sold subject to the condition that it shall not, by way of trade or otherwise, be lent, resold or otherwise circulated without the publisher's prior consent in any form of binding or cover other than that in which it is published and without a similar condition, including this condition, being imposed on the subsequent purchaser.

Cover photograph by Slide File
Cover design by Poolbeg Group Services Ltd
Set by Poolbeg Group Services Ltd in New Baskerville
Printed by The Guernsey Press Ltd,
Vale, Guernsey, Channel Islands.

About the Author

W.A. Harbinson is author of the best-selling novels *Genesis* and *Revelation* as well as a number one US best-selling biography of Elvis Presley. Harbinson was born in Belfast and presently resides in West Cork.

*For Stan & Dorothy Rickwood
on their 50th Wedding Anniversary*

Chapter One

She saw the shadows of the tombstones in her eyes, but refused to give in. Instead, she leaned forward, elbows resting on the dressing table, forcing herself to look at the face she did not wish to see.

"Yes," she said aloud to that disturbing reflection, "you are Jennifer Birken. *Me.* Sixty years old, dear."

Informed so many times that old age brought its own rewards, such as peace of mind, pride, and the wisdom of experience, she felt cheated and betrayed, stripped of her dignity, left unprepared for the fears that kept her awake at nights.

It was all in the mirror.

Her face was too lined, the skin like faintly yellowed parchment, the proud cheekbones like stones in parched earth. The once generous lips were puckered, the good teeth were not her own, and the eyes, though still as green as jade, were no longer clear. And grey hair – naturally – now too thin for proper grooming, though mercifully cropped short to allow for the wig that usually covered it.

It happened so fast. You blinked and youth was gone.

Only childhood seemed to stretch out forever. The rest passed far too quickly.

She smiled bleakly, shook her head in self-reproach, then glanced about her. The apartment was older than she was – and that seemed impossible.

A tremor passed through her and she took a deep breath, then fought back by turning herself into another person, at least for another day.

First foundation cream and make-up, followed by carefully pencilled eyebrows, then lipstick to fill out her puckered lips – a bit garish for someone her age, but not *too* much so. She soon looked like someone else – indeed, almost human – but she wouldn't really feel like a new person until her grey hair was hidden.

A sixty-year-old redhead.

The wig she picked out was the colour of her lipstick, and she held it above her like a crown, recalling the coronation of her beloved Queen Elizabeth II, then ceremoniously lowered it onto her head, pressed it into position, and tucked in a few rebellious strands.

Now, in the mirror, she saw another woman – a lively old tart whose green eyes were sparkling, the crimson lips and red hair in competition for instant attention.

She looked like a valiant old soul, all set for a good time.

"All you need is a dress," she said.

The dress, in black satin to match her stockings and high heels, was enhanced by a gold-buckled belt and string of large pearls.

She examined herself front and rear, with great care, like a model, then nodded approval and left the bedroom. After glancing through the window at Shepherd Market,

Departures

which was busy, she looked around the small, charming apartment, her last home on earth.

The lounge was filled with bric-a-brac and exquisite paintings by unknown artists – her modest hopes for the finer things of life gathered into a feathery nest. One breath and you could blow it away, her gossamer dreams going with it.

Deciding to have a gin and tonic, she turned towards the drinks cabinet.

The pain was sudden and unexpected, a knife slicing through her, and she doubled up, clutching at her stomach, helplessly gasping. Dazed, almost blinded, groaning through gritted teeth, she hurried back into the bedroom to grab a phial of pills from the dressing table. Her hands were still shaking when she tapped two tablets into her sweaty palm. After swallowing them without water, she gritted her teeth, sank into a chair and waited for the pain to pass. Which it did . . . eventually.

"Oh, God," she said. "Thank God!"

Yet when her disarrayed senses came together again, she had to choke back the dread of what was happening to her.

It still seemed unbelievable.

Wondering if she could bear it, she clenched her fists on the dressing table, glared at her own reflection and whispered "Damn you!" In defiance, she lit a cigarette and walked from the room.

After pouring a gin and tonic, she sat in front of the TV set, hoping to distract herself with the news. There, on the small screen, in colours emphasising the positive, an exotically beautiful young lady with radiantly empty eyes was saying: "And now for some news from the United

States . . . It was announced today that Hollywood screenwriter, Bill Eisler, who recently won a Pulitzer Prize for his first novel, as well as an Academy Award for his own screen adaptation, has been named winner of the British Film Academy's Special Award for a lifetime's contribution to cinema. This is the first time that these three great awards have been made to the same person within the one year, so Mr Eisler will be coming to Britain next month for the British Film Institute's annual Academy Award dinner. We now go over to Paul Evans in Los Angeles . . ."

As the newsreader dissolved into a static-streaked image of two men seated between plastic plants in a television studio in Los Angeles, Jennifer felt her heart racing and heard that name repeating in her head: *Bill Eisler! Bill Eisler!* She leaned farther forward, put on her spectacles, and squinted at the man being interviewed.

She was seeing a ghost.

"Oh, Bill," she murmured, "it can't be . . . I don't believe . . ."

But he was there, right in front of her. Aged by forty years, but definitely him . . . silvery-haired, still handsome, and speaking just as he had done way back then, answering the questions in a pleasant, unhurried manner.

After confirming that he would fly to England to collect his award, he was cut off and replaced with the first newsreader.

"And that," she said, "was Bill Eisler, whom we shall doubtless see again, when we televise the British Academy Award ceremonies next month. Now for some local news . . ."

Departures

Jennifer inhaled, trying to calm her racing heart. She blew the smoke out, watched it drifting across the screen, then torn between disbelief and exhilaration, she switched off the TV set.

She sat a long time, smoking and drinking, contemplating, trying to put her spinning thoughts into order. Eventually, squinting down through her spectacles, she started to write.

Chapter Two

∾

Bill Eisler climbed into the rainbow-coloured dune-buggy that was parked in his driveway overlooking the ocean, and drove down a steeply winding road to the beach below.

Staring at the Pacific, noting the glint of sun on water, he said, "How can that woman lie in bed when all this is available?"

Then he thought of the letter he had received yesterday and his heart skipped a beat.

What should he do?

Relieved to park at the end of the steep road, he began his weekly jog along the beach.

He did so breathing deeply, enjoying the beating wind, appreciating the smooth-sloped dunes, the gulls gliding over the waves, the Santa Monica Mountains eerily beautiful under a purple haze.

Normally he used this weekly run as a distraction – enjoying the golden girls, the muscular young men, the people with metal-detectors; even the odd wild-eyed freak staring up at the fleecy clouds – but this morning he hardly saw them, since his thoughts kept circling like the gulls above . . . around that unexpected, startling letter.

"God damn it," he murmured, shaking his head as he ran, trying to focus on his conflicting emotions, feeling far too emotional. "I still can't believe it . . ."

The gulls circled above, communicating across the sky, reminding him of the phrases in the letter that still made his heart race . . . *Saw your television interview . . . could not believe you were still alive . . . thought you were killed in the war . . . so thrilled to realise . . .*

At first he'd thought it was a hoax, but other phrases all too quickly made it clear that it had to be genuine . . . *Your hotel in Kensington . . . tea at the Ritz . . . our one trip to Cornwall . . .* Bill, still running, his eyes dazzled by sunlight, recalled London in wartime, the German planes and falling bombs, Jenny's face illuminated by blazing buildings as his shadow fell over her . . .

"No," he whispered, slowing down. "I don't think I can take this."

Gasping, he touched his toes, then took another deep breath and turned back, trying to block out his thoughts.

When he saw some young girls, lean and bronzed, almost naked, he winged back to another time and place and that wonderful English girl. Caught between pain and delight, he almost groaned aloud, but thought of Maureen, felt a spasm of guilt, and ran even faster.

Arriving back at the dune-buggy, he wiped the sweat from his face, then drove up a winding track and along the main road, eventually turning into his driveway, not far from the cliff-top. He cut the engine and sat on for a moment, looking over the home he'd bought two years ago. Though expensive, the house had been bought with the income from his last produced screenplay, based on the true story of a family of wet-backs struggling to survive in North Hollywood. He had been a social worker before becoming a writer. Ironically, it was his knowledge of the city's deprived that had made him a wealthy man.

He hadn't planned it, but that's how it had worked out.

Sighing, he climbed down from the dune-buggy, patted it affectionately, then climbed stone steps to the patio, where Maureen was having breakfast by the swimming-pool. Wearing slacks and a short-sleeved shirt, slim legs crossed as she buttered toast, she was framed by ocean and sky, her long red hair shining.

"I eat while you exercise," she said, "and I'm *still* thinner than you. Explain that, my genius."

"I don't want to cross swords with a third-generation Irish-American. You're God's blessing upon me."

"You look exhausted. You better sit down and eat. Slimmer's toast with unsalted butter. Orange juice on the side."

She lowered her gaze and bit into a slice of toast, her brow furrowed in concentration as she read the *Los Angeles Times*.

"Any interesting news this morning?" Bill asked, to escape his thoughts about Jenny Birken and that unexpected, startling letter from London, England.

"No. Just the usual misery and political madness. Any news in the mail?"

He hesitated. "No. Not a thing."

As if sensing his distraction, Maureen closed her newspaper, brushed some strands of hair from her forehead and turned green eyes upon him.

Departures

"Have you spoken to Denholm yet?"

"Yes, at seven this morning."

"And how's the weather in London?"

"Early afternoon there and the autumn leaves are falling. Denholm said it was nearly as dark as Finland."

Maureen shivered. "And how *is* the wicked Denholm these days?"

"He sounded as urbane as always and sent you his love."

"That old charmer hasn't changed. And what did he say about your movie? Did *he* think you should try to make it in England or raise the finance right here?"

"He thought we could raise it there and said he'd help me out. He's going to try to raise a lot of interest before I arrive."

"Have you decided when you're going?"

"Yes, in about a week. The British Film and Television Academy award ceremony takes place in September, but I want to be there at least four or five days before that. Denholm thinks the publicity about the award can only help with the finance."

"I *still* think that with your recent run of awards, you could raise the finance right here."

"We've been through all this before, but let me repeat myself. Since this is a movie about the love between an English woman and an American, it's imperative that the whole thing be produced and shot in that country. I also happen to believe that this should be a modest movie, because only by sticking to a small-budget screenplay can I direct it and *remain in control*. Do you understand, Maureen?"

"You don't have to sound so testy, Bill."

"OK, I'm sorry."

Maureen smiled and squeezed his hand. "Methinks I doth protest too much. You're right. You should do it. I'm just being a bitch because of my own frustrations about work. Your anger is justified."

"I'm not angry, I promise. Not because of your comments. I'm more annoyed because you've never been to London and yet refuse to come with me."

He felt hypocritical saying it. He hadn't told her about Jenny Birken and that very strange letter.

"You know why I won't go," Maureen said. "I'd just be in your way. I'd love to go with you, but I'd rather do it when you've nothing else to do. What with trying to raise finance for your movie, then the Award Ceremony and the publicity, I'd probably be left on my own too much to really enjoy it. Don't worry. The next time . . ."

He knew what she was thinking. Formerly a New York stage actress, she'd moved to Los Angeles ten years ago in what had turned out to be a vain bid to make it in the movies. He'd met her shortly after he'd sold his first screenplay – when she was facing the bitter fact that she would never become a star and needed something else in her life. They'd had a brief, joyous affair and married quickly, without regrets – but, since then, his career had soared while hers had virtually sank into oblivion. She hadn't worked since they were married, but as his success had grown, taking him away from home more often, she had developed a growing desire to get back into acting.

"Would you be willing to go," Bill asked, "if it meant the chance of getting some work in London?"

Maureen glanced sharply at him.

"Denholm didn't just send his love. He also asked if

you were still interested in working – and when I told him you might be, he said he'd found a couple of good roles for you."

"Me? In *London*? Are you kidding?"

"No, I'm not. According to Denholm, the Royal Shakespeare Company's planning a stage revival of *A Streetcar Named Desire* and has persuaded Equity to let them use an American actress in the part – and, since you've already played it on the New York stage, he thinks you'd stand a good chance."

"You flatter me," she responded.

"Anyway, you're a well-known stage actress, you *have* played the role, and if you managed to get this part with the RSC, it'd gain you a lot of prestige and put you back in the race."

"And the other part?" she asked, growing visibly more excited.

"The very opposite. The mature, rags-to-riches heroine in an original Anglo-American television costume-drama series to be shot by a commercial TV company in London – a role that wouldn't give you too much prestige with the critics, but *could* make you a star with the public. Denholm's spoken to the casting directors and they both want to try you."

"You mean I'd have to audition?"

"It's been a long time, Maureen."

She brushed the hair from her eyes. "You think I can do it?"

"Let's face it: you'll be up against some tough competition from other actresses, so there's no guarantee of success. You'll have to decide if you want to risk failure – but I think you should."

"Then I'll try it." She tugged him close and kissed him, then stood up and gazed around in a trance of delight.

"I have to go for a shower," she said. "Oh, God, London at last!"

She blew him a kiss and hurried into the house, leaving him alone by the pool, his gaze fixed on the sea below. Surfers swept in on the waves, joggers loped along the shore. The gulls that were circling above were as wild as his thoughts.

Jenny Birken was still alive. She had written that she wanted to see him and he trembled to think of that. How much had he loved her? Too much for his own good. Yet that love had been safely in the past, a gossamer memory. The Jenny he had known was no more. Like him, she would have aged. The lovely English rose he had loved would bloom no longer.

Did he want to see her? Yes, dammit, he did. He had to see her, no matter what the risk, because the heart has its reasons.

Realising that he was a sixty-two-year-old man kept alive by his passions, he stood up and followed Maureen into the house.

"What fools we all are!" he whispered, wiping tears from his eyes.

Chapter Three

∽

Slumped in an armchair, gazing around the house she loathed, Carol felt a lot older than forty.

This home had become her prison and she wanted to escape, but each time she heard Mark crying upstairs, she was convinced, by the strength of her love for him, that she would never be able to leave.

She hated the weekends. During the week she had her work and was well away from John, but the weekends, which she was forced to share with him, seemed to go on forever. Not that "share" was the proper word. They hadn't shared anything for years. John spent as much time as possible out of the house, playing rugby or golf, using both as an excuse for a lot of drinking with friends who were as bad as he was. It was killing her slowly.

Snapped out of her bitter reverie by the sound of John's car, she instantly filled up with tension, then went to the window.

Autumn leaves were falling from the bleak trees to the hedgerows, covering the lawn and driveway. Beyond the garden was Pond Square, once the green of Highgate

Village, its 19th century houses rendered colourless by London's grey sky.

John stood unsteadily beside his red Porsche. Once a smoothly handsome man, he was running to fat, his florid face revealing that he drank too much in general and had certainly been drinking heavily at lunchtime. He closed the door of the Porsche gently, almost stroking it as he did so, then straightened up and walked towards the house.

Carol's heart lurched in despair at the sight of his unsteady gait. She turned back to the room and lit a cigarette. The front door slammed shut, John swore, something fell, then his footsteps advanced along the hall and he entered the lounge.

"You just knocked something over," Carol said.

"I didn't break it. Stop worrying." Flushed and sullen, he went straight to the drinks cabinet, poured himself a Scotch with soda, swirled it around in the glass and drank too much with one gulp. "So, where's my lunch?"

"Don't you think you've had enough to drink?"

"Don't start *that* again, Carol."

"I can't help it. You look awful."

"*You're* no oil-painting, darling."

"There's no cause – "

"Don't give me that wounded look. I just want my lunch, thanks."

"I haven't made you lunch," she told him, growing more nervous. "I *assumed* you were having it at the pub."'

"Well, I wasn't."

His blood-shot eyes were hard beneath prematurely grey hair; flushed, with full lips and jowls, he looked constantly angry.

Departures

"You were getting drunk, as usual, with those rugby-playing, beer-swilling philanderers who think they're grown men."

"They *are* grown men. They simply like a good time. And stop sounding so damned superior. You're forty years old, your only child is a bastard, your mother runs a nightclub that could pass for a brothel and she dresses like a Piccadilly whore. What have *you* got to crow about?"

"Don't you *dare* speak about my mother in that manner! And please stop calling Mark a bastard!"

"I repeat: What have *you* got to crow about?"

"Not much. I have *you* for a husband, after all. It isn't something to boast about."

"Watch it, Carol. Be *careful*."

She felt the tension knotting her stomach, a slight seizure of panic. *I won't let him hit me again*, she thought, wondering how a marriage could go so wrong, hurt that love died so easily.

"Anyway," he said, "I don't know why you're complaining. It's a perfectly harmless way of passing the weekend, so why nag me about it?"

"You don't have to be so blatant about – "

"Christ, here we go again." He shook his head in mock despair. "Just because I've met a few old girlfriends at the pub now and then – "

"I'm sorry I can't take your philandering as lightly as your stockbroker friends. Some of whom also think it amusing to make passes at me."

"If that kid upstairs – "

"He isn't. You haven't a friend I'd respect that much. One drunkard in my life is enough. And your friends are like you."

"I don't know how you can criticise *me* for having the odd affair when you have that little bastard upstairs. And as for drinking, given the presence of that kid, I should think I've good cause."

"God, what a hypocrite! You were practically an alcoholic long before I even embarked on my one affair – so don't say Mark caused it!"

"Just tell me who that bastard's father is."

"*You're* the bastard!" she spat at him.

He slapped her face.

"Damn you, don't hit me!"

He threw his drink in her face instead. It was more shocking than a blow. When she opened her weeping eyes, she saw him grinning and that was too much. She slapped his face. He hit her back. She was burning and blinded by tears when she hurled herself at him, raining blows on his chest.

"Whore!" he whispered as he punched her. She collapsed and was jerked up by her hair and then slapped repeatedly. When he let her go, she fell to the floor and curled up in a ball.

"I'm going out for another drink," he said breathlessly, above her, "and I want no complaints when I come back. Now get off the floor."

"No! Go back to the pub and leave me alone."

"That's just what I'm doing."

He walked off, slammed the door, and started the Porsche. Only when she heard him driving away did she sigh with relief.

She stayed curled up like a ball, too exhausted to move, wiping the tears from her cheeks and recalling the past.

It wasn't too easy. The past was another kingdom. She must have been in love with him once, but it was hard to imagine . . .

Thank God for David.

Just thinking about him gave her the strength to stand up, determined at last to leave for good.

The packing was easy, since there was little she wanted. After filling two suitcases, she put Mark in his carry-cot on the rear seat of the car, then hurriedly locked the house and drove away, already feeling much younger.

Yes, thank God for David.

At a standstill in the usual traffic-jam in Earl's Court, Carol glanced at the pavements packed with exotically clad young people and thought of how, when in a state of despair over her failing marriage, she had been taken by her friend Patricia to an antiques fair in Chelsea and there casually introduced to David.

In contrast to John's more formal stockbroker image, David was a mop-haired, casually dressed man ten years her junior who had, over drinks with her and Patricia in a nearby pub, charmed her with his good humour, slightly bohemian personality and obvious interest.

Under Patricia's sardonic gaze, Carol had shamelessly exaggerated her interest in antiques and agreed to let David escort her to an antiques fair in Alexandra Palace the following weekend. After that fair, over lunch and a bottle of wine, David had told her, with a grin, that he didn't think she had much interest in antiques at all. When she blushed, he laughed at her embarrassment.

After that, they saw each other on a regular basis, and she soon learned that he'd originally wanted to be a painter, had married too young, been divorced five years later, and then, realising that he lacked the talent to be an artist, had gone into the antiques business instead. Moderately successful and content with his lot, he lived happily in a cluttered apartment above his shop in King's Road, Chelsea, and also worked behind a stall every weekend in the Chelsea Antique Market.

Carol soon fell in love, began her affair with him, and enjoyed the happiest months of her life.

Now, turning into King's Road and driving in the direction of the Chelsea Antique Market, she heard Mark gurgling contentedly behind her and swelled with pride.

Parking illegally in the only space she could find, she pulled the carry-cot out of the car, then hurried along the crowded pavement, past the usual Saturday afternoon gangs of punks, with their vividly-coloured hair, leather gear and chains, as well as the customary gawking tourists. Holding Mark in front of her, she managed with some difficulty to push her way through the densely packed market until she arrived at David's stall. He looked scruffily attractive in corduroy trousers, hush-puppies, shirt and thick pullover. When he saw her, his brown eyes widened in surprise. Then he ran his fingers through his dishevelled hair and gave her a grin.

"Well, well," he said, "what a surprise! And with little Mark, too! What's the occasion?"

"I've left John for good."

"No joke?"

"No, David. I've moved out."

"Uno momento," he said, ignoring the startled customers, then cupped his hands like a megaphone over

his mouth and bawled, for all his friends to hear, "Hey, I've just won the war!"

While some stall-holders applauded and others shouted jokey remarks, David rushed around to Carol, kissed her, and said, "Hold on! Look after the stall. I'll be back in a minute."

He rushed from the emporium, leaving Carol behind the stall. Some of the dealers waved at her. Embarrassed, she waved back. Mark was clenching his fists and kicking, so she distracted herself by fiddling with his blanket and stroking his cheek. Her heart was racing and she didn't know where to look, but she was blindingly happy.

Another round of applause announced David's return. He hurried up to her, beaming like a schoolboy, holding a bottle of cheap champagne.

"You've *really* left him?" he asked her.

"Yes."

"Terrific!" he said. He walked around the stall and removed the price tags from two of his fine-cut glasses, wiped them clean, then uncorked the champagne. When the cork burst out of the bottle there was more cheering and clapping from the other dealers.

Giddy with happiness, Carol took the glass from David and let him pour champagne into it.

"To us," he said.

They touched glasses and drank, doing it quickly, inviting drunkenness. Carol wanted it to go to her head and make this magical day shine.

She closed her eyes when David kissed her. His lips were moist and warm. When she heard someone calling her name, she opened her eyes again.

Someone was waving at her – another stall-owner,

Myrna Plowright. She waved again and indicated the phone on the wall near her head.

"Looks like a call for you," David said.

"It could only be Mother," Carol replied. "Only she knows I come here."

"The redoubtable Jennifer Birken. You better go and speak to her."

Already slightly drunk, Carol kissed him on the cheek, then put down her glass and crossed the crowded emporium to take the phone from the duffle-coated Myrna.

"Hello," she said. "Carol speaking."

"This is your mother, dear. Please prepare yourself for a shock. The police have just paid me a visit and told me to find you."

"The police?"

"John's been involved in a car crash. Driving home from the pub. He was drunk and crashed into another car. I'm sorry. He's dead."

Carol stared across the emporium, through a drifting skein of smoke, past the bobbing heads of the packed, jostling people, and saw David holding up Mark, who was kicking and smiling.

She stared at them for a long time, cold, too shocked to move, and heard her mother calling her name repeatedly as if in a bad dream.

Chapter Four

～

"I'm so glad you girls volunteered to come with me," Jennifer whispered. "Otherwise I don't think I could have stood it. You've all been so considerate."

Marjorie obviously hadn't heard her and was staring aroundthe chapel at John's relatives, but Barbara and Doreen nodded solemnly. They were good girls,really, and had obviously tried their best, but it had to beconfessed that their clothing was not too appropriate, alittle on the gaudy side to match their well-painted faces.

John's relatives stared hard when they arrived, but no words had been spoken.

Carol, poor dear, while looking attractive in black, was trembling and as white as a sheet, not being used to this kindof thing. Thank God, then, that John was out of sight in his coffin, up there, beside that priest with the sweaty brow. The priest read from the bible, his voice a somnolent droning, a noise disturbed only by the sobbing of John's mother and sister.

Frankly, Jennifer wasn't too keen on John's relatives, which was one of the reasons she had invited her gaudy girls to come here with her. Also, funerals reminded her of mortality and this wasn't the time for that.

"Is the furnace behind those curtains?" Doreen asked.

"Yes," Jennifer whispered.

"I've never *been* to a cremation before and I feel kind of funny."

"There's nothing to it, my dear."

Concerned that Carol might have overheard Doreen's naïve remarks, Jennifer glanced sideways at her, but Carol was still staring straight ahead, her face as white as a sheet. Apart from that, she looked quite pretty. You'd never guess she was forty. She didn't look a day older than David, who had been so good to her.

Which was more than you could have said for the corpse.

As she glanced to her left, she noted how the mourners had instinctively formed themselves into two different groups, John's relatives and friends at one side of the chapel, Carol's friends spread thinly along the pews on this side. It was clear from the frequent sidelong glances that most of John's relatives (all terribly respectable, dirt swept under the carpet) were discomfited by the presence of Jennifer and the girls from her club.

Rendered drowsy by her painkilling tablets, Jennifer was still alert enough to extract some amusement from that particular brand of segregation.

"I wish he'd get it over with," Doreen said, indicating the droning priest. "He just goes on and on."

"Shush!" Barbara whispered, embarrassed. "Show some respect, Doreen."

Distracted by the whispering, Carol glanced at them.

Jennifer took note of the anguish in her face and was once more bemused.

In death, John had gained Carol's forgiveness for all he had done to her.

What was love, exactly? A form of insanity? Jennifer wondered as the priest finished his droning and led them all in a prayer. Jennifer bowed her head obediently, moved her lips but said nothing. She dwelt instead on the fact that at this very moment an aircraft was bringing her first love out of the distant past.

That aeroplane would be approaching London soon – and Bill Eisler was on it.

Excitement and dread swept through her, shaking her leaf and bough, but passed away when she raised her head again and opened her eyes.

The curtains had finally been drawn back to reveal the furnace, and while the epicene priest started droning again the coffin moved into the flames on some kind of conveyor belt.

Not having been to a cremation before, Doreen sucked in her breath and gripped Jennifer's hand. Carol trembled, covered her mouth with a handkerchief and started to weep.

Jennifer hugged her, trying to console her. She couldn't help remembering what a swine John had been, and found herself wondering once more about the nature of love.

It was, at least to most women, a realm of self-sacrifice.

Yet had she, Jennifer, sacrificed herself for Bill Eisler? If he had not died, or at least disappeared so completely, would her love have endured for so long? And how could she, an old woman nearing death, even think in such terms?

You must be kidding yourself, my dear.

As the coffin slid into the furnace, Jennifer hugged Carol again, then glanced at Doreen, Marjorie and Barbara, taking note of their heavy make-up, unsuitable clothing and cheap, gaudy jewellery. Even when trying to look sorrowful they had the laconic air of women who have little more to learn. She wondered what they would think of her romantic recollections of a man she had known, body and soul, forty years ago.

They would think her mad.

Well, madness came with old age. It was a form of protection. She accepted this wisdom as the curtains closed across the furnace, hiding the grim reality of death.

The priest said his final prayer, then hurried outside, pulling a cigarette from his pocket while the mourners followed him out as quietly as possible, some of them weeping.

One of those sniffing back tears was Doreen, who, with her peroxide blonde hair, false eyelashes and gaudily painted lips, looked like someone who had just stepped off the stage of the London Palladium.

"It was just like being in church," she explained, as she dried her eyes with a handkerchief. "I feel almost religious."

"Oh, God," Carol sobbed, "I just can't stop crying. *Why am I crying?*"

Jennifer hugged her and led her along the aisle, towards the door of the chapel.

"It's all right," she said. "It's perfectly natural. John was your husband, after all, and that must count for something."

When they reached the hall outside, John's sister, Belinda, detached herself from the embrace of her weeping mother and, clutching her handbag as if protecting it from thieves, said, "How *dare* you bring these people here! They're an insult to my brother's memory. You have no right to – "

"These ladies are friends of Carol's," Jennifer interjected grandly, "and are here to lend her moral support. They are friends of *our* family."

"They're just whores from that awful club you run. You have no right to – "

"*Whores?*" Marjorie said, her face reddening. "Did she call us *whores?*"

"These ladies are *hostesses* from my club," Jennifer said, "and have not come here to be insulted by you or anyone else."

"For God's sake," Carol said, removing the handkerchief from her face and looking even more shocked, "this is no time for – "

"Don't *you* say anything!" Belinda snapped, glaring fiercely at Carol. "You've done enough already! John's friends told me that he only got drunk because he had another fight with you. He got drunk because he was upset – and then he tried driving home. *It was your fault, you bitch!*"

Shocked, Carol gasped and stepped back. Jennifer, outraged, was about to slap Belinda's face when her father, clearly embarrassed, tugged her away, whispering, "For God's sake, Belinda, this isn't the time or place to – "

"She drove him to it!" Belinda shrieked, struggling to

break free from her father. "Her and that crazy cow of a mother with her nightclub and whores. It was her fault! You *know* it was!"

Then she burst into tears again, burying her face in her father's shoulder as Marjorie said, "*Who's* a whore? *I'm* not a whore!" Carol, grabbing Jennifer's arm, whispered, "Oh, God, please get me out of here! I can't stand all this!"

"Yes, Carol," Jennifer said, putting on a posh accent. "I can see we're not wanted here."

Once outside the crematorium, in the chilly grey morning, Carol bowed her head and burst into tears again. "How could she say those things?" she sobbed. "She practically accused me of murdering him!"

Jennifer's girls were busy lighting cigarettes.

"Don't take any notice of her, luv," Barbara advised. "She's just a malicious cow."

"Frustrated," Doreen added. "I know the signs. She's not getting enough."

"And that John was a bastard anyway," Marjorie observed. "He got what he deserved."

When Carol's head snapped up, Marjorie realised what she had said, slapped a hand over her mouth and blushed deeply. Jennifer took Carol firmly by the elbow and said, "Come on, dear. Let's get out of here."

Carol had stopped weeping, but was obviously still shocked. She let herself be bundled into Marjorie's car without saying a word. When the rest of them had clambered in behind Carol, Marjorie drove off.

Looking at Carol, Jennifer found it hard to grasp that this mature, stricken woman was the child who had sat on her knees in what seemed like only yesterday.

Departures

Time moved like the wind, invisible, inexorable, and you suddenly looked back over your shoulder and wondered where it had gone. It had certainly gone for her, since death's shadow now fell about her, making her dwell too often on how casually and brutally it struck down the good and the bad, the bright and the dull.

Death was like love: an indefinable dream. Always present, it never really existed, except in the heart and mind. It was here and yet not here. Pleasure and pain combined. It touched the soul, but destroyed common sense to make slaves of the free.

Carol had once loved John, but that love had turned to hatred. Now that he was dead, her blighted love filled her with guilt.

The car left the crematorium, went around the roundabout, then raced along the North Circular Road, heading back to the West End. Jennifer looked past Carol's profile at the grey world outside. She looked at the cloudy sky and thought of Bill Eisler, up there in an aeroplane.

He was coming to London.

What did she want from him? Was it material or emotional help? Was she trying to regain a lost dream or exploit what had been?

She didn't really know, so she reached out for the hand of her daughter and patted it lightly.

She would soon be speaking to Bill Eisler and could hardly believe it.

Chapter Five

∾

January, 1944. The war was nearly five years old, Jenny was eighteen, and the present was vastly more exciting than anything in her past.

Born and bred in Cornwall, in the south-west of England, she had spent most of her time on her parents' small farm in the lush green hills high above the Atlantic Ocean. Four months before she had enlisted in the Women's Auxiliary Air Force, undergone her basic training on an air base in Cambridgeshire, then was posted directly to London as a WAAF driver for the Department of Information in Whitehall.

LACW Jennifer Birken was billeted with other WAAFs in a disused school in the East End, not far from the streets where Jack the Ripper had once prowled. She spent her working hours driving military officers between the Department of Information in Whitehall and their various hotels, schools and boarding-houses in the great war-torn city.

She was initially overwhelmed by a London at war, with its sandbagged doorways, air raid shelters, blackened, skeletal ruins and mountains of rubble. This city at war was like no other place on earth, always covered in a pall of black smoke, rubble constantly sliding, fire-engines ringing their bells as they raced through the busy streets. By day the city was grey and black, its bombed buildings like charred stage sets; but at night it changed dramatically, became vividly unreal, air-raid sirens wailing, Ack-Ack guns roaring, searchlights webbing the black sky above the barrage balloons where the Spitfires harried the German planes. She saw collapsing buildings, walls of flame, fountains of sparks, dark smoke billowing above the ruins as the earth roared and trembled.

"People may be suffering and dying," Lily Monaghan told her, "but let's face it, we all love this war. It's not the sort of thing you like to admit, but it's the bloody truth, luv."

Certainly it was true for most of the WAAFs whom Jenny lived with. They were quartered in large dormitories in the school in Whitechapel. They ate and slept together, sometimes forty to a room, worked long hours and rarely got a full night's sleep – and most of them played as hard as they worked, aware that each day might be their last.

By day the thousands of troops seemed intent on their war work. By night they were a restless mass that rolled in great waves up and down the Strand, around Piccadilly Circus, through the blacked-out streets of Soho, braving the bombs and incendiaries, ignoring the air-raid sirens and guns, in order to drink and dance, find a woman, fall in love, before dying on land and sea, or in the air, in the full flush of youth.

Jenny's girlfriends loved those men, flirted with them, were seduced, shed tears when the men said goodbye or simply failed to return.

"They're such sweet boys," Lily said. "No more than schoolkids. You take their clothes off and find skin 'n' bone and you've just got to cuddle them. They're our heroes, the poor dears."

Lily was Jenny's best friend: a rough-tongued East Ender, big, brassy and sentimental, her hair bleached blonde and her lips always painted as red as a rose. Cynical and flirtatious, suspicious and sentimental, she treated men as if they were little pets and then threw herself at them. She took Jenny under her wing, amused by her innocence, and introduced her to the city's night life while also protecting her.

"Oh, blimey!" she said. "You're just a poor country girl who hasn't a clue. You've got a lot to learn, darlin'!"

Which was certainly true.

Jenny was shy, unsophisticated and romantically inclined, initially shocked by the casual promiscuity of her many new friends. Yet soon, under Lily's protective wing, her shock turned to amusement, a guarded fascination, and though remaining a virgin she became involved with various men, learned what she needed to know, and gradually immersed herself in the social whirl of London's West End.

London's pubs and clubs were hidden behind black-out curtains, but were always packed and noisy. Men and women in the uniforms of a dozen different countries passed like ships in the night, briefly here and then gone. The war encouraged quick couplings, heightened emotions, defiance. Jenny soon had to confess to Lily that she too was enjoying it.

"Get yourself a Yank," Lily told her with a wink. "They're the ones with all the goodies. They've got chocolate, ciggies, alcohol, nylons and lipstick – you name it, they've got it. And the Yanks, the pets, are so generous when you show them affection."

Jenny managed to resist the Yanks. She occasionally flirted with some of them, but felt herself surrendering gradually to the war's heady atmosphere. The air-raids came most nights, turning the city to flame and smoke, and when the Ack-Ack guns pounded, when the sky filled with flak, tracer bullets and brilliant flares, filling the night with sound and fury, the most modest person was bathed in the radiance of glory. Then ordinary men seemed extraordinary, common souls became uncommon – and Jenny sensed that this illusion (she was convinced it was that) was the one that presented most danger and could lead her to foolishness.

So she decided not to take anyone too seriously; determined not to let the romance of war blind her to commonsense.

"Don't kid yourself," Lily told her. "You're just shy, that's all. But sooner or later you'll fall for someone – and when you do, you'll fall harder than me, 'cause you're the serious kind."

Not as liberated as Lily, but taking her cue from her, Jenny learned to drink and smoke, to hold her own in conversation, and to flirt without becoming too involved or giving too much away.

"You think I'm shameless," Lily accused her, "but I'm not – I have my principles. It's just that this war's not going to last and these times won't come round again. Do you remember *before* the war? God, wasn't it *dreary*? And what do you think will happen when the war ends and the Yanks go back home? We'll be back to respectability, to home and hearth and sipping tea; we'll have nothing to look forward to but marriage to some nice, decent bore. So God bless the war. God bless the Yanks. And let's go out and find them!"

Shocked by Lily's promiscuity, amused by her intrigues, and envious of her confidence and insatiable lust for life, Jenny tried to emulate her, realised she couldn't do it, but went out with her as often as their separate shifts permitted, taking pleasure from her rumbustious presence and mischievous tongue.

"I've finally weaned myself off the Yanks," Lily confessed to her one evening. "I've found this really delicious creature. He's an RAF pilot called Denholm Wilding and I think he's a dream. He spends most of his furloughs in this great hotel in Kensington – it's filled with pilots and correspondents and a lot of odd women. He's as wicked as Sodom and Gomorrah, but utterly charming. I want you to meet him."

"Anytime," Jenny said.

The hotel in Kensington was indeed an extraordinary place. Its bars and restaurant were always packed with pilots, sailors and soldiers of all ranks, their girlfriends and prostitutes, and the correspondents, mostly from overseas, who were covering the war.

The correspondents lived in the bars and were highly visible. They listened constantly to the radio, argued about what was said, took notes, clung to the telephones and eyed up the ladies. Some were civilians, others worked for the armed forces. Most of them were pals of the pilots and navigators whose young eyes were filled with death's darkness and the light of defiance.

Denholm Wilding was such a character, a dashing rake with a sense of theatre, a Spitfire pilot who was two years older than Jenny but seemed twice her age. The Spitfire pilots lived off their nerves and were never truly off duty, always waiting for the telephone to ring and call them back to the field. They were very young old men, flying constantly, run ragged, covering their intimate knowledge of death with hard drinking and impassioned womanising. Yet Denholm still stood out among them, seemed more colourful, less doom-ridden. Before the war he had been an actor and it showed in his manner. He was handsome, flamboyant and charming, if disturbingly cynical.

"A virgin from the country!" he exclaimed theatrically when Lily introduced Jenny in the packed, smoky bar. "As fresh as a flower in a field in May. George, two more G and Ts! We're all dying of thirst here."

Denholm had just turned twenty, but seemed at least thirty. He looked particularly attractive in his flight-lieutenant's uniform, but drank like a fish, smoked like a train, laughed too loudly and rarely stopped talking.

Jenny soon came to like him, but was always wary of him. He had flown too many sorties and shot down too many planes. He had escaped death narrowly so many times that he now believed in nothing but instant pleasure – the here and now; the available.

"You're so innocent," he told her. "You have a sense of morality. You believe in your past, have faith in the future, and refuse to give yourself to the moment in case it betrays you. You believe in life, Jenny, not in death, but only death is invincible – and this being so, you should give me life by sharing my bed."

"No, thanks," Jenny said.

She knew that he meant it – that he wanted to seduce her – and knew also that Lily was aware of it and chose to ignore it. Although smitten by him, Lily was wise in the ways of men, and knew, as she often acknowledged to Jenny, that Denholm couldn't be pinned down.

"He likes my body," she confided to Jenny, "my big breasts and wide hips, the fact that I'm taller than he is and a bit simple minded. Denholm likes easy women, the kind who dote upon him – like me – but he fancies you because you're a virgin who needs to be broken in. He believes in nothing, you see, except his casual pleasures; he's too busy trying to stay alive to work at anything else. A womaniser? God, yes, he is – but what else has he got? What have *any* of these poor buggers got except the promise of death?"

A defiance of death was what kept them all alive. Jenny saw it in the hotel, in its packed lobby and bars, in the many pubs and clubs and loud conversations that drowned out the wailing of the sirens, the explosions, the growling planes. Denholm seemed to know them all, everyone, everywhere, but though he showed them the night life, introduced them, flirted with them, he always circled back to the hotel in Kensington, which seemed like his only home.

"I like the journalists," he explained. "They believe in nothing but the news. They stop believing in the goodness of their fellowman when they pick up their pens. The only things they believe in are drink, food, sex and death. *Real* men, my dears. Priceless!"

So the noisy hotel in Kensington became a home-from-home, a place for garrulous conversation and romantic intrigues. Men came and went like nameless characters in a play, speaking in many different tongues, flirting and drinking between missions, then abruptly disappeared, often never to return. They often died in their Spitfires, Lancasters and Flying Fortresses over France and Germany and Italy. Yet sometimes, as with Denholm, they returned many hours later, looking older and weary, until the food, alcohol, conversation and women brought them back to the land of the living.

No one talked about the ones who didn't come back. Those who disappeared ceased to exist, might never have been.

"If some day I walk out of here and fail to return," Denholm said, "just have a drink on me. I've left a certain amount of money with the barman to cover the bill. No tears, my darlings, no regrets – just have a drink and a laugh. We're not worth more than that."

But they *were* worth more than that, and knew it, as did Jenny. She found herself drawn to their company like a fish to the water. She resisted Denholm's advances, encouraged his liaison with Lily, had platonic relationships with various young men, and managed to convince herself that the war was fun and that death, which came to so many, would not intrude upon her.

But it did in the most brutal, unexpected way.

At the beginning of March, just three months after she had arrived in London, her parents wrote to say that they were taking a brief holiday from the farm in Cornwall. They were coming to visit her. Jenny arranged to meet them at Paddington Station but was late in getting there. When she finally arrived, she found a scene of chaos. Firemen, ambulance-teams and a horde of ARP workers moved in and out of the smoking concourse. When she asked what had happened, she was informed that two of the platforms had been hit by bombs.

An hour later, she was told that her parents were among those who had died.

They were buried in Cornwall. That time was a nightmare, offering Jenny nothing but grief and guilt. Weeks later, back in London, still in deep shock, she went through the motions of living while quietly dying inside herself.

The war had been a gift to her, an unprecedented adventure, one excitement after the other, a realm of pure pleasure. Now she was filled with guilt, haunted by her own survival, because in enjoying the war, she had ignored its grim reality: the fact that many were finding death and anguish while she had her good time.

She retreated into herself, stopped going out with Lily, and spent most of her free time lying listlessly on her bed, taking succour from the darkness, listening to the terrible sounds of the nightly air-raids. She often felt the bed shake when a bomb exploded nearby, saw the crimson glow of flames through the windows of the large room; and decided hopefully, when black smoke indicated a fire nearby, that she stood a good chance of dying and would surely deserve it.

"Enough's enough," Lily said after weeks of this

performance, her big eyes filled with indignation in a frame of blonde hair. "It's not your fault they died. A lot of poor buggers died in that air-raid and a lot more are going to die tonight – and none of it's your fault."

"I was *enjoying* the war."

"So you should. You're young enough. *I'm* enjoying the war. I think even *Denholm* enjoys it. An awful lot of us are going to be bored stupid when it's over, and no matter how brutal that seems, it's the truth and you know it. Now stop pitying yourself and get off that bed and let's go out for a good time."

"I can't, Lily,"

"You can. Denholm's found a new friend, a US Air Force journalist, and he's just as much a virgin as you are. I want you to meet him."

"I can't."

"Get up, damn you!"

Cowed by Lily's vehemence, Jenny did as she was told: putting on her uniform, collecting her gas-mask, and following her voluptuous friend into the war-torn night.

They were both off-duty, but Lily took her jeep anyway, driving fearlessly through the streets in defiance of the air-raid and finally braking to a halt outside the hotel in Kensington and hurrying between its black-out curtains to the bright lights inside.

"*This* is what you need," Lily told her. "This is your therapy."

And indeed, Jenny felt that she had come home.

The lobby was packed as usual. Around the piano in the far corner a lot of drunken men and women were singing the words they hoped were true . . . "*We're gonna hang up our washing on the Siegfried Line . . .* " The air was filled with cigarette smoke, a blue haze in white light, and Lily waved left and right, gave a wink, waved again, then led Jenny straight to the bar.

Denholm was there, leaning languidly against the counter, in the company of RAF Flight Lieutenant Anthony Barker, whom Jenny knew, and a slim, shyly smiling corporal in the uniform of the US Army 8th Air Force.

"Ah, ha!" Denholm exclaimed. "Here comes my girl! And with a once-familiar pretty face in tow. Welcome back, Jenny. Come close and be ravished. You both know Anthony Barker, aerial-navigator par excellence; and his friend here, dearest Jenny, this Yank, is Corporal Bill Eisler. A newcomer to our group, a brilliant young author, he is being wasted as an Air Force correspondent. So what will you drink, girls?"

"We'll both have gin-and-tonics," Lily said, then glanced sternly sideways. "And no arguments, Jenny."

"No arguments," Jenny said.

"Billy-boy," Denholm said to the shy young American, "this pretty little thing is Lily's friend, Jenny Birken. Alas, she is not keen on Yanks – but *you* might change her mind. George, two G and Ts for the delectable ladies. And be quick about it!"

Instantly touched by the American's embarrassment over Denholm's introduction, Jenny studied him boldly and was very taken with him, seeing innate gentleness in his mild, hazel eyes, which made her want to reach out and stroke his thin, thoughtful face.

Surprised, even shocked, by this impulse, she felt compelled to make fun of him.

"Bill *what?*" she asked.

"Eisler," he replied.

"A brilliant young author," she said before she could stop herself. "So what do you write when you're not being wasted as an Air Force correspondent?"

He coughed into his fist, looking at the floor as if wanting to dive into it, then reluctantly raised his eyes and murmured, "Just a few unpublished short stories."

"Just a few unpublished short stories," she repeated, unable to stop herself. "Ah, yes, I see . . ." And nodded, as if deep in thought, then leaned slightly towards him. "Are they . . . *naughty*?" she asked him.

He stared at her, speechless, then blushed brightly from neck to forehead – and as Denholm roared with laughter, as Lily beamed and Anthony smiled, Jenny gazed at Bill Eisler, lost herself in his shy gaze, and realised in a flash of magical comprehension that he was reaching out to grasp the emotions she was feeling for him.

Chapter Six

∽

"A green and pleasant land," Bill said, leaning across Maureen and gazing down through the window as the Concorde banked over Heathrow Airport and the flat fields around it. "Just as I remember it."

"Memories can be deceptive," Maureen replied. "It was a long time ago, Bill."

He fell back into his seat, grinned at her, tightened his safety belt. "England doesn't change very fast. It has a long history. The English tend to cling to that history – and it all looks the same down there."

"Be prepared for a few disappointments."

"Yes, Maureen. I'm listening."

Her concern amused and touched him, and he patted her wrist, forced to contain his excitement as the Concorde descended towards that green and pleasant land which for so long had lingered in his memory. Maureen was right, of course – memory could be deceptive and he had to be prepared for changes – but emotion was stronger than logic and could not be suppressed.

Departures

He would soon be seeing Jenny, the first woman he had truly loved, and his heart raced with excitement and nervousness each time he thought of that.

"It's surprising," Maureen said, gazing thoughtfully down through the window, "that you haven't managed to get back here before this – not since the war. I mean, you've done so much travelling – we've *both* travelled so much – and yet we've never managed to get to England, which you wanted to see so much."

"Just one of life's accidents. Our travels were mostly related to work and that was all in the States."

Maureen smiled. "Well, we're finally here – and I'm very excited."

"Me, too, Maureen."

Yet he still felt guilty because of his planned reunion with Jenny, so was relieved when the Concorde finally landed, to let him escape, with the other well-heeled passengers, into the pearly light of the English morning.

"Isn't it strange how memory plays tricks on us?" he said when they had collected their luggage, walked unchecked through customs, and were following their porter along the crowded terminal, towards the exit. "I was waiting to see something I'd remember from my previous arrival here – and it wasn't until we entered the terminal that I realised my arrival during the war had been at Southampton Docks."

"Premature senility," Maureen replied. "My day will come."

He had to smile at that. "No doubt about it. But I do feel pretty strange. I mean, this airport doesn't look a bit like England. We could be back in LA."

"Don't panic. I'm sure we're in England. The customs

officers, even when they stopped people, were very polite. And they had English accents."

"I *did* notice that much."

He was still in a good mood when they left the terminal and were led by the porter to a line of people queuing for taxis. He had wanted a black cab – he still remembered them with fondness – and was disappointed to get an ordinary Ford with a driver whose English was suspect, his eyes crossed, his face pockmarked.

"Is this England or New York?" he asked Maureen as the taxi moved off.

"Keep your voice down!" she whispered back.

Grinning, Bill glanced out the window as the motorway became a busy road lined with Tudor-styled houses.

"There you are," he said, pointing. "*That* looks like England!"

"Damn, it really *is* pretty here," Maureen replied with rising excitement. "Just like Denholm's postcards! I didn't think they'd still have that kind of architecture outside tourist areas. And that carpet of leaves around the trees... It's just like a movie-set!"

Bill couldn't help laughing, though he was thrilled as well. "Just as I remembered it," he said, sinking back into his seat and reaching out to squeeze Maureen's hand. "Real picturesque!"

Then it all changed, the Tudor houses disappearing, giving way to increasing traffic and visibly polluted air – exhaust smoke from leaded petrol; more black smoke from industrial chimneys – in a road that ran straight as an arrow between prefabricated factories, warehouses of steel and concrete, rows of crumbling council houses with clothes flapping in back yards, garages and supermarkets on pavements strewn with rubbish, and stores with plate-glass windows that reflected the snarling traffic that had slowed to a snail's pace.

Picturesque, it was not.

The driver slammed on the brakes, making Bill and Maureen jerk forward. When they managed to sit back, adjusting their clothing, the driver smacked the steering-wheel with his hand and uttered an oath.

Having boasted to Maureen about the politeness of the English, Bill was taken aback.

"*What* was that?" he asked.

"Fookin' afor!" the driver snarled.

"Pardon?"

"Afor!"

"*What?*"

"*The fookin' A-4!*" the driver exclaimed, raising his hands in despair. "Always fookin' jammed up!"

"I don't think – "

But Bill didn't finish his sentence, since the car suddenly shot ahead, gears grinding, the driver muttering, and Bill was thrown to and fro, then back into his seat. He glanced at Maureen and sighed.

"Dumb coont!" the driver muttered, braking sharply and banging his horn with a clenched fist. "Shouldn't be allowed ona fookin' road!" he added loudly, pressing his foot down again.

"He's not English!" Bill whispered.

"I think he is," Maureen replied.

"The sonofabitch can't be," Bill replied. "The English just don't behave this way!"

"Right," Maureen said, sounding distraught.

The remaining journey took forever. The taxi crawled through dense traffic, stopping and starting in violent spasms, while the driver continued snarling curses, not caring who heard him. Then, when trying to get rid of the stench of stale ash and beer, Bill rolled his window down and the poisonous smoke from the truck ahead billowed into the cab, making him and Maureen cough, as well as causing the driver to curse even more vehemently.

"Fookin' filth!" he exclaimed when the smoke finally cleared. "This friggin' city's dyin' on its fookin' feet!"

At least the scenery changed, becoming seedily sophisticated, the houses as Bill had remembered them, if less glamorous – decaying. Then a busy high street, shop-windows filled with fashionable clothing, then a side-street lined with restaurants and more shops, leading up to the hotel.

The taxi stopped with a jolt.

"OK, mate," the driver said, looking relieved and lighting a cigarette. "This is it. Yer 'otel. Very nice an' all, guvnor."

He climbed out of the car, placed their suitcases on the pavement, stretched himself, loudly cracked his knuckles and said, "Thirty pounds, thanks."

Bill glanced at the meter. It didn't appear to be working. He looked back at the driver, who was wearing a torn bomber-jacket and denims, and said, "I don't think so, buddy. I think fifteen should do it."

"What aboot the tip?"

"The fifteen includes the tip."

"Are ya accusing me of tryin' to cheat ya, Yank? I mean, don't fookin' try it on!"

Departures

"Please, Bill!" Maureen whispered nervously.

"Fifteen pounds," Bill insisted.

"Fookin' Jesus," the driver said, "a Yank tight-fist! OK, fifteen quid."

He snatched the money from Bill's hand, climbed into his car and slammed the door. "I hope ya both git mugged," he shouted, "ya tight-fisted shites!"

Then his car screeched and made a tight turn and raced away from its own smoke.

Bill glanced at Maureen and saw the shock in her eyes. He looked around for the doorman and instead was confronted by a filthy, dishevelled woman, surrounded by four children, who stuck her hand in his face and said, "A couple of quid fer the childern. *One* pound, mister. Some *pence*, at least!"

"Oh, Lord!" Maureen muttered.

"Where's the doorman?" Bill asked, shoving some coins into the beggar's hand and glancing up at the hotel. It was just as he remembered it. Solid Victorian and pretty grand. It only lacked the doorman in gold braid who had always stood there.

"I don't think there *is* a doorman," Maureen said. "Let's take the cases ourselves."

"Are you kidding?" Bill said.

"I won't stand here another second, Bill. Now let's get inside."

Bill glanced at the dishevelled beggar and her four filthy children, looked along the street at its expensive shops and restaurants, then shrugged, grabbed both of their suitcases and led Maureen inside.

Walking through the open doors he thought of Jenny and was shrivelled with guilt.

Yet he still felt excited.

And was disappointed again.

The hotel was not the place it had been. Most of the original furniture had been replaced. The oak-panelled walls had been covered with a hideous flock wallpaper, pillars of artificial marble soared up from a floor of fake Italian tiles, the new furniture was sparse and functional, scattered around glass-topped tables, and a large portion of the original lobby had been filled in with slick "tourist" shops.

It looked just like the airport.

"Very nice," Maureen murmured.

"Well, it's not exactly *the Savoy*," Bill replied ineffectually. "But as I told you, I wanted to stay here because this is where I was during the war. Of course it's changed. It wasn't like this at all. I mean, it's . . ."

"Yes, Bill. I understand."

She glanced left and right, her eyes slightly out-of-focus, retreating from what appeared to be an extraordinary number of residents, most of them a little on the shabby side and making far too much noise.

Maureen sighed in despair.

Bill checked in at the desk. He had to wait a long time. A lot of people were bawling in many different languages and the desk clerks, both wearing stained black jackets, dealt with them like a pair of somnambulists, their pale faces managing to express little more than disdain.

When Bill's turn finally came, he wasn't treated much differently, but eventually, after quarrelling about whether or not he had booked a room, he actually managed to sign in and obtain his room key.

Departures

"Fourth floor," the desk clerk said, practically yawning. "The lift's to your left."

"Right," Bill said, taking Maureen by the elbow to lead her away. Then he stopped when he noticed that no one had made a move towards his luggage.

"The cases," he said.

"What about them?" the desk clerk asked.

"Isn't someone going to take them up for us and show us the room?"

The desk clerk raised his eyebrows. "*Show* you the room? I'm afraid, sir, that if you *don't like* the room, there are no others available."

Bill sighed. "OK. Do you at least have a porter?"

"Not really," the desk clerk said, but raised his right hand to snap his fingers and wave someone over.

It was a teenaged bellhop, wearing a badly stained, frayed uniform, his sleepy face scarred with acne, his jaws working on gum.

"Please escort this lady and gentleman up to their room," the desk clerk intoned with studied indifference. "And take their suitcases."

The sleepy bellhop stopped chewing. "I ain't s'posed to carry luggage," he said. "That's a job for a porter."

"We *don't have* a porter," the desk clerk replied.

"No one told me I'd 'ave to lug friggin' luggage. I should git more for this."

"You'll get a kick up the arse if you're not careful. Now take these people *and* their suitcases upstairs."

"I'll report this," the bellhop responded, reluctantly picking up the suitcases. "Don't fink I won't, mate!"

"You do that," the desk clerk said in a glacial manner. Then: "Next! Who's still waiting?"

Bill felt disillusioned and angry, saw that Maureen was mortified, stood beside her, hemmed in by their luggage, in the small, dark elevator. The bellhop chewed his gum, blew bubbles and burst them, and tunelessly muttered what was obviously some kind of pop song. When the doors of the lift opened again, he picked up the suitcases, grimacing melodramatically, and led them along a corridor whose wallpaper and carpet were of an old and decidedly worn vintage.

The same wallpaper and carpet that had been there during the war.

Shocked and disorientated, suddenly hurled back to the past, Bill vividly recalled Denholm, Lily, Jenny and himself, all much younger and in uniforms, entering and leaving these very rooms in a turbulent, more pleasant age. He almost stopped walking, but Maureen tugged his hand, and he followed her automatically, getting his breath back as the surly teenage bellhop opened a door and showed them inside.

When Maureen slipped him some pound coins, he grinned cockily and hurried out, not waiting to see if they wanted anything.

"Terrific service," Bill murmured.

The room had been modernised and was blandly inoffensive, with a double bed, chipped television set, and a rudimentary bathroom.

There was no space to walk around.

"Very nice," Maureen repeated.

"It's a lousy room," Bill replied. "I can't even believe this is the same hotel."

"It's not *that* bad, honey."

"Don't patronise me," he replied, feeling bitterly

disappointed. "The hotel *I* stayed in was beautiful, a regular museum-piece, and had staff so considerate and polite you were walking on air. This joint is a *tourist* trap. At least that's what it's become. Godammit, I really need a drink – and I need it *right now*!"

He phoned through to room service, was given the same desk clerk, asked for a bottle of Johnnie Walker, two glasses and a copy of the menu.

"Sorry," the desk clerk said. "No such thing, I'm afraid. We don't have room service and the restaurant was closed down years ago."

"The *restaurant* was closed down?"

The desk clerk laughed indulgently. "Too many tables for too few customers. Our clientele prefer to eat out. For the ethnic variety, I gather, as well as the price."

"What about *breakfast*?" Bill asked testily. "I mean, we *were* assured that's included."

"Which it is, sir, of course. And if you'd taken the trouble to look at the inside door handle, you would have found a brown-paper bag, probably hanging there right now, marked *Petit dejeuner*, *Frühstuck*, *desayunar* and *breakfast*. Simply read the instructions, tick the square facing the preferred breakfast, as shown on the attached card – limited, I fear, to croissants or sandwiches – and hang the bag with card on the *outside* door-handle with, or without, the do-not-disturb sign. Anything else, sir?"

"Yes. Connect me to the Savoy Hotel. I'm moving out right this minute."

"You'll still have to pay for one day and night here."

"I will."

"Very good, sir."

The phone went dead. Bill studied Maureen's face.

She was staring at him in an unfocused, wavering way, as if embarrassed on his behalf and trying to avoid his gaze.

"You don't have to – " she began, sounding forlorn. "I mean, it's not that . . ."

"What the hell," he said, "it's not that important. Let's go somewhere better – a place *you* deserve. And let's do it this second."

Before she could argue, he picked up the suitcases and lugged them laboriously towards the door. When Maureen opened the door for him, he gratefully walked out, dropped the suitcases again, glanced up and down the grim corridor and shook his head ruefully.

"You can't go home again," he quoted. "And I should have known that. You can't bring back the past."

Then he picked up the cases and started resolutely towards the lift, hoping that his embarrassment and disappointment didn't show in his face.

"Godammit it!" he whispered.

Chapter Seven

~

Bill's first experience of Great Britain, in March, 1944, was the unattractive view of Southampton docks from the deck of the ship that had transported him, with hundreds of other American troops, across the Atlantic. Bill had spent most of the voyage in a heightened state of awareness composed of the fear that the ship might be attacked by the Germans and disappointment that this hadn't actually happened.

He had also spent much of the journey in a state of extreme self-consciousness, too much aware of the fact that most of the other young men in the ship, stacked like sardines one on top of the other in their bunks, were destined to take part in the great battle to free Europe while he, though a US Army 8th Air Force flight-lieutenant, was going to England as a non-combatant.

He would write about the battles to be fought by these young men all around him.

He would cover their dying.

So, he was uneasy, but also quietly proud, being twenty years old and considering it an achievement that after a mere two years as a cub reporter on his local newspaper, in Norman, Oklahoma, he had managed to get all the way to England as a journalist in uniform.

And those grey docks in front of him, with their rusty pylons, ugly cranes and sandbagged warehouses, were his gateway to the country he yearned to see.

He was filled with excitement.

This only increased when he transferred from the ship to the train that would take him and the others to London. Again, the troops were packed in like sardines, in every compartment and corridor, and soon the carriages were filled with cigarette smoke and resounding with conversation and laughter.

The train moved out of the docks, and soon the sandbagged warehouses and grey streets beyond gave way to fields more green than anything he had seen before; then quaint little villages, cottages with thatched roofs, cattle and sheep.

Bill could hardly believe that at last he had arrived in the land that had given birth to Shakespeare, Dickens, Pepys, Coleridge and Ben Jonson – the land of his dreams.

He, who aspired to be a writer, was thrilled beyond words.

Then it gradually changed. He saw the first of the ruins, broken walls, scorched timber, then hillocks of rubble and smoky air as the train approached London.

Bill was shocked. He did not understand how anyone could have survived such widespread, awesome devastation. It didn't seem possible.

But miraculously they *had* survived and, when he left the station, swarmed around him in their thousands: men and women of many nationalities, most of them in uniform, others in normal clothes but with tin helmets on their heads, hurrying across the busy roads, dodging through traffic that included many troop trucks, and filling the restaurants, cafes and pubs as if the war didn't matter.

After reporting to his superiors in a stately building off Whitehall, near Big Ben, the House of Commons and Westminster Abbey, he was pleasantly surprised to learn that he would be living with other foreign correspondents in a hotel located not far from the Royal Albert Hall and Kensington Gardens.

"You'll have a good time," the officer-in-charge informed him. "It's a non-stop party out there. I only wish I could join you, kid."

It was not the kind of remark that Bill could relate to a city at war; and indeed, so busy were the streets, and so casual the appearance of the people, that he would have had trouble accepting that there actually was a war . . . until, being driven towards his hotel in Kensington, he saw more bombed buildings, sandbagged doorways and gun-emplacements, and the barrage balloons floating overhead at the end of their cables.

"It doesn't *seem* that there's a war going on," he said to his driver. "Everyone looks so unconcerned."

"Why be concerned when there's no way to avoid it?" the pretty WAAF corporal replied. "There are air raids just about every night – and you can't avoid *them*! 'Ere's the 'otel, sir."

It was an old and stately building with leaded glass doors, brown-panelled walls covered with exquisite paintings, and chandeliers shedding their light on

Victorian furniture, velvet drapes and potted plants. It was also a hive of activity, filled with men and women of different nationalities, most wearing uniform.

Its upstairs rooms were largely taken over by journalists, with every corridor and public room under the care of immaculately attired staff, who seemed eminently capable of creating order out of chaos and ensuring that the clientele's needs were met with the minimum of fuss.

Bill loved it.

And he soon learned that the city *was* at war. That evening, having gone to bed early to recover from his journey, he was jerked out of a sound sleep by the wailing of the air-raid sirens. Shocked by the noise, he was even more disturbed when the sirens were followed by the rumble of bombers overhead, the blowing of whistles, then the pounding of the Ack-Ack guns in Kensington Park, and finally, the deafening thunder of exploding bombs.

He practically fell out of bed, then pulled his blackout curtains aside and looked into a darkness that was being coloured dramatically by jagged sheets of flame, fountains of sparks, and a gigantic, constantly changing web of crisscrossing searchlights. The floor beneath him shook and the windowpanes rattled. There was roaring, wailing, booming and the hissing of water. Then he let the curtains fall back into place and ran from the room.

He hurried downstairs to the lobby, saw the black-out curtains covering the velvet drapes, then was stunned to observe that the bar was packed with noisy revellers, many singing, *"Oh Johnny! Oh Johnny! Oh!"* around a lively piano.

Bill entered and pushed his way through the crowd to the counter, where he tried in vain to order a drink.

Luckily, an ebullient RAF flight-lieutenant dropped a hand on his shoulder and exclaimed theatrically, "A newcomer! Buy this poor Yank a drink! A pint of best for my friend, John!"

"Sorry," Bill began, as the barman pulled an ornate pump handle to let beer spout into his glass. "I was trying to order, but he didn't seem to notice me. I mean, I – "

But the handsome flight-lieutenant simply beamed more widely and introduced himself with: "Denholm Wilding. Flight-lieutenant. RAF Bomber Command. And this is Flying Officer Anthony Barker, who will pay for your beer."

"My pleasure," Anthony Barker said with grave sincerity, thrusting his hand out. "And you are . . . ?"

"Bill Eisler," Bill replied, shaking the hands of Barker and Wilding in turn. "I'm a correspondent with the US Army 8th Air Force. I – "

"Just arrived today?" Wilding asked.

"Yes."

"And staying here, in this grand hotel?"

"That's right, Denholm."

"An excellent place to be located, old son. Alas, *we* are located in the wilds of East Anglia and can only come to London when we're free, this being most weekends. And naturally we always stay here – so convivial, dear boy."

There was a high wailing sound outside the hotel, followed by a fierce explosion. The floor shook beneath Bill's feet, dust drifted down from the ceiling, and since he had almost ducked while his friends remained unperturbed, he covered his confusion by asking, "Do both of you fly?"

"Yes, old son. Lancasters. I'm a pilot – and Anthony, now paying for your beer, is my hopefully trustworthy navigator. Have you *had* English beer before?"

"No."

"Here you are, then. Let it wet your dry throat."

Bill drank his first English beer. It was warm and tasted bitter.

"It's called 'bitter'," Wilding explained, as if reading his thoughts. "Always ask for best bitter and you'll obtain the best beer. Now have a good swig, old son."

Bill drank deeply, his eyes stinging from cigarette smoke, and immediately felt flushed and slightly unreal.

"It's good of you – " he began.

"Not at all, old son," Denholm replied. "We like to welcome our allies to this little bar. You know the saying we Brits have about you damned Yanks – 'Overpaid, over-sexed, and over here' – and I don't want your sensitive soul to be cut by such words."

"Gee, I – "

"Of course it's *true* that you're overpaid, over-sexed and over here! But you *do* have the contraband – "

"Pardon?"

"The chocolates and cigarettes and other luxuries," Anthony Barker informed him.

"And so," Denholm continued, his handsome face flushed, "Anthony and I are understandably keen on our American allies."

Another bomb exploded nearby. The building shook,

more dust fell. This time, anaesthetised by the English beer, Bill was proud of his self-control.

"Gee," he said, "and you guys actually *fly* those bombers! What's it like over Germany?"

"Hell on earth," Anthony said.

"We're in *the air*," Denholm corrected him. "Actually, it's all really *too* boring. Now *journalism* – that sounds *much* more exciting! We English love words, m'boy."

"*I* love words," Bill replied, feeling good, being drunk. "I've wanted to write since I was fourteen years old. That's why I always wanted to come to England – particularly London. Most of my favourite writers lived here."

Denholm patted his shoulder and beamed at the barman. "Three more pints on our American friend, John. And have one for yourself!" He turned back to Bill. "A burgeoning novelist, eh? Well, you're in the right hotel. Not too far from here, in De Vere Gardens, lived Robert Browning and Henry James. Also close by is Young Street, where Thackeray not only lived, but also hosted a reception for Charlotte Brontë, after the success of *Jane Eyre*. Ezra Pound lived just across the road in Kensington Church Walk; John Stuart Mill and Bernard Shaw's mistress, the vivacious actress Mrs Patrick Campbell, lived in Kensington Square; and of course Lord Byron and Charles Dickens both frequently attended the soirees held in Holland House, just up the road. One could go on forever, old chap – and that's only *this* area!"

"You seem to know a lot about writers," Bill said. "Is it one of your interests?"

"Well – "

"He's an actor," Barker said, rubbing his bloodshot

eyes. "Can't you tell that, old chap? His interest in words goes no further than speaking them until we're all deaf."

Denholm laughed heartily at that.

"A *real* actor?" Bill asked.

"Oh, a little bit here, a little bit there – "

"Mostly in the *provinces*," Barker clarified, "in cold, draughty town halls."

"A little rep' and so forth," Denholm continued, unperturbed, "but nothing to get excited about, old son, and not much future in it. More important is what's happening here and now: all those ports – " he indicated the ladies around them – "in this turbulent storm of war. Drink, sex and survival – now, *they're* worth fighting for! So drink up, Billy-boy!"

When Bill finished his beer, someone bought him another and the crowded bar seemed to close in to warmly enfold him. Outside, London burned. When the bombs fell, the floor shook. The pianist continued playing, the group around him were still singing, and the other men and women became blurred as Bill's drunkenness deepened. And since death was outside, being alive in here seemed magical, making him talk as he'd never done before, until his words became jumbled.

When he awakened the next morning in his bed, he could hardly believe it had happened.

And he had his first hangover.

His new life in England was frantic and fascinating, not giving him too much time to be alone or suffer homesickness. In preparation for the impending Allied invasion of Fortress Europe, the British Isles had been turned into a huge armed camp, as Bill saw

Departures

when he was sent here and there to report what was happening.

Large-scale military exercises were taking place in the south; fake concentrations of dummy ships and troops, designed to fool the enemy, were to be found all over the countryside; airborne and amphibious landings were being rehearsed almost daily; thousands of British, Commonwealth and American troops were already being moved to the assembly points along the coast; and the enemy was being softened with day and night raids against marshalling yards, airfields and military positions in Germany and occupied France.

Bill was plunged into a world such as he could never have imagined when surrounded by the wheat fields of Oklahoma.

There were no wheat fields in London. The sun rarely shone here. Yet when he saw the smouldering ruins, the water geysering up from burst pipes, the flames flickering brightly in billowing black smoke, he was filled with an odd exhilaration that could not be denied.

"You're part of the war, now," Denholm told him. "You're one of us, old son. You may be a mere Yank, a vastly privileged ally, but like us, you're risking life and limb in pursuit of your calling. By the way, you *did* bring some goodies from the PX? Where's that dear paper bag?"

Enthralled by his work, Bill ran himself ragged, but spent nearly every evening in the hotel's lively bar, with its hard drinking aircrews, noisy sailors and soldiers, flirtatious WAAFs and circulating whores, where Denholm Wilding and Anthony Barker were spending most of their furlough.

"We normally only get here on weekends," Barker explained, "but we were due for two weeks off and couldn't think of anywhere better to spend it. We're both bachelors, you see, so what more suitable place could we be in? This is where the world meets."

"Particularly in the lower regions," Denholm clarified. "One must *not* sleep alone, old son."

"I sleep alone," Bill confessed.

"My heart breaks for you, dear boy. So where's our little paper bag of goodies? Without you, we would *suffer* so!"

Bill had learnt that because of "rationing" the British suffered great deprivations, notably in the line of certain luxuries, such as chocolate, cigarettes and sheer nylons. And since the Americans had free access to all the things the British lacked, Denholm was keen to use him to obtain what he required from the PX.

"In return for nylons," he told Bill, "or even the odd Hershey bar, Lily will be extraordinarily generous. Have you met Lily, Bill?"

"No, Denholm, I haven't."

"That's because she hasn't *been* here," Barker explained. "But she's coming this evening."

Bill liked Lily Monaghan the minute he met her. Wearing the uniform of the Women's Auxiliary Air Force, she had bleached blonde hair and brightly painted lips, talked with what Bill assumed was the famous "Cockney" accent, and was clearly simple-minded, good-natured and out for a high old time.

"Oh, goodie!" she said, after being introduced to him. "Another American pilot!"

"Actually, I'm not a – "

Departures

"Bill's a novelist," Denholm interjected with a bland expression.

"Actually, I'm not – "

"He's a *novelty!*" Lily said. "A perfect little angel, he is. I could just *eat* Americans!"

"Lily's a WAAF driver," Barker explained, "and as such gets to drive a lot of Americans, most of them officers."

"And so generous," Lily added. "Denholm tells me *you're* generous as well. So nice to meet you, Bill!"

Denholm gave her a gin and tonic. The air-raid sirens wailed outside. Lily sighed, her breasts heaving impressively, and said, "Here comes bloody Jerry again. You'd think they'd give it a rest some night."

"It's *you* they're looking for, Lily."

The sirens continued wailing. The German planes were approaching. The Ack-Ack guns in the park started pounding, then the first of the enemy bombs exploded south of the city.

"All right, Denholm," Lily Monaghan said, "take your hand off my bum. We're not in your bedroom yet!"

Denholm laughed and removed his hand. Anthony Barker smiled laconically. Bill blushed and felt a sudden surge of love for his new friends, aware that Denholm and Lily made an unlikely couple, yet understanding what attracted them to one another.

They both had a lust for life.

"He's a romantic, our little Yank," Lily said. "I can tell just to look at 'im. He wouldn't *dream* of putting his hand on my bum. He wants to hold hands in candlelight."

"How pitiful," Denholm said.

Bill saw a lot of Lily during the following fortnight,

since she came to the bar most evenings, obviously to see Denholm. And listening to their saucy banter, seeing their drunken eyes and quick smiles, he found himself trying to imagine the terror their laughter was hiding.

In Denholm's eyes, Bill saw an exhaustion and dread that could not be expressed; and when he studied Anthony Barker, much quieter, more laconic, he would try to imagine him and Denholm in their Lancaster bomber, flying through the flak and gunfire of the deadly skies of Europe, following the flares of the pathfinders, to drop their bombs on the oil plants of Leuna, Magdeburg and Politz.

"Hell on Earth," Barker had said.

Bill knew it was true and sensed that Lily also knew it. He was convinced that this big girl, who seemed simple and sincere, loved the airmen from the depths of a compassion that would never be stated.

"Haven't you got a girlfriend, darlin'? she asked Bill. "I mean, you look like you *need* one."

"Billy-boy," Denholm said, "is in love with his Muse. He is going to be a *writer*, dear Lily, which is why you can't read him."

"I *can* read him," she replied. "He's as sweet as pie, he is. He's just a bit shy, is all, so we'll have to find him a soulmate."

"No, thanks," Bill said. "I'll find my own soulmate. I'm just too busy to do it right now, since I'm reporting the war."

"*What* war?" Barker enquired.

"*I* don't see any war, do you?"

"No, Denholm," Lily replied, as the sirens wailed and the bombs fell. "He really *does* need a girlfriend – and if he gets me some chocolate and stockings, I might even find him one."

"The chocolates and stockings are guaranteed," Bill promised, "on the condition that you don't hinder my growth by helping me out."

"Agreed," Lily said. "Do you like the name 'Jenny'?"

"Why do you ask?"

"I have this friend," Lily replied. "Another WAAF driver. From Cornwall, as pretty as a picture, and just right for the likes of you."

"The likes of me?"

"The sensitive type. Jenny's sensitive as well, too good for this riff-raff here" – she indicated Denholm and Anthony – "and right now she could really do with someone decent."

"Where *has* Jenny been lately?" Anthony asked her.

"Her parents were killed three weeks ago, when those bombs fell on Paddington Station, and since then the poor thing's been in a state of shock, blaming herself because her parents were on their way to visit her. Now she hardly ever leaves the billet, except when going to work."

"Poor girl," Anthony said.

"Of *course*!" Denholm exclaimed, ignoring the bad news. "Why didn't *I* think of Jenny? She's so sensitive, even *I* haven't had her, so she's just right for Billy-boy!"

"No soulmates," Bill responded. "You promised me, Lily. Otherwise . . ."

"No nylons, no Hershey bars," Anthony said. "Without which, life is meaningless."

"I don't care," Lily insisted. "I'm going to drag her back here soon. She used to love coming here – "

"In a limited way," Denholm clarified.

" – and since she can't stay in those barracks forever, I'm going to get her back to the real world."

"You promised!" Bill reminded her.

"It's nothing to do with you, Yank. Jenny was coming here before *you* showed up – and I'm simply going to make her do so again, for her own good. On these grounds, you can't refuse me my little goodies – and I *do* think you're sweet!"

She blew him a kiss.

The following day, Bill was working late and had to make his way back to his hotel by foot. The night sky was webbed with wavering searchlights and filled with barrage balloons, German bombers and the harrying Spitfires: a bizarre *son et lumiere* spectacle; a chaotic, catastrophic devastation that made his heart race.

He entered the hotel in Kensington and went straight to the bar, which was, as usual, crammed with men and women in uniform. Some drunks were singing *"We're gonna hang out our washing on the Siegfried Line,"* and the air was filled with cigarette smoke, a blue haze in white light.

Denholm was leaning languidly against the bar, talking to Anthony.

"Ho! Ho!" he exclaimed, waving a hand in welcome. "Here's our young American friend! Is that Lily's bag of goodies under your arm, Bill?"

"Yep."

"She isn't here yet."

As Bill placed the bag of PX purchases on the counter, Denholm looked towards the entrance, broke into a wicked grin, and waved his free hand. "Ah, ha!" he said boisterously. "Here comes my girl! And with a once-familiar pretty face in tow. Welcome back to the land of the living, Jenny. Come close and be ravished!"

Bill turned around to face Lily and Jenny Birken. He saw Lily's bright smile, then a moon-shaped, piquant face, very pale, surrounded by black hair, with eyes as green as jade, looking at him as if looking into him.

Introduced to her, he took her hand in his, felt its delicacy and warmth, but dropped it hastily, as if he'd been scorched. Then her voice, soft and shy, as sweet as honey, accented, resounded through him to capture him completely and run away with his racing heart.

"Bill *what?*" she asked.

It was love at first sight.

Chapter Eight

∽

"Don't get your knickers in a twist," Marjorie said in her forthright manner, patting her blonde hair and staring with wide-eyed sympathy at Carol. "Men aren't worth shedding tears for, darlin', even when in their graves."

"Well, *really*!" Barbara exclaimed, shocked by Marjorie's thoughtless comment. "I should think you'd have something more sympathetic than *that* to say, so shortly after the funeral."

"I didn't mean – "

"It's all right," Carol interjected. "I know what you mean."

"We'll soon be opening," Jennifer said deliberately, "so why don't you girls join Doreen and get yourselves ready?"

"Good idea," Barbara said. "We've been talking all afternoon! Come on, Marjorie, let's go."

Marjorie stubbed her cigarette out in the ashtray, then patted Carol's hand. "I'm really sorry," she said, "but you'll survive. We all do. And maybe it's been for the best. Try to look on the bright side."

"Thanks, Marjorie. I will."

Both women stood up and walked across the club, towards the dressing room at the back, while Carol smiled wanly and rubbed bloodshot eyes.

Jennifer glanced distractedly around the empty club with its mock Dickensian decor, Victorian furniture, settees in crimson velours, and antiques supplied by Carol's boyfriend, David. The barman, James, wearing a striped shirt and polka-dot bow tie, was preparing for the evening while the cleaning woman, Rhoda, with a scarf around her head and a cigarette between her lips, was taking the chairs off the tables and putting them back on the floor.

"Are you all right?" Jennifer asked.

"Yes," Carol replied, "I'm fine. I just can't believe that he's really gone, that he's out of my life for good." She sighed. "I feel confused. I don't know *what* to think."

"You don't know what to think because you feel grief for a man who mistreated you. We all feel obligated to the dead. It's one of nature's mean tricks."

"He was my *husband*, Mother."

"Only on paper, dear. In practice you scarcely had a real marriage."

"You mean his promiscuity?"

"Yes – *and* his other cruelties. I don't have any time for men who beat their wives – and just because they've passed on, I can't pretend to virtues they never had."

The observation made Carol flinch, but she nodded agreement. "Before David, I had rotten taste in men, didn't I?"

"Yes," Jennifer said.

"Because I never had a father?"

"You *did* have a father, but I suspect that growing up without him had a bad effect on you. They made fun of you at school because he was missing. That hurt you and made you solitary and, later, susceptible to older men."

"Most of whom were bad choices."

"Not necessarily bad; though you were certainly drawn to married men, which is why you made a bad choice with John. He'd been married before and had a lot of confidence, and so, being drawn to experienced men, you fell into his clutches."

Carol sighed. "I suppose you're right. I thought it was so romantic – my father, a pilot, being shot down during the War – but later, at school, when I was being made fun of, I started yearning for someone to replace him. God, the trouble that brought me!"

Jennifer smiled, though she was feeling uneasy, aware that Bill Eisler was now in London and would soon be in touch.

Did she dare to confess that?

"At least I found some comfort here," Carol said, indicating the dimly-lit club with a wave of her hand. "That's why I still love this place." As a child, she had spent most of her free time here, helping out in various ways, fetching tea and coffee, and she had certainly received much affection from Jennifer's girls, as well as an education based on real life, rather than books. "I don't know what I'd have done without Marjorie and Barbara and Doreen. They gave me a lot more than they'll ever know. A kind of family, in fact."

"They're not bright enough to know," Jennifer said. "But you're right: they *did* give you that. They have everything John's family lack: the kind of knowledge that only experience brings. Which means they have heart."

Carol still looked pale and drawn, her dark beauty defiled by pain, and Jennifer swelled up with guilt over the lies she had told. She had wanted to tell her daughter the truth; but since Carol had been a child in less liberated times, Jennifer wasn't sure how she would take the news.

Rhoda, the cleaning woman, emerged from the kitchen, where she had been putting away her things. She approached the table, her shoes scuffling on the floor, since she rarely raised her feet properly, and wriggled into her ragged overcoat as she stopped in front of them.

"I'll be off," she said, squinting down at Jennifer through a cloud of cigarette smoke, the smouldering butt still between her lips. "Should I leave the front door open when I go?"

"You might as well, Rhoda."

Without touching the cigarette with her fingers, Rhoda inhaled again, blew another cloud of smoke and said, "Real sorry about your 'usband, Carol. Try to be brave, luv."

"Yes, Rhoda, I will. And thanks."

"Not at all."

As Rhoda shuffled away, Doreen emerged from the dressing room, patting her piled-up hair, tugging down her skin-tight, blood-red dress, rehearsing a sensual pout and fluttering her false eyelashes. She, also, stopped in front of their table to gaze down on Carol.

"OK, luv?" she asked.

"Yes, Doreen, I'm fine now."

"The shock's sometimes delayed," Doreen advised her.

"You can't be too careful, luv."

"I'll be all right, Doreen."

Doreen glanced across the room, to where a shaft of light poured into the lamp-lit gloom. "The door's open already, I see. Ah, well! Another evening of conversation and romance. I'm growing old being beautiful."

She smiled knowingly at Jennifer, waved at Carol, then tottered off on stiletto heels to take a seat at the bar.

Jennifer yearned for a cigarette. She was starting to feel nervous. Bill had written back to her from Los Angeles, saying how surprised he was that she was still alive and living in London and promising to have lunch with her, if business permitted, during his first day in the city. He had said that he would ring her in the morning to confirm the arrangements.

Tomorrow morning, in fact.

Jennifer yearned for a drink, something stronger than the wine, but was distracted when Carol leaned towards her with a tremulous smile.

"I've asked you before, but you've never given a proper answer, so – "

"Why, since your father was killed, did I never remarry?"

"Yes, Mum, that's the question."

Jennifer shrugged. "I don't know."

"But you had lots of menfriends."

"Yes. Most of whom you resented and treated abominably – which may be your answer."

"The fact that none of them, in my estimation, never matched up to the father I never knew?"

"Correct," Jennifer said.

"So you didn't marry again because of me?"

Departures

"Perhaps."

"I doubt it. I think that if you'd found a man you wanted, you'd have married him anyway."

"Maybe. It's difficult to say. I *will* say that your father was an exceptional person – which probably made me judge other men too severely."

"Was he also handsome and gallant?"

"Yes, he was."

"Then you did the right thing."

"Good," Jennifer said. "I'm glad you think that. And I'm even happier to know that at least you've got David waiting for you. I like him. *Everyone* likes him. So you should go and see him right now and forget all this nastiness."

"No," Carol said, "I can't. John was *cremated* this afternoon. I love David, but to go and see him this evening would be positively scandalous."

"You and I are a scandalous couple," Jennifer said. "Now go see that man."

Agreeing with a sigh that displayed her true needs, Carol walked out of the club, leaving Jennifer alone at the table, surrounded by the world she had regained from the pain in her past.

The loss of Bill Eisler.

Chapter Nine

"It's delicious," Carol said, staring across the candle-lit table at David, in his small flat above the King's Road in Chelsea.

"My latest dish," he replied, raising his glass of wine to her. "*Fagioli all 'Uccelletto,* which means beans cooked in small birds. It's an old Tuscan dish. Dried white beans, peeled potatoes, cloves of garlic, olive oil, sage leaves and lots of black pepper. They *should* be toscanelli beans, which of course they are not; but the wine, a Carmignano, comes from the region, so that should make up for it."

"I always feel embarrassed when you cook for me. Not because you're cooking, but because I can't. It's something I never learned."

"Like mother, like daughter – and your mother, efficient in so many ways, is not one for the kitchen."

"Yes, you're right there. She can fry an egg or boil potatoes, but not much else."

"Looked after you, though."

"Yes, David, she did."

"And made a very good job of it."

"Is that a sly compliment to me?"

He grinned. "I suppose so."

He was a handsome man and in the candlelight looked romantic, his hair long and attractively untidy, his brown eyes filled with warmth.

"Where and when did you learn to cook so well?" Carol asked him.

"When necessity called," he replied. "It was after my divorce, when I was first living here alone and found myself eating out of tins, with the odd boiled egg thrown in. So, it was *that* kind of necessity. However, I think it was also something to do at the time – a form of distraction, a new interest, to keep me from brooding about the divorce and my feelings of loneliness. Then, of course, I started travelling a lot to Tuscany to buy antiques, eventually purchased my holiday villa there, and became a lover of Tuscan food. So *something* good came out of my divorce – if only the cooking."

"You never told me why your marriage broke up."

"Well, it wasn't as bad as yours – no mutual loathing and violence. We just married too young and discovered we weren't meant for each other. I thought I would be a painter, she was studying law, we saw less and less of each other and just drifted apart."

"You simply agreed to call it a day?"

"More or less. We were hardly seeing one another, were both unfaithful on odd occasions, and eventually, when I decided to give up painting and sell antiques – which would force me to travel and keep me away from home even more – she suggested, in her pragmatic way, that we sit down and have a little chat. Which we did –

and agreed that we should separate. We sold our house in Hampstead, split the proceeds down the middle, and arranged the divorce without animosity."

"Do you still keep in touch?"

"We send each other cards at Christmas and on birthdays, but apart from that, nothing. Separation is easier without children, so that loss was our gain."

"Speaking of children, how's Mark?"

"No need for worry there. Lorraine will treat him like a king until we get to him."

"Your sister's sweet," Carol said. "Your *whole family* is sweet. Is that why you are?"

"I'm only sweet to certain people," he replied, grinning, "and you're a weak spot. And it's so nice to see you smile again. Where there's pleasure, there's hope. Was it really that bad?"

"You mean the funeral?"

"Of course."

She blushed when recalling it. "Yes," she told him, "it was. I tried not to cry, but did. Then I despised my own hypocrisy – shedding tears for a man I'd loathed – and to top it off, John's sister, Belinda, attacked me after the service for letting the girls from my mother's club attend. She described them as whores."

"What had you thought of Belinda *before* that?"

"I always loathed her."

"So why worry about what she said at the funeral?"

"Guilt, I suppose. Because she practically accused me of having caused John's death; and since our fight made him leave the house to drive drunkenly back to the pub, I certainly feel a *little* bit responsible."

"That's nonsense, Carol. John drank all the time. He

also hit you a lot. That day, he hit you again and stormed from the house. Hardly *your* fault!"

"Oh, I know it wasn't *really* my fault . . . But still, I feel guilty. Maybe because of my relationship with you. I'm a puritan at heart."

David finished off his food, pushed the plate aside, then leaned across the table to hold her hand.

"You needed someone in your life," he said, "because he wasn't really in it. You needed someone who'd treat you decently, because he mistreated you. In short, you needed someone to love you, because he never did." He squeezed her hand, his gaze steady and tender. "There's nothing to feel guilty about, Carol. You can let your guilt be buried with John and call it a day. Now let's go to bed."

She wept as they made love, but was shedding tears of joy. She received him because she wanted to *be* him or lose herself in him. His naked body was her blanket, his hard limbs were her shield, and his lips, which spoke eloquently in silence, returned her numbed skin to life. She lost and regained herself, surrendered to him to be touched by him, was so touched and drawn back from the darkness of her stifling despair.

"Come inside me," she whispered, wanting another child by him; and when he came, she did so at the same time, then subsided beneath him. He lay upon her, remaining inside her, until they both got their breath back.

"Am I too heavy?" he asked.

She chuckled. "Don't move!"

"It's a lovely way to spend the evening," he said. "My dinner pales in comparison."

She licked his cheek, feeling wonderful. "Perhaps I

was *inspired* by your cooking. One never knows in these matters."

She traced his smile with her fingertips. His hair lay upon her face. The light from a street lamp by the window fell obliquely across them.

"I'll have to remember that," he whispered, "and keep up with my cooking."

She patted his naked spine, he slid off her, and then she turned into him. "You're a real treat to eat," she said.

His smile broadened as he snuggled closer to her, his hand on her stomach.

"Do you *really* want another child by me?" he asked.

She closed her eyes and ran her fingers down his arm and felt like weeping with love for him.

"Yes," she said, "I think so. But not now, in these circumstances. It's too early to even consider it, let alone discuss it. God, I shouldn't have said that!"

She squeezed his hand and he kissed her shoulder. "It just slipped out, Carol. Indiscretion in the heat of the moment – though I *am* glad you said it. I think you should marry me."

"*Now?*"

He chuckled. "No, not now. Neither this week nor next. When a reasonable period of time has passed. Will you marry me then?"

He was staring steadily at her, so she glanced up at the ceiling, torn between her doubt and longing.

"I can't answer that, David."

She felt him shift slightly, so squeezed his hand again. "Don't be hurt, David. I don't mean it the way you think. I love you – and you know what I feel for Mark – but this isn't the right time. I've been bruised too much by men.

Departures

My one marriage was a disaster. You and Mark are the best things in my life, but another marriage could kill that."

"It wouldn't."

"It might." She sighed and swung her legs off the bed, then turned back to kiss him. "I'll think about it," she said. "In the meantime, I've a lot to sort out. Don't feel hurt. I love you."

She kissed him again, then dressed herself in the darkness, while he lay on the bed, silently watching her, his gaze loving and sad. When she finally left the flat, he waved at her, his smile touched with unstated pain.

"You're still beautiful!" he called out quietly to her.

"You're not bad yourself," she said.

Chapter Ten

∽

When the telephone rang, Bill was standing by the window of his room in the Savoy, looking over the Thames river at the bright lights strung along the South Bank. Picking up the phone and giving his name, he was pleased to hear the voice of his old friend, Denholm Wilding.

"Settled in, have you, old boy?" Denholm asked with a trace of mirth.

"Yes, Denholm."

"I thought you intended staying in our old hotel in Kensington – to relive the past."

"Our old hotel is no longer the one we knew. Why didn't you warn me?"

"Because I didn't know, old son. Unlike you, I'm not smitten by nostalgia, so I haven't gone back there since the war. Really bad, was it?"

"Damned awful, Denholm. It's been gutted and rebuilt and is geared for tourists. No restaurant. No service."

Denholm laughed. "So now you're in the timeless grandeur of the Savoy. I bet Maureen is pleased!"

"She sure as hell is. So how are you?"

"Excellent. In good health. Making money hand-over-fist. And looking forward to discussing your movie in an informal manner. What about lunch tomorrow?"

"I have an appointment at lunchtime. Would your evening be free?"

"I'll have to cancel some beautiful people, but if you promise to bring Maureen along – "

"I do."

" – then let's make it the Garrick Club."

"Sounds terrific."

"Can I say hello to Maureen?"

"She's in the bath."

"Go and rub her back, old son. Give her my love. And since it's late, I better ring off now and let you get a good sleep. Eight o'clock tomorrow evening?"

"Fine."

"Goodnight, Bill. Have sweet dreams."

Bill put the phone down as someone knocked on the door. Opening it, he let the waiter carry in a tray containing the light supper he had ordered. When the man had gone, Bill sat down to eat.

He could hear the water gurgling out of the bath and Maureen humming a song.

Reminded by Denholm's invitation that he would be having lunch with Jenny Birken the following day, Bill gazed guiltily across the dark river, to where the audience was pouring out of the Royal Festival Hall, some of them boarding the brightly lit boat by the pier in the river. Lights were strung along the South Bank and across the great bridges; and the sky, which he had imagined as always cloudy, was resplendent with stars.

"It's beautiful, isn't it?" Maureen said, emerging from the bathroom, wrapped in a blue towel-robe and letting her hair down.

"Yep, it sure is."

He pretended to study the river while contemplating Jenny Birken. The thought of seeing her excited him, but made him nervous as well, because he didn't know what she would be like now, nor what she would think of him. Also, since Maureen had been told that he would be visiting Anthony Barker, when in fact he would be seeing Jenny, he felt thoroughly ashamed of himself.

"I'm already in love with London," Maureen said, taking the chair facing him and brushing strands of hair from her eyes. "It all looks so . . . *solid* . . . so *civilised* . . . And this hotel is a dream come true."

"Sorry about the first one."

She chuckled with ripe amusement. "I'm sorry for *you*, Bill. You must have been so disillusioned. The expression on your face told it all – a fond memory turned sour."

"The world moves on, Maureen."

"Are you *very* upset?"

"No. In fact, it's funny, when you think about it. That was Denholm on the phone and he was certainly amused that I was harbouring such fond memories of the place – no nostalgia for Denholm! Incidentally, he sends you his love and has invited us both to dinner tomorrow evening."

"And was Denholm his usual, urbane self?"

"My hotel may have changed, but Denholm hasn't. For urbane, I'd say cynical."

Maureen chuckled again, then tucked into her light supper. Taking his snack in silence, Bill gazed out at the

Departures

river, along its glittering length, and felt quietly excited at the thought of making his movie here, particularly since his screenplay had been based on his affair with Jenny in this very city. Then he felt nervous again, wondering what Jenny would be like now, and was glad when the supper was finished and he and Maureen could go to bed.

But he couldn't sleep – the hours were all wrong – and when Maureen rolled lightly against him, he knew that she, too, was restless.

Her hip pressed against him, her breasts warmed his arm, and he rolled over until he was facing her. Their bodies met. Maureen moved her fingers over him. He felt aroused, or imagined being so, and let his hands find her softest spots. The sound of her breathing quickened and she kissed him on the lips. He was suddenly short of breath, tense with need, near to tears, and started raising himself above her, looking into her green eyes. After a while he let his breath out, releasing thwarted emotions, and felt a kind of grief, deep despair and humiliation, then fell back beside her, where he had been, to look up at the ceiling.

"I'm sorry, Maureen. I can't do it. I thought I could, but I was wrong. It's all in the mind now."

Maureen took hold of his hand and squeezed it affectionately. "It's OK. It's not that important."

"It is to me," he told her. "It reminds me that I'm ten years older than you and the difference is showing. I'm old. You're still young."

She raised his hand to her face, pressed his fingers against her cheek. "That doesn't matter, Bill. Not as much as you might think. What matters is what we feel for one another – and this doesn't change that."

"It does, Maureen. Godammit, it must! Sooner or later, you'll become dissatisfied or I'll become more frustrated."

"I love you, Bill. You know that. And *that's* all that matters."

"Christ, you're too good to be real."

"Yeah, right!" She chuckled throatily. "Now let's get some sleep. OK?"

"Agreed."

He took her into his arms, kissed her forehead and stroked her, then lay beside her, holding her hand, his heart racing uncomfortably. She fell asleep quickly, but he failed to do the same, and eventually, still troubled, he slid out of bed and went to the window overlooking the river. When he turned on the lamp on the table, Maureen opened her eyes again.

"You can't sleep?" she asked him.

"No, Maureen. It's jet-lag."

"No, it's not, Bill. You're still brooding about your age and what you feel is your failure. Please stop it. It's senseless."

"It's not senseless to me. I still *want* to do it. I sometimes actually *think* I can do it, but I can't and that kills me."

"It doesn't matter. I didn't marry you for that. That was only part of it."

"We tried to have a child. We failed and now it's too late. Do I forget that as well?"

"Yes, Bill, you forget that."

"Don't you feel resentment?"

"No, I don't think so. At least, no more than I resent other things – my career – God knows what else. *You* wanted a child, Bill. Perhaps even more than me. That's why you do all that social work – to make up for the loss."

"Yes, Maureen, that's right."

"We didn't have children – that's too bad. But it isn't the end of life. Other people suffer a lot more – as you of all people surely know."

"You really don't mind about the other?"

"No, Bill, I don't. Now I'm going to sleep contentedly in this bed while you read a book. OK?"

"Right, Maureen."

He heard her loud sigh, then the silence enfolded him. He gazed across the river, which reflected the stars, and saw the lights on the other side winking out, one by one. He looked on in a trance, filling up with love for Maureen; but then thought of Jenny, recalling her vividly, so tiptoed across the room, quietly withdrew her letter from his jacket pocket and returned to the table. He put his spectacles on, opened the letter and stared at it in wonder.

The words were a blur. There were tears in his eyes. Not seeing the words properly, he saw her face instead, as it had been all those years ago, pale and piquant, framed by dark hair, her gaze bright and mischievous.

For over forty years he had lived with the conviction that Jenny Birken, the girl he loved, had been lost in an air raid. Now, gazing down at her letter, he had to wipe his tears away, before her words, written in a faltering hand, could take shape and have meaning . . .

Dear Bill,

I hardly know where to begin!

I realise that this letter will come as a shock to you, since I am sure you have forgotten me completely – and certainly, while I have not forgotten you, I confess that I never thought it possible I would find you again.

I am Jennifer Birken.

As you may recall, I was a WAAF driver in London during the war and you and I had a relationship which was, so I thought, deeply involving for both of us.

We were, I sincerely believe, in love.

As you may now remember, we lost touch with one another after you left London to take part in the invasion of Europe in June, 1944. Shortly after your departure, I was wounded in an air raid, hospitalised for many months outside London, then shipped as a bed-patient back to Cornwall, where I originally came from.

By the time I was fully recovered, which took many months, I had lost track of you completely and thought that you had died in Europe.

This evening, I saw you on television – and I can scarcely believe it.

Yet of course I do believe it – and it's so thrilling to realise that –

No! I cannot say what I feel. What can one say after all these years? What can one write?

Naturally, what we were, or what we did when we were young, has little to do with either of us today. However, while I appreciate that you and I now lead separate lives, I could not resist writing to let you know that I am still alive and living right here in London – and, also, to let you know that when you come to London, as planned, I would like to meet you again.

I need to see you, dear Bill.

Does that sound rather silly? Please don't take it that way! I am aware that the past is past, that you are a different person (as I am) and that this letter might be a rude intrusion into the life you have made for yourself since we lost each other. Nevertheless, I do have reason to see you and would deeply appreciate it if we could, without embarrassment or guilt, meet at least once during your stay in London.

I remember you with nothing but the deepest affection,
And remain,
Yours truly,
Jennifer Birken.

Bill studied the letter, choking up, his heart racing, then folded it neatly, not wanting to crumple it, and returned his gaze to the river. He saw a pale moon reflected in the rippling black water, then looked up at the sky, still resplendent with stars, and was shocked to realise that it was the very same sky under which, in a very different age, he and Jenny had found love.

He could not bear to look at Maureen, who was now sleeping soundly, but neither could he keep himself from recalling his most touching adventure.

Love's singular blossoming . . .

Chapter Eleven

∽

"Bill *what?*" WAAF driver Jenny Birken asked him in the crowded bar of his favourite hotel in Kensington, in April, 1944.

"Bill *Eisler*," he replied, feeling flustered, aware that Denholm Wilding, Anthony Barker and Lily Monaghan were all grinning at him.

"Are you the writer Lily told me about as we came here?"

"Well, I'm not really a – "

"A magnificent talent!" Denholm proclaimed grandly. "Slightly immature, but sensitive. His short stories have been widely discussed in the best American magazines. A writer of promise, they said."

"*Please*, Denholm," Bill practically stuttered, feeling hot with embarrassment. "That's not true at all. I mean, I'm really just a correspondent, and I – "

"A brilliant young author," Jenny said, with a mischievous smile. "So what do you write when you're not being wasted as an Army 8th Air Force correspondent?"

Burning even brighter, Bill coughed into his fist and

glanced uneasily at his wickedly grinning friends. He wanted to sink into the floor, but heard himself muttering pitifully, "Just a few unpublished short stories. I . . ."

"Just a few unpublished short stories," Jenny repeated mockingly, then stepped closer to look up at him and ask him if the stories were *naughty*, by which she meant sexy.

Bill thought he would die, but then he caught the tone of their laughter, felt hands slapping his back, and suddenly felt that he had found the best friends he might ever have.

"No," he said, "they're not naughty. At least I don't think so. I mean, that word isn't used in America. What does it mean?"

"*Touché!*" Denholm exclaimed, raising his glass in a mock salute as Jenny, with an utterly charming smile, said, "Well, it is nice to meet you, Bill, after all Lily's told me."

"Complimentary, I hope."

"I can't possibly betray her confidence."

"Just tell me I'm not evil," Bill said.

"No, Bill. *Denholm's* evil!"

The evening dissolved into laughter and drunken camaraderie as Bill proceeded to lose himself in Jenny, seduced by her modest beauty, and, even though he was drunk, by the pain he saw lurking behind the humour in her radiant eyes.

Death, as he had already discovered, was something nobody talked about.

"Life," Jenny said, "must be wonderful in Oklahoma, but I thought it was just the title of that musical with all the wonderful songs."

"It's a bit more than that," Bill informed her, "but the musical's good as well."

"Did you see it?"

"No, but I've read about it in the New York papers."

"Never believe what you read in the papers," Anthony observed. "You, being a writer, should know that, but we'll forgive and forget."

"You're so cynical," Lily told him.

"He's just educated," Denholm riposted. "And if *you* had been educated, Lily, you would not be so sweet!"

Lily giggled at that. "You think I'm sweet, Denholm?"

"You have lovely eyes, m'dear," Denholm intoned, ogling her bosom. "I am mesmerised by your virtues."

Lily giggled again, but Jenny sighed melodramatically.

"Jenny doesn't approve of me," Denholm explained to Bill, "because she thinks I'm amoral."

"A *moral*?" Lily enquired.

"Let's say *immoral*," Anthony suggested, "and make life much simpler."

Bill had to laugh. He noticed Jenny's cat-like smile. Confused again, he ordered more drinks, waited patiently for them to come, distributed them and gratefully sipped his, avoiding that green gaze.

"You're not writing short stories for the Army 8th Air Force," Jenny said, her voice slightly accented and sensual, "so what do you do?"

He shrugged, feeling foolish. "I'm a correspondent for official publications. I write about the war and the personalities in it. I interview people, collect information, and put it all together into articles that'll hopefully hearten the good folks back home, not to mention the troops."

"Propaganda."

"Not exactly."

"What a dreadful waste of talent," she said, "even though in a good cause."

Bill's cheeks burned again. "I don't think – "

"She's teasing you," Denholm interjected. "She's stirring the pot, old son."

"You're a driver?" Bill asked her.

"Yes. The Women's Auxiliary Air Force. I drive officers here and there, from HQ to various bases, so I get to meet lots of men and find out what's going on."

"It must be dangerous," Bill said.

"You mean the air raids?"

"No, the officers." Denholm laughed at that one. "I'm told that the higher the rank, the more keen the ladies."

Jenny didn't bat an eyelid. "That could be true, but I wouldn't know. Since I only *meet* the higher ranks, I don't have a wide choice."

"Which is why we're socialising with you lot," Lily explained, then laughed hysterically, clinging to Jenny for support and wiping tears from her eyes.

"It's not the officers the women like," Anthony said. "It's the Yanks. Overpaid, over-sexed and over here – the war's only real winners."

He wasn't being offensive. Bill knew that and grinned. "You guys make me feel so lucky," he said, "I'm going to drink to that."

"Come on!" Denholm exhorted, raising his glass. "Let's drink to the Yanks! Let's get *drunk* for the Yanks!"

"I'll second that," Anthony said.

They all touched glasses and drank. The alcohol went to Bill's head. The warmth of Jenny's smile made him glow with a sublime, inner radiance. Lily giggled in fits and starts, brushing blonde hair from flushed cheeks, and Denholm slid his arm around her waist and rested his head on her breasts. Anthony leaned against the bar, golden-haired, aristocratic, squinting through the drifting cigarette smoke at the crowded piano. Voices were raised in song again, singing *"The White Cliffs of Dover"*, and Bill felt at one with them, losing his old self, finding the new, and then caught the steady gaze of Jenny Birken and was helplessly drawn to her.

Her parents had been killed and she had spent a month weeping, yet now her pained eyes were bright with mischief, her smile was utterly dazzling. Bill felt drunk and filled with yearning, brimming over with the need to love, and knew then, in that noisy, smoky bar, that he would not, must not, let this lovely girl slip from his grasp.

When she and Lily left the hotel, he felt almost bereaved.

Luckily, she returned with Lily every evening of that week, by which time Bill had worked up the courage to whisper, "Would you come to dinner with me some night? Just the two of us together. Well away from the prying eyes and ears of this bunch of gossips."

"Why do you want me away from prying eyes and ears? Are your intentions dishonourable?"

"They might be."

"Oh, all right," she said.

They saw one another regularly after that, meeting in cafes and pubs, attending the theatre and cinema, or walking around the city, when she showed him the former homes of the writers he had most admired when still an adolescent in Oklahoma.

"The East End," she teased him, "is where I stay with Lily. Jack London *and* Jack the Ripper were very creative there. But you'd probably like Hampstead better. Keats had his home there. I can take you to the consulting rooms of Conan Doyle, the Cadogan Hotel of Oscar Wilde, or even to the George and Vulture pub, off Cornhill, where Mr Pickwick and Sam Weller often repaired for relaxation and Dickens himself spent much of his time. I am at your command, sir!"

"You seem to be well-read," he observed. "Are all the English this literate?"

"We have a heritage, you poor Yank."

"I want to inherit *you*, Jenny."

"I won't ask you what you mean by that, since it sounds dreadfully impertinent. What's life like in Oklahoma? Are the men mostly big, tough cowboys with guns, boots and stetsons?"

"Not really, Jenny. It's an agricultural area. The men sit on machines, not on horses, and they don't carry guns."

"Ah!" she exclaimed, smiling brightly. "That's why you're so gentle."

Too gentle by far! He could not get up the nerve to kiss her, though he desperately wanted to.

"*Are* you gentle?" she asked him.

"I'm not a psychopath," he replied. "I mean, I don't tear the wings off butterflies or swing cats by their tails."

"Are you shy?"

"Stop it, Jenny!"

"I think you're shy. You and Denholm are opposites in more ways than one."

"What ways?"

"The ladies. Denholm's really quick with the ladies. He

has the need to possess every woman he meets – and he's very successful."

"Was he successful with you?"

"No," she said, squeezing his hand. "But I'm glad you're concerned."

"How else are Denholm and I different?"

"You believe in goodness, but Denholm doesn't. You're terribly moral where he's immoral. You have faith in the potential of human beings whereas Denholm mistrusts them."

"I like him," Bill insisted. "I somehow trust his cynicism."

"That's because he has the charm of the born actor – *and* the skills to go with it. He knows exactly how to address his audience and draw them into his web."

"You think he's done that with me?"

"He likes you, Bill – more than most, I think – but only on his terms."

"*You're* the cynical one," Bill told her.

She chuckled. "Perhaps."

"So never you and him?" he asked more anxiously.

"No," she replied.

"And Lily?"

"Oh, yes. Lily has lots of men, loves them all, or so she claims, but deep down she's besotted with Denholm and probably hurts over him. She's sweet and terribly good-natured – so Denholm will probably hurt her, sooner or later."

"I don't think so."

"I do."

Bill started putting his arm around her. She fitted into him very nicely. He explored the city to discover her, to learn how to infiltrate her, and felt her presence permeating him even as he dissolved into her.

"You'll be a fine writer," she told him.

"You're prejudiced," he replied.

"Perhaps, but I'm convinced that I'm right – you have that look in your eyes."

"That look is lust, Jenny."

"No, Bill, it's romanticism. You're one of those men who has to dream and then make the dream real."

He finally embraced her one evening, in the doorway of a Victorian school in Whitechapel, where she and Lily were billeted with the rest of the WAAF driving pool. They didn't kiss, but put their foreheads together, and he just leaned against her, pressing into her, short of breath, while the air-raid sirens wailed dementedly and aircraft growled overhead. He explored her body with his hands while burning buildings collapsed nearby, and smiled nervously and stared at her, the smell of smoke in his nostrils, and felt the tears springing to his eyes as he told her the truth.

"I love you," he said.

She didn't reply, but simply nodded and pushed him back, then smiled more shyly than before and opened the door and hurried inside.

The city burned all around him.

He fell in love in that burning, in the midst of death and destruction, and glowed with an ethereal heat in that great conflagration.

"I love her," he whispered.

She hadn't replied, but he took that for a good sign, since the next time they met, when they embraced, he felt her presence more surely. They had a beer in a Soho pub and did not discuss the previous evening, but when they left, arm in arm, to join the others in the hotel in Kensington, he was convinced that his declaration of love had not been forgotten.

And at least she seemed happy.

"Ah!" Denholm exclaimed, grinning broadly, his eyes bloodshot, when they joined him in the familiar, crowded bar. "Our two lovebirds! What a pleasant surprise! We see you less than hithertofore and are most disconsolate. More than that – deeply wounded!"

"Stop it, Denholm," Lily admonished him, flashing Jenny a supportive smile. "You're just jealous 'cause your two weeks leave is over and East Anglia beckons."

"East Anglia?" Bill asked, a little slow on the uptake.

"Afraid so, old chap," Anthony said, his elbows propped up on the bar, his smile weary and sad. "Duty calls, and so forth."

Jenny glanced at both men, then her troubled gaze fell on Lily. Bill sensed their shared fear, that emotion they never mentioned, and then thought of bombing missions over Germany in the dead of the flak-filled night.

He felt oddly guilty.

"Don't look so glum," Denholm said. "After all, you now have Jenny! And besides, we'll be back most weekends to keep our eyes on you."

"Great," Bill said. "Terrific."

The people around the piano were singing *"We'll Meet Again"* and a pretty WAAF, clinging to a flight-lieutenant, was weeping profusely.

"How embarrassing," Denholm said.

"I think it's nice," Lily said.

"And will you cry for me this evening," Denholm asked her, "when I leave for the wars?"

"I dunno. I might. Buy me another couple of drinks and I'll flood the place, which should give you a good laugh."

"You wrong me, Lily."

"No, I don't, Denholm. You'd *like* me to cry – you'd enjoy it – but you'd also laugh at me."

"So have another gin and tonic, Lily. I want to see floods of tears."

"That's not funny," Jenny said.

Denholm didn't stop smiling, but his gaze fell upon her, his eyes red from lack of sleep and a lot of drinking, but still bright and perceptive.

There was a short silence between them, emphasised by the clamour around them, then Lily cleared her throat, brushed the hair from her face, offered a slightly out-of-focus smile and said, "So let's all get drunk before you leave. *Very* drunk! Let's get *really* drunk!"

"Let's do that," the laconic Anthony agreed. "Let's drink away our final hours of freedom and be wicked with it."

"Let's do *that*," Denholm said.

Lily giggled hysterically, Denholm ogled her heaving breasts, and Jenny shrugged as if defeated, then smiled and tugged Bill closer to her. Anthony ordered more drinks and Denholm started telling jokes. The people around the piano were singing, *"Room Five-Hundred-and-Four"* and there was laughter and shouting and the sound of breaking glass, and for once, perhaps because the sky was cloudy, there was no German air raid.

Bill got very drunk indeed, told his friends he would miss them badly, and became even more maudlin when he thought of Denholm and Anthony in East Anglia: climbing into their Lancaster, taking off in the black night, crossing the dark English Channel and flying over France, then heading into the dangerous skies over the Ruhr.

He glanced at his friends, who seemed too young, too unconcerned, then looked at the others in the bar, overwhelmed by their fortitude.

Denholm left the bar with Lily. She had to practically carry him. He kept turning around to wave and losing his balance and falling back into her. Anthony also had to be carried. He was sleeping against the bar. Bill and Jenny managed to waken him and carry him out. He had lost coordination, but they supported him between them, to half-walk, half-drag him across the riotous lobby, then up the well-trodden stairs and along to his room.

He sobered up a little, then. "Denholm's right next door," he told them. "He does not sleep alone, as I do this unfortunate night. That means I will have no rest. His lovely Lily will shriek and moan. I will fall asleep and waken up screaming, thinking the end has come. Ah, well, such is life!"

He laughed and fell into his room, rolled about in the darkness, found the bed as Bill turned on the light and Jenny studied the floor. Bill didn't bother undressing him, simply removing his jacket and tie, then rolled him onto the bed and covered him up with the blankets.

At that moment, Lily moaned in the adjoining room – and Jenny walked out.

Anthony laughed and closed his eyes and then said,

Departures

"Thank you, dear boy. Your concern for me, while truly appreciated, should be directed elsewhere." And he waved his hand to indicate the open door. "Your beloved Jenny has left!"

Bill left the room, slamming the door shut behind him, then hurried along the empty corridor and back down the stairs. Jenny was crossing the lobby. He reached out and took her hand. She tugged it away and kept walking until she was outside.

"Jenny, what – ?"

"I wish to go back to the barracks," she said. "Please fetch me a taxi."

"What's wrong?"

"I need a taxi."

"I know, but what's wrong?"

"What's wrong is that you won't fetch me a taxi. Shall I do it myself?"

She started across the pavement, but he quickly tugged her back. "OK, dammit, I'll get you a cab! Just wait here. OK?"

"Of course," she said. "Naturally."

He stood by the kerb and tried to wave down a taxi. When he glanced over his shoulder, she was tapping her foot, so he turned away and kept waving his hand until a taxi stopped for him.

"Can I take you back to the barracks?" he asked her.

"If you wish," she said primly.

He slipped into the seat beside her, closed the door as the car moved off, then felt the dead weight of the silence that had fallen between them. Looking through the window he saw the railings of Kensington Park. The sky above the lawns was low and cloudy, with not one star in sight.

"Is it me?" he asked finally.

"No, Bill, it isn't you. I'm sorry, but I promise it isn't you. I just got upset."

"Because of Denholm and Anthony?"

"Yes."

"They were just drunk, that's all."

"I know that, but it doesn't make any difference. To them everything's a cheap joke – and Lily's worth more than that."

"They don't mean any harm. They just don't take things too seriously. Dammit, Jenny, they go out there, they drop their bombs on Germany, they get killed off like flies in those raids and so they have to laugh at it."

"*And* at Lily," she replied. "And probably at me. And we forgive them for the reasons you've just stated, and they know that and play on it. God, yes, I sympathise! I know what they go through. But that doesn't give them the right to be so cynical and hold us so cheap."

"They don't."

"Denholm does. Anthony doesn't, but Denholm does. And I don't think it's the war and the constant threat of death. No, I think it's just Denholm, it's his nature, and that's what upsets me."

Bill glanced out the window. The taxi was passing through the West End. Shaftesbury Avenue was packed with troops who were swarming to and fro, slipping in and out of darkness, through doorways surrounded by sand bags, behind black-out curtains.

"Maybe Denholm *is* cynical," he said, "but what the hell, Jenny? He's a good friend for all that."

"To you?"

"To both of us."

"Perhaps I'm just not sophisticated enough to appreciate his urbane ways. I'm just a poor, simple country girl."

"All right, Jenny, that's enough!"

"You admire him. I know *that* much. So just remember this . . . I won't be treated by you the way Denholm treats Lily. I won't be made fun of or talked down to. Do you understand that?"

Shocked, he just stared at her. Her gaze was fierce and steady. Passing behind her, as the taxi moved through the City, were broken walls, skeletal buildings and piles of rubble – the mounting debris of war.

"How can you say that?" he asked her. "How can you talk to me this way, after what I said last night?"

"You mean I owe you for that?"

"Godammit, Jenny, what is this?"

She turned away to gaze out the window.

"I'm a virgin," she whispered.

Struck dumb, he just stared again. She shivered once and then was still. She was wearing her uniform, the peaked cap on her head, and he studied her exposed neck, her shoulders and spine; saw the gas mask strapped around her, now resting on her hip, and trembled and raised his eyes to the ruins slipping by in the darkness.

At that moment she seemed so frail, so defenceless, he wanted to die for her.

"So am I," he confessed instead.

He thought he heard her sniffing, and she certainly raised her head, then turned towards him, smiling tenderly, her eyes softened by his statement, to take hold of his hand and lightly stroke it.

Nodding solemnly, she leaned back against the seat and took a deep breath. She stared straight ahead, still smiling with silent pleasure, and passed the rest of the journey hardly moving, breathing evenly, while Bill, overwhelmed by love's confusion, did not dare to speak.

Eventually, to his relief, the taxi stopped in Whitechapel, outside the grim Victorian school that was now a WAAF barracks.

"'Ere we are, guvnor," the driver said. "Do you want me to wait for you?"

"Yes, thanks," Bill said.

He followed Jenny out and saw her hurrying towards the school. The building, large and ugly, was remarkably untouched, though surrounded by more blackened ruins and mountains of rubble. The Germans attacked this area a lot and that thought was disturbing, but he reached out for Jenny, turned her towards him, and saw her eyes gleaming.

He gazed at her in a silence fraught with tension and increasing embarrassment. Then he pulled her into him, closed his eyes, and took a deep breath.

And finally kissed her.

Her lips were moist and tender, pressing tentatively against his, withdrawing, pressing searchingly this time, then withdrawing for good.

She stepped back and smiled at him.

"Goodnight, Bill," she said.

She stepped backwards into darkness, quietly closing the door, and he turned away, breaking into pieces, and returned to the taxi.

Departures

Then he heard the door opening, heard her calling his name, and turned around to see her beckoning him towards her. He hurried back to stand before her, holding his breath, almost dying. She leaned forward, holding him by the shoulder, to breathe into his ear.

"I love *you*!" she whispered.

This time, when she closed the door, he stood there a long time, unable to imagine a future that did not have her in it.

Chapter Twelve

∽

Bill was feeling guilty when, after a sleepless night thinking of his first love, he kissed Maureen on the cheek, wished her good luck, and watched her being driven off along the Strand in a taxi, heading for Harrod's, where she would spend the morning shopping before her first audition that afternoon.

He felt that in his night of recollection he had somehow betrayed her.

He also felt nervous. While pretending to wait for Maureen downstairs in the Savoy's lobby, he had in fact rung Jenny to confirm that they could meet today for lunch at the Dorchester. Jenny had not been home, but he had heard her voice on the ansaphone, no longer softly sensual, but high-pitched, abrupt and shaky – an old woman's voice.

Checking his wristwatch and noting that he had two hours to spare, he hailed a cab, directed the driver to the Whittington hospital in Archway, North London, then settled back in the seat, wishing that he had not tried to regain his past through a meeting with Jenny.

Departures

He didn't want to see her as she was now.

Nor did he want her to see him.

He was glad to escape the taxi and walk into the old, decaying hospital in Archway. After checking at the reception desk, he had to walk for what seemed like miles, along a draughty corridor that had holes in the linoleum, to a ward of such depressing drabness it almost made him feel ill.

Anthony Barker's golden hair had turned grey and stringy, his sardonic gaze was dulled, and his lengthy battle against the pains of arthritis had erased his aristocratic good looks and replaced them with too many lines on drawn, yellow skin. He was sitting up on the bed, his swollen fingers resting on his lap, but raised his head when Bill stopped beside him.

"Hello, Anthony," Bill said.

Anthony stared at him in silence, his dulled eyes slightly puzzled, then, when recognition came, his smile made him look younger. "Bill!" His voice still sounded youthful. "You actually came! I didn't believe it would happen." He offered his hand, but changed his mind and jerked it away before Bill could shake it. "The arthritis," he explained, shrugging apologetically. "If you shake my hand I might scream. Here, take this chair."

Bill glanced around the ward. Most of the patients seemed fairly old. He saw tubes, plasma jars and limbs in traction, so sat down with reluctance.

"Well, I won't say you haven't changed," he told Anthony, who nodded agreement.

"That's fair enough, Bill. You're looking a bit healthier than I feel and otherwise you've aged quite well. When did we last meet? Eight years ago? It seems a lot longer now."

"Yes, Anthony, it does."

"And who would have thought, during those sunny days in 'Frisco, that this bloody disease was waiting to claim me and put paid to my future?"

"You can't fly forever, Anthony. Even as a commercial airline pilot, you'd have had to retire soon."

"Yes, I know. But I was planning to run a charter aircraft company. Now even that hope is gone."

"You mean there's no way they can cure this?"

"No, I don't think so. I've a severe case of rheumatoid arthritis, which they think is incurable. I take tablets to dull the pain, but they have unfortunate side-effects. All in all, I can't say I'm a ball of fire. I also surrender too often to excessive self-pity, so let's talk about something more pleasant – the good old days and so forth."

"I don't think I'm up to a discussion about the good old days," Bill replied, thinking about his forthcoming lunch with Jenny.

"Then let's talk about you instead. Did you come with your wife?"

"Yes, You've never met her, have you?"

"No."

"She's very beautiful, but ten years younger than me. I'm now at that age where the difference is noticeable, and I can't say I'm finding it a thrill."

"You mean *she* makes you feel bad?"

"No, not at all. On the contrary, she's wonderful. It's just that . . . Well, to be truthful, I'm not too good at it any more – and although she insists that she doesn't mind, I feel bad about it." Anthony rolled his eyes, but Bill ignored him. "There's also the unfortunate fact that we don't have any children and that Maureen's career went into a decline. It's causing some problems."

"She was an actress, wasn't she?"

"Yes. Pretty successful on the New York stage. She went to Hollywood, had a pretty bad time, then met me on the Warner lot, the day I sold my first screenplay."

"In other words, you were going up as she went down."

"Right. Now she wants to get back into acting, which is something I understand. If I seem a bit nervous, it's because I'm hoping, with Denholm's help, to fix her up with a good role here in London. She's going this afternoon to the first of two auditions, but if both end in rejection, the damage caused might be more than our good intentions were worth."

"That's a chance you'll have to take," Anthony said.

"Yes, I guess so."

Bill lowered his gaze, ashamed of himself, aware that although he was feeling uneasy about Maureen, he was even more nervous about the lunch that was rapidly approaching.

"How's Denholm?" Anthony asked. "His usual amoral, witty self?"

"He never changes. Aren't you in touch?"

Anthony shrugged. "Oh, you know Denholm: always on the hop. Running here and there; doing this and that. An energetic, entertaining, self-centred man who rarely dwells on the past. Out of sight, out of mind."

Bill sensed a slight edge of bitterness, which he chose to ignore. "When did you last see him?"

"About five years ago. At that squadron reunion you managed to avoid by being in LA. I was OK, then. At least the arthritis was just starting. I thought it was just middle age, a little stiffening of the bones, and that I could cure it by getting more sunshine. How little I knew!" He sighed and glanced reflexively at his crippled hands, then looked up again. "Anyway, I seemed fairly normal, Denholm was his usual self, we both had a very good evening, then went our separate ways. But since I never married and Denholm did, it sort of placed us in different worlds."

"Denholm has always lived like a single man."

"But his friends don't, dear boy."

"And since then?"

Anthony shrugged again. "I haven't seen him since then, though I often see his name in the papers – the big financier, backing the more glamorous industries, such as TV, the movies, and advertising. But I also see *you* on TV. Overpaid, over-sexed, and over here – things haven't changed much." Bill laughed, remembering that old phrase. "Anyway," Anthony continued, "you always *did* say you were going to be a writer – and you finally made it. I'm glad for you, Bill."

"Why?"

"Because you earned it."

"A lot of luck, Anthony."

"I survived the war by luck, but I also earned it – luck's only part of it. As for you, you didn't sell out. You wrote for the movies, certainly, but you wrote about vital issues; and from what I've read, you also do important social work – so you've earned your good times."

Bill smiled to cover his embarrassment. "I may have selfish reasons. I get a lot of the material for my screenplays from the unfortunate souls I help. Maybe that's why I do it."

"I don't think so, Bill. You were always the one with high ideals. The one we all liked to tease."

"I enjoyed it."

"I know." Anthony smiled, but even that seemed to hurt him. He shifted uneasily on the bed, pulled his hands up, cursed softly. "So, this movie you're planning to make with Denholm?"

"It's actually based on my experiences with you guys during the war. Truth is, I don't think I'd have progressed beyond local journalism if I hadn't been inspired by those few months in London. I have to admit, it was a great experience. War is evil, but it has its good points. And I suppose that's the movie I want to make: about the war's good points."

"Ah, yes, they were surely the days! All of us together in that hotel . . . Will you make us immortal?"

"No resemblance between persons living or dead – that much I can guarantee."

Anthony chuckled. "Yes, I believe you. All fiction, of course." He dragged his crippled hands laboriously across the white sheet, then moved them back again, intrigued by their uselessness. "I wonder what happened to Jenny," he said distractedly, "after she vanished from London during VE day? Did you ever find out?"

"No," Bill lied.

"You were very much in love, as I remember."

Bill sighed. "Yes, I was." He glanced around the ward, distracting himself from his dishonesty. "This hospital's very *old*," he said, "and depressing as hell. It makes me ill just to look at it."

Anthony put his head back, winced with pain, then managed a chuckle. "How true!" he said. "I feel I'm in a

Charles Dickens novel – *Bleak House* or *Hard Times*. It's tolerable when one is asleep. When awake, it's a bad dream."

"Can't you go somewhere else?"

"No. I can't afford private treatment."

"Would you be better off elsewhere if you *could* afford it?"

"Perhaps. Here, they're understaffed and short on finance. They just can't keep up."

"I think you'd feel a lot better in more pleasant surroundings. Tell you what . . . I have an old pal, a Harley Street specialist in bone diseases. I'm going to give him a call, get the name of a hospital that specialises in your kind of problem, then have you transferred there for private treatment and some second opinions. You might be surprised."

"Very kind of you, Bill, but I really can't afford to – "

"It's on me. Let's say it's for old times' sake."

"I really can't – "

"Please, Anthony, I insist. It's the least I can do."

Anthony put his head back, closed his eyes, and took a deep breath.

"I'm at your mercy," he said.

"Great. Thataboy!" Bill reached out to squeeze Anthony's shoulder, but remembering his condition, he stood up instead, preparing to leave. "I have to run," he said. "A business lunch. But I'll be in touch soon. OK?"

"OK, Bill."

"Adios."

"I'll be seeing you."

Remembering that old song, Bill smiled and left the

ward, then hurried out of the hospital and waved down a taxi.

He sighed, feeling forlorn, as the taxi, crawling through dense London traffic, made its way to the Dorchester.

Yes, he was nervous, not knowing what to expect, so when he arrived at the hotel and took his seat in that grand restaurant, he ordered a large Scotch, drank half of it too quickly, and felt his heart leaping each time an elderly woman came through the door.

Jenny was late.

Very late.

Then, suddenly, there she was.

Bill's heart almost missed a beat.

Chapter Thirteen

It was shock.

Jenny came towards him on the arm of the *maitre d'hotel*, tottering on high heels, tugging distractedly at a Victorian black-lace dress, wearing across her shoulders what looked like a dead animal, and blowing a cloud of smoke from brightly painted lips in a heavily mascared face.

Bill didn't realise for a moment that this creature was his guest, but when he saw the bemused *maitre d'hotel* (not the mere table waiter, he noted) bearing down on his table, his heart started beating again, though his spirits did not rise.

"Darling!" the creature called out from a distance, her voice resounding above the babble of the other diners. "You haven't changed a bit! You look positively, absolutely divine, dear! *Do* let me kiss you!"

She jerked her elbow out of the helping hand of the *maitre d'hotel* and leaned over Bill, filling his nostrils with a tropical jungle of perfume and planting a sticky kiss on his blushing cheek, then said, "There! How did that feel?"

"Very nice, Jenny."

"*Jennifer!*" she corrected him firmly. "All my friends call me *Jennifer!*"

After staring sternly at him, she broke into a gaudy smile, then turned to blow smoke in the bemused *maitre d'hotel*'s plump face and said, "Well, my good man?"

"Certainly, Madame! Of course!"

While Bill removed the lipstick from his face with his napkin, the *maitre d'hotel* hastily pulled Jennifer's chair back. When she was seated, he snapped his fingers for service and then hurried away, clearly keen to return to his proper duties by the restaurant door.

"What's *that* you're drinking?" Jennifer asked.

"*What?*" Bill said, embarrassed. "Oh, Scotch."

"Not good at lunchtime, darling. Too harsh on the liver. I'll have a Campari with soda – and the menu, of course!"

"Yes," Bill mumbled. "Of course."

Hardly able to look at her, he ordered the drink from one waiter and was given two menus by the other. Not wishing to appear rude, he set the menus on the table beside him and forced himself to gaze directly at his guest, whose broad, vividly painted lips were no longer smiling.

"What a cheek!" she exclaimed.

"Pardon?" he replied, his heart sinking when he saw that this was definitely Jenny Birken, her face now cadaverous, her skin like ancient parchment, her lips thin and brightly painted, a blonde wig on her head.

Only her eyes were unchanged, still bright-green and

lively; though he sensed that there was something desperate about them as they focused upon him.

"When I arrived," she said, "and gave the *maitre d'* your name, he tried to have me escorted here by a common waiter – a mere boy, if you will! Well, I soon changed *that*, didn't I!"

It was not a question, but a statement, given at great volume, and it made a few of those at the nearest tables turn curiously towards them.

"Yes," Bill said. "I noticed."

"Service isn't what it used to be," she replied. "Not even here. So how are you, Bill, dear?"

Her smile was tremulous and unnatural, making him squirm. "I'm fine," he said. "I – "

"Waiter!" she snapped, turning her head and glaring at him. "Where's my *aperitif*?"

"I believe it's coming, Madame," the waiter replied. "In fact, I see that – "

"Ah, good!" Jennifer said, breaking into a purple smile as the other waiter returned with her drink. "Excellent!" When the waiter handed her the glass, she indicated that he should stay a moment. She sampled the Campari, sighed and muttered, "It'll do!", then waved the waiter away with her free hand and beamed brightly again. "So, Bill, how are you, dear?"

"I'm fine. I – "

"Perhaps we should order the food, darling. You know *how long* they take to serve one in these dreadful hotels." She picked up the menu. "Most *impressive*!" she said.

Bill glanced uneasily around him, then at the menu, while his guest put her menu down, lit one cigarette with the butt of another, blew another cloud of disgusting smoke and perused the menu again.

"It's all terribly English," she said, without looking up. "That's why I suggested this place – because it's so English."

"Yes," Bill said, "so I noticed."

"Of course, now that it's a *tourist* attraction, God knows what the food's like!" She stared haughtily at the offended waiter. His spine stiffened visibly. "I'll have the smoked salmon, then the roast beef, and then the plum pudding. I want everything well done. And you, Bill, dear?"

"The same, thanks."

"How very adventurous of you. And shall we wash the meat down with a little red?"

"Yes," Bill muttered.

"Nothing *too* expensive, darling! I've been here before and the prices are quite atrocious! Just make sure that what you get is as rich as blood and has a good punch, ha, ha. What about a bottle of – ?" She rattled off a name in French and Bill nodded agreement.

The waiter retreated, looking relieved, leaving Bill alone with her.

There was a brief, tingling silence.

"So, dear Bill," she said in a rush of smoky air, "tell me everything you've been up to."

"Well, I – "

"A Hollywood screenwriter! How exciting it must be! I suppose you know all the stars and have sumptuous gatherings."

"Not really. I actually live fairly modestly with my – "

"Of course, Americans can't act, can they? I mean,

they're strictly *personalities*. They can't speak and have precious little bearing – all that mumbling and scratching. Not *my* thing at all, I'm sure!"

Bill hardly knew what to say. He was still feeling embarrassed. He was also ashamed of his self-consciousness, but could not help himself. Her voice was so loud, it was making a lot of heads turn, and when they did, what they saw was this . . . *actress;* this tartly dressed up, histrionic old lady blowing smoke like a train.

Bill wanted to hide.

"You go to the movies a lot?" he asked, desperate for something to say.

"No. Hardly ever. Television at home is so much more civilised, don't you think?" – the question was purely rhetorical – "and of course the quality is so much higher here than it is in your country, don't you agree?"

"I wouldn't know, Jenny. I – "

"Jennifer," she corrected him, looking stern.

"Sorry," he said, finishing his Scotch. "I've never really thought of you as Jennifer. Back then, it was Jenny."

"It was not."

"It was."

"You know that simply isn't true, Bill. The name 'Jenny' is common."

"I like it."

"I do not."

"OK, Jennifer, I'm sorry. Memory plays tricks on us all. It was just a mistake."

She beamed with pleasure. "Of course, Bill."

But it wasn't a mistake. He knew damned well it wasn't. He had never called her 'Jennifer' in his life – at least not until now.

"Bread, Madame?" asked the waiter who had materialised beside her.

"Is it extra?"

"No, Madame."

"Very good. I'll have brown, thanks. No, I won't – that bread doesn't look fresh. Please remove it." When the waiter had departed, Jennifer offered another ghastly smile and a cloud of blue smoke. "Standards definitely are falling, dear. Even here. They get so many Americans with their notorious bad taste."

Bill couldn't believe his ears. He wondered if she was joking. He forced himself to look at her, saw purple lips pursed primly, and noted that the brilliant green eyes held that odd luminosity. She didn't appear to be joking.

"Salmon, Madame?" the next waiter asked.

"Of course!" she snapped. "I ordered it! And let's hope it's a lot fresher than the bread."

She talked incessantly through the salmon and Bill didn't interrupt her, feeling too dazed and disbelieving. She also talked throughout the main course, hardly stopping for breath, managing between the food and careful sips of the red wine to inform him that London had changed terribly since he'd last been here, that standards had slipped dramatically, and that tourism, which propped up London's economy, was also destroying it.

"The Japanese with their cameras, the Germans with their bad manners, the noisy French and Italians and Spanish, plus half of uneducated Asia *and* American crassness. It's too much, dear. It really is."

"*I'm* American," he reminded her.

"But you're exceptional," she informed him.

"Otherwise, we wouldn't be sharing this table, as we once shared our past."

So the subject was actually mentioned. She was on the plum pudding by then. She had offended the waiters and caused whispering at nearby tables, but finally, the past had been mentioned, which made it real for the first time.

Perhaps also for her.

She went silent for a moment, looking vaguely embarrassed, pushed the remains of her pudding aside and lit up a cigarette. She blew the smoke sideways, away from him for a change, then let her gaze wander around the enormous Grill Room, as if looking for old friends.

Bill used the opportunity to study her. He felt more sane in the silence. He tried to see the girl he had loved, to find the Jenny in Jennifer, but the face that was now turned in profile possessed nothing familiar.

Only the eyes – the vivid green eyes – were the same as they had been.

Almost, but not quite.

They possessed a new, oddly unfocused intensity . . . as if gazing inward . . .

Perhaps she was mad.

Bill could hardly recognise her – perhaps slightly; no more – and he felt a great sadness and disappointment when she turned back towards him.

Her green eyes were wet, staring tragically at him, and she reached across the table to take his hand and squeeze it affectionately.

Her skin was dry and seemed cold.

"Darling, Bill," she said, loudly. "It *is* wonderful to see you again. When I saw you on TV, I simply couldn't believe my eyes – you, alive and well! I felt that I was going to faint, so great was the shock. And delight, of course. I wept tears of joy. I couldn't sleep for days after, being flooded with old memories, thinking repeatedly of those few months we had together – the hotel in Kensington, the Dome of St Paul's Cathedral, tea at the Ritz, our trip to Cornwall – and I felt so sad and happy at once, I surely knew what my tears were for. We *were* in love, weren't we, Bill? So deeply and truly. And I remembered it all, every moment, every detail, and then wrote to you, feeling that I was talking to you, that you really were that close. And now, here you are!"

Bill felt more embarrassed than ever, convinced that what he was witnessing was a performance, rather than the real thing. Certainly that painted mask was a disguise for more than age; and as he studied it carefully, intrigued by those tearful eyes, he sensed that there was something theatrical beneath the emotion.

Which only made him feel more let down.

"I think I should tell you," he began, anticipating complications, "that I'm married now, and I – "

She squeezed his hand again. "I know, Bill. You told me so – "

"I did?"

"In your letter. But please don't worry, Bill. I harbour no illusions. I understand fully that we are not what we once were. I also know that we cannot re-live the past or get back what we've lost. That was not the point of asking to see you. So please relax, dearest Bill."

She released his hand, inhaled on her cigarette, glancing at the other diners with disdain before looking back at him.

"So," he ventured, being offered a chance to speak, "you said in your letter that shortly after I was shipped out to Europe, you were wounded in an air raid, hospitalised for some time, then eventually sent back to Cornwall."

"That is correct, Bill."

"And clearly you recovered."

"Yes, Bill, completely."

"OK now, are you?"

"Of course. Don't I *look* fine?"

"You look wonderful," he lied. "You really do. Still beautiful, Jenny."

"Jennifer."

"Sorry – Jennifer."

"Thank you, Bill," she said with an odd formality. "You always were sweet."

"Are you married?"

She looked sad. "No, Bill, I'm not."

"You *never* got married?"

She blew another cloud of smoke, wiped a tear from her eye, looked melodramatically tragic and said, "No, dearest Bill, I did not. I have never been married."

She stared at him almost accusingly, then sighed and continued.

"Oh, I came close a few times, almost said 'yes' once or twice, but in the end, I just couldn't do it – I always backed off."

She sniffed again, wiped her moist eyes with a handkerchief, then looked deeply wounded.

"I have to confess, it was you, Bill. I was in love with your memory. You were the finest, the *only* love of my life and I couldn't forget you. So, I never married. I lived alone all those years. When my wounds had healed, I left home and returned to London, where I kept to myself and lived as a poor, single woman, taking on any work I could find. It was difficult, Bill, *very* difficult, but at least I survived."

Her eyes were still moist, her painted lips were trembling, and she sniffed back more tears.

Bill started to warm to her. He almost saw the Jenny in Jennifer. He thought of what she had once been, what she had meant to him, and decided that the passing of time had not destroyed everything.

Jenny lived inside Jennifer. That lost girl had not died. The goodness and courage that had first drawn him to her still existed in that old woman's spirit.

He reached across the table to take her hand. Then he smiled at her.

"You wrote in your letter," he said softly, taking care not to offend her, "that you had a specific reason for seeing me."

She slipped her hand out of his, inhaled on her cigarette, blew a cloud of smoke across the table and smiled boldly at him.

"Because I need money," she informed him. "And who *else* could I turn to?"

He was utterly speechless.

Chapter Fourteen

∽

After shopping in Harrod's as a way of passing the morning, Maureen returned to the Savoy, luxuriated in the bath, then dressed in a skirt and jacket of simple grey and ivory elegance, enhanced her good legs with matching high-heels and went down to catch the limousine that the TV company had thoughtfully sent for her.

Since the TV company was in the West End, the journey did not take long and soon she was walking through swinging doors into a lobby constructed like an atrium and designed to impress. It was mostly glass and steel, with white marble floors and abstract paintings, and the girls behind the white computers on the gleaming white desks were all young and pretty and mostly blonde-haired to match the decor.

It did not seem like a place for creative work. It looked more like a bank.

Rendered even more nervous by this ostentatious flaunting of wealth, Maureen presented herself to the white-shirted guard in the lobby and was directed, with

Departures

no trace of a smile, to one of the desks. A pretty blonde stared up at her, dismissed her and turned away, concentrated instead on the flickering screen of her computer and asked, as if speaking to herself, "Yes? Can I help you?"

"I've come to see Richard Postman."

"Who?"

"Richard Postman. The director."

"Oh, right. Just a mo'." The girl picked up a 'phone, pressed a button, hurriedly covered the mouthpiece with her hand and whispered, "Who *are* you?"

"Maureen Kennedy," Maureen replied, remembering to use her professional name. "I'm an actress. I – "

"Right." The girl waved her hand, telling Maureen to be silent, then announced her to the other end of the line and put the phone down. "Take a seat," she said. "He won't be long. He's busy right now."

"But I have an appointment for two o'clock – "

"He's busy. Can you *please* take a seat?"

Taken aback by the girl's impatience, Maureen took a seat near the swinging doors, hoping that her blushing wouldn't show and wishing that Bill was here with her.

She waited a long time. She had never waited that long before. She tried reminding herself that she wasn't well known any more, that her days of glory were past, but she still felt a touch of resentment at being treated off-handedly.

Did she really want to go through with this? Right now, she wasn't sure. She knew only that she was unhappy, dissatisfied with her life, and that having no children to look after, she needed something to do. She was about to turn fifty, but felt younger, *looked* younger; and though time was an increasingly precious commodity, she was letting it slip past.

She needed more than Bill's love and a good marriage to keep her engaged.

Yet, as she waited . . . and waited . . . she remembered what it was like to be an actress . . . and started feeling misgivings.

Eventually, the blonde waved her over to the desk and told her to present herself on the second floor.

"Mr Postman's assistant will be waiting for you," she said, "when you get out of the lift."

"Thank you."

"No sweat."

It was a silvery metallic lift, its floor richly carpeted, with background music playing from hidden speakers as it carried her up to the second floor. As she stood there, alone, she started wishing she hadn't come. Then the lift stopped. The door opened and she hurried forward, almost bumping into the smiling man who was standing in front of her.

"Whoops!" he exclaimed in a feathery whisper. "Not too eagerly, dear-heart!"

He grabbed her by the elbows, flashed his perfect teeth, let her get a good smell of his *eau de cologne*, then slipped his cravat off his loose-sleeved shirt and said, "Maureen Kennedy?"

"Yes. I'm sorry, I – "

"I'm Terence – Mr Postman's personal assistant. This way, my angel!"

"Please call me Maureen."

"Of course, pet!"

He waltzed her through an open-plan office filled with

steel-framed glass partitions, more typists and computer operators, then down a flight of stairs and into a crowded control-booth. The engineers at the console glanced up when she entered, but immediately, without waiting to be introduced, went back to their work.

"Have you met Richard before?" Terence asked without looking at her, his admiring gaze focused instead on the studio below.

"No," she said.

"He's a monster," Terence said. "An absolute tyrant. But he's so *creative*, a genuine *artiste*, that one has to forgive him. That's him – that one there."

He was pointing down at a well-fed man who, wearing a white shirt with matching pants and tennis shoes, and with his black hair waved and greased in the fashion of the 1950s, was melodramatically bawling out a young actress wearing a 19th century dress. Bathed in the hot brilliance of the arc-lights, the actress was sobbing and dabbing at her tearful eyes with a handkerchief, but the director continued bawling and waving his hands, while the technicians, standing behind the TV cameras, were either grinning or looking bored.

Even in the safety of the control-booth above the studio, Maureen shared that girl's humiliation.

"He seems a little temperamental," Maureen muttered.

"Oh, he is, sweet! So talented!"

It was not Maureen's view that temperament necessarily went hand-in-hand with talent, but she kept her opinion to herself as Richard Postman screamed one last time at the weeping actress, violently kicked the basket of flowers at her feet, then stomped out of the studio, slamming the door shut.

When the technicians broke into applause, the sobbing actress jumped up and fled.

Terence turned to Maureen and flashed his perfect teeth. "Isn't he *wonderful*?" Then he hurried to open the door of the control booth and await his master's arrival.

Postman arrived soon enough, wiping his sweaty brow and saying, "Christ, I can't take much more of this! That one practically *lisped*!" He brushed past Maureen, glared down at the studio and said, "How did the bitch sound from up here? Never mind! I don't want to know! I need a glass of iced water. *Terence!*"

"Yes, Richard!"

Terence gave him a glass of water. He drank it down in one gulp. When Terence handed him a towel, he wiped the sweat from his face, took a deep breath, stared stonily at Maureen and asked, "Who are you?"

She wanted to slap his face, but instead just gave her name. He smiled then, without charm, handed the towel back to Terence, was given a cigar and had it lit by his assistant, then leaned against the bench by the console and said, "Of course! Maureen Kennedy! You've come to discuss the role of – "

"I thought it was an audition."

"We haven't got that far yet. This is just a preliminary discussion about the role – *and* to ascertain if it's worth going further with you."

"Oh," Maureen said, feeling crushed. "I'd thought – "

Postman put his head back and blew a stream of smoke at the ceiling. "Of course I've heard of your work," he said. "Mostly the New York stage, wasn't it?"

"I did a little movie work as well, but – "

"It didn't last long, right?"

"Right," she said, humiliated.

"Too mature for stardom, were you?"

"I got married," she responded.

"That doesn't show too much dedication – giving it up just for marriage."

"We all go through these phases."

He actually smiled at that, but again without charm. "So," he said, "you want to make a come-back and work in TV."

"I wouldn't exactly call it a come-back," she said. "I was never *that* well known."

"Very honest of you to say so."

"Not at all."

"Have you ever worked on TV?"

"Yes, a little. The odd supporting role or guest spot – up to about five years ago. All of it in Hollywood, naturally."

"Naturally!" Postman said.

Maureen looked around her. The technicians were still at the console. They were smoking and staring at her and Postman with bored curiosity. Down below, in the studio, the technicians were filing out through the door, doubtless going for tea.

"Excuse me," she said to Postman, "but could we conduct this interview somewhere else? I'd like to sit down."

"I don't have the time," Postman said, "and this won't take long."

"We have ten minutes," Terence said.

Maureen sighed. "Is this where you'll be shooting the mini-series?"

"Only some of it," Postman replied. "Just a few interiors. This is an Anglo-American production, with money also coming from Europe. It's a three-generational saga about two 19th century wine-producing families – one in France, the other in California – so we'll be doing a lot of location work in France, which is advantageous tax-wise. We have a shooting schedule of three months, commencing early next year. Do you think you could manage that?"

It was a lot longer than Maureen had anticipated. Three months away from home. Three months away from Bill. And, even worse, three months in the hands of this egomaniac.

Thinking about it, her heart sank.

"Yes," she said, indecisively.

"You sound hesitant."

"I'm not. Denholm sent me the script – "

"Denholm Wilding! Mister Money!" He and Terence both laughed.

" – and I think I'd be good in the role. Katherine Brennan is my age, she's from an Irish immigrant family, her vineyards are in California, and, like me, she is . . . childless."

"Ah, yes," Postman replied with a smirk, "that's a very good point. You'll understand *that*, at least!"

The condescension was insulting and made her cheeks burn, overlaying her humiliation with an anger that at least gave protection.

"Of course," Postman continued, blowing smoke and studying the ceiling as if in deep thought, "an awful lot of home-grown tomatoes *also* want this part, and since the production is so prestigious they'd work practically for free."

"I won't work practically for free," Maureen replied, "but at least I'm American."

Postman glanced at her, then blew more smoke at the ceiling. "British actresses are so well trained," he said, "they can adopt any accent."

It was clear to Maureen that what was at issue was not her talent, but her willingness to crawl to her director. She had suffered this before, with so many, so many times, and the thought of having to do so again was too much to bear. She wanted to return to acting, she *needed* it, but perhaps not this badly.

"I'm sure an American actress would be much more convincing," she said, "and I *know* I can do justice to the role. *Please* try me out, Mr Postman."

"Richard. We don't go in for formality here. Just call me 'Richard'."

"Please try me out, Richard."

She was ashamed of herself, could hardly believe that she had said it, and felt the nausea rising in her stomach as her cheeks started burning.

And when Postman sighed, as if making a momentous decision, she felt even worse.

"Well," he said slowly, savouring each of his golden words, "I suppose, if you're *that* keen, I should at least give you a chance . . . You'll audition?"

"That's what I came here for."

"When do you fly back to LA?"

"In ten days."

"What about Friday, then, for the audition? Say, eleven a.m.?"

"That would be fine."

"See you then."

"Right, Mr Postman – I mean, Richard. I'll see you on Friday."

"*Ciao*, baby!"

"Thank you."

Terence waltzed her out of the booth, back across the open-plan office, then showed her into the lift and waved her goodbye. The descent was an eternity. She felt as if she was suffocating. She had been reminded, brutally, of the humiliations of her old profession, and so was very glad to make her way back out into the street, where she stood for a time, too shocked to move, her confidence already in tatters, her conviction collapsing.

She wanted Bill there, beside her.

Chapter Fifteen

~

Greatly relieved to have escaped from the Grill Room, but still in a state of shock at being hijacked by his past, Bill led Jennifer out of the Dorchester and stood beside her on the pavement of Park Lane. The afternoon was dismal, the wide road jammed with traffic, and Hyde Park, at the far side of the road, was sulking under low clouds.

"A taxi, sir?" the doorman asked.

"Yes, thanks," Bill replied.

"No, thank you, my good man," Jennifer loudly contradicted him. "We are within walking distance of my home, so take your begging hand elsewhere."

Balanced precariously on her ridiculous high heels and not helped by too much wine, she took hold of Bill's arm and started walking him along the pavement of Park Lane, towards Piccadilly.

"I picked the Dorchester Grill, dear Bill," she explained helpfully, "not only because it's so English, but also because it's close to where I live."

"Where's that?"

"Shepherd Market. It's an elegant little square in the heart of Mayfair, filled with restaurants, pubs, and high-class prostitutes. You'd need a fortune to buy there now, but I've been lucky in that regard. I'm a sitting tenant in a small flat – sorry, apartment – above a wine bar. It can get noisy in the evenings, but being busy it makes me feel safe. And it *is* lovely to be able to live there, in the midst of the rich, most of whom are foreigners."

"What's a sitting tenant?"

"A tenant who can't be thrown out or have his or her rent put up."

"Ah," Bill said. "I see."

In fact, he felt like screaming. Apart from her hysterical performance during lunch, her shameless request for money had made him feel so totally exploited as to render him speechless.

A forty-year-old romance down the tubes.

"Let me get this straight," he said, being obliged to walk with her along Park Lane. "As you said during lunch, you've been running some kind of club in Soho – "

"A *gentleman's* club," she reiterated firmly.

"Right, a gentleman's club, running into heavy debts. If you don't find twenty thousand pounds pretty soon, you'll be declared bankrupt and your club – your sole means of survival – will have to be repossessed."

"Yes, Bill dear, that's correct."

"And you want me to give you the money, right?"

"Wrong. I want you to *lend* it to me."

"But you've no idea how you're going to repay it."

"That's certainly correct. But I repeat that given a little time, I think the club can survive."

Departures

"I still don't understand why the club's not making money. It certainly *seems* busy."

"It's Colonel Qadaffi, dear. He has the Americans terrified. My business depends on tourism, mostly American, and at the moment your fellow countrymen, never renowned for their courage, are keeping well clear of Britain because of Qadaffi's threats of reprisal. Once this whole thing dies down, the Americans will return, as loudmouthed as before, and then hopefully my business will pick up again."

"How many times do I have to remind you," Bill said, "that *I'm* an American?"

"Oh, be quiet, Bill. Stop being so sensitive. You *know* I think you're quite different. But *most* Americans . . . Oh, dear!"

As they turned into Piccadilly, Bill had the urge to run away, but couldn't do so because of the Jenny he had loved all those years ago. She was still here, in Jennifer, clinging unsteadily to him, and though he felt exploited, he could not disown what she had become, nor pretend she was someone else.

The love he had felt in 1944 lived on in him still.

He owed her something for that.

Nevertheless, what she was asking was outrageous and had to be dealt with.

"Can't you just get a loan from the bank," he asked, "until things pick up again?"

"No, Bill dear, I can't. My credit is overdrawn."

"And you can't remortgage the property?"

"I'm mortgaged up to the hilt already."

"So if you don't find that twenty thousand pounds you'll definitely go bankrupt?"

"Yes, Bill, I'm afraid so."

"That's an awful lot of money."

"That's why I'm asking *you*, Bill."

The impertinence was shocking. It also made him feel degraded. He had carried the memory of her all these years, shouldered the secret guilt of his enduring love for her, and was now faced with the knowledge that her sole reason for seeing him was to use him.

"It's a lot to ask for, Jennifer."

"I don't have a choice, Bill dear. Either I sink or I swim. Believe me, I need it."

"I'm sure you do. But please bear in mind that if I even considered giving it – "

"Lending it!"

" – I wouldn't be able to do so without consulting my wife."

"No!" she snapped. *"Definitely not!"*

She let go of his arm and stepped away from him. "You *can't* tell your wife! Don't even consider it! How can you explain this to your wife without telling her about us? No, Bill, you *definitely* cannot tell her. *I forbid you to tell her!*"

"But, dammit, Jenny – "

"Jennifer!"

"Twenty thousand pounds, Jennifer! I'm not sure I can afford that kind of money – or even that I should lend it if I could. Dammit, why should I?"

She walked closer to him, eyes flaring. "You can afford it!" she whispered angrily. "I've read all about you. You can certainly lend me that amount without suffering unduly. And since you can do it, you *should* do it. You owe me at least that much for the worst years of my life, when I thought I'd lost you forever. I was in need then, Bill, and there was no one to help me. Now, when I'm in even worse trouble, I *can* be helped by you. How can you *refuse* me?"

"I might have to," he said.

She stepped back, looking shocked, started to speak but changed her mind, then turned away and started up Half Moon Street. Then she stopped, tottered sideways, practically fell against the wall, and doubled up, clutching at her stomach and gasping for breath. She let out an anguished moan.

Bill hurried up to steady her. "Are you OK?" he asked.

She waved her hand impatiently. "Don't worry, I'm fine. It's just a minor, rather embarrassing complaint. Nothing to worry about."

"Are you sure?"

"Yes, I'm sure, Bill."

She took a deep breath, straightened up, breathed more evenly, then shook her head. "My, my, how embarrassing! I'd better be getting home now! Thank you, Bill. I'm sorry to have troubled you. Please forget I ever existed."

She looked like she was hurting – even her tears seemed real – so when she started to walk away again he impulsively stopped her. "Please, Jennifer! One moment!"

Though hurt and disillusioned by her exploitation of their love, he was haunted by the feeling that whether play-acting or not, this Jennifer, who had once been his Jenny, was in certain ways genuine.

"OK," he said. "I'm sorry. I'm being a bit ungracious. You just took me by surprise, that's all, and now I feel pretty bad. What the hell! What can I lose? Let me think about it, Jennifer. Tell you what: let me come to your club and look the place over. How does that sound?"

"You don't have to – "

"Yes, Jennifer, I do. So what's the address?"

She opened her handbag and withdrew a card. "Here it is," she said, giving him the card. "We're open from five in the evening. Could you make it tomorrow night?"

"Sure," he said. "I think so."

"I'll see you then, Bill."

"Yes, Jennifer."

She looked thoughtfully at him, eyes bright yet touched with darkness, then leaned forward, kissed him on the cheek and hurried away – a still sprightly, distinctly flamboyant figure, giving life to his past.

Chapter Sixteen

Jennifer waited a few minutes, then glanced back along Half Moon Street and, taking note that Bill had disappeared, retraced her steps to Piccadilly. After checking again that he had gone, she hailed a taxi and asked for Highgate.

She heaved a sigh of relief when the taxi moved off.

While the pain had subsided, she still felt badly shaken by the intensity of the attack she had suffered – more so because of being reminded that her remaining days were numbered and destined to be filled with pain. Nevertheless, she felt deeply ashamed of her embarrassing performance in the Dorchester, even though she was aware that it had been caused by her nervousness at meeting Bill after so many years. To make matters worse, she was also feeling guilty over the shock she had given him by asking him, more blatantly than she had intended, to lend her the money.

He had reacted as if his face had just been slapped, then looked disillusioned and deeply wounded.

It had made her feel dirty.

Sighing, she glanced out as the taxi turned into

Frognal Lane, moving uphill between imposing Victorian houses, under trees shedding brown leaves, then along narrow, winding roads. She thought of Bill and felt rotten, having hurt him so badly, destroying his faith in her, making him think she was a parasite, trying to live off old memories.

Why hadn't she just told him the truth? Because it could have been dangerous. She couldn't tell him just yet, since he wasn't the only one who could suffer. There were others to think about . . .

"Damn!" she whispered, admonishing herself. "What a mess it all is!"

Closing her eyes, she felt her heart racing, so breathed evenly to make it slow down. She opened her eyes to the trees and rolling fields of Hampstead Heath, and was reminded of Cornwall, green hills above the sea, where she and Bill, for one blissful weekend, had found exquisite happiness. Then she glanced down at her shrinking, blue-veined hands and shuddered with grief.

There was not much time left.

"Whereabouts in Highgate?" the driver asked her.

"Just drop me off by the Green, please."

"Right, luv," he replied.

He pulled up at Pond Square, which no longer had a pond, and she clambered out, paid him, and stood there until he had driven off. She glanced around the square, at the old, pretty houses, then walked up the garden path to Carol's house.

The front door was open. Instantly made nervous, she entered the house . . . and found Carol in the lounge, sitting at the *secretaire*, leafing through a pile of papers, ghostly in the gloomy light of the beautiful, old-fashioned room. She looked up when Jennifer walked in, then smiled wanly at her.

"Oh," she said, "it's you."

"I got a fright when I saw the open door. I thought it was burglars."

"No, just little old me."

"You should close the door, Carol."

"I normally do. I just forgot. And burglars, I'm beginning to think, would be the least of my worries."

Jennifer glanced around the room, taking note of the packing crates and wrapping paper. "What do you mean?"

Carol picked up some papers, made a fan out of them, then let them fall like the autumn leaves. "I've just been going through John's papers and can confirm what I told you before: things don't look good. Can I pour you a drink?"

"No, thanks. I had some wine at lunchtime and my stomach was hell."

"*Wine* at lunchtime!" Carol smiled as she stood to pour herself a sherry. "What *was* the occasion?"

"Just an old friend," Jennifer lied. "You wouldn't know her. So, what's the problem?"

Carol had a sip of sherry and sat down at the cluttered *secretaire*. "As you know, John liked us to live in style – a big house, the flash cars, all the travelling, his active social life, and so forth."

"He certainly liked to spend what he earned."

"That's the problem. He was spending a lot *more* than he earned. That twenty thousand pounds overdraft I mentioned is just the tip of the iceberg; it also seems that he's been overdrawn constantly for the past few years, has other gambling debts and loans, and recently, to pay some of them off, cashed in his insurance policies, leaving me with nothing but responsibility for the remaining debts."

"Dear God," Jennifer said, which was no help. "And the house?"

Carol shook her head despairingly. "His debts are shocking. Much worse than I'd thought. If I sell the house, that'll certainly cover *most* of them; but it'll still leave some to be dealt with. And then I have to live on a day-to-day basis, as well as look after Mark. So, as I told you before, I'm going to have to *earn* money."

"You're *already* earning money," Jennifer reminded her, "which is something, at least."

"You can't get out of debts with a normal wage – which is why I need my own business." She sighed. "God, I could kill him. He's dead, but I'd *still* like to kill him. On top of the funeral, this is just another nightmare."

Jennifer's heart went out to her. To distract herself from John's ill-treatment, Carol had taken a job as a chauffeuse with a company running a personalised service in expensive car hire. Excited by the possibilities, she had wanted to start her own company, but John had refused to let her do so, which had made her desperately unhappy. Now, even in death, John had ensured that she would not find the money she needed to start her own business. He might haunt her for life.

"Twenty thousand pounds," Carol said distractedly. "It didn't seem that much. I thought I could borrow it against the house, but now I haven't a hope."

"Something is bound to turn up," Jennifer said, "and in the meantime, you have other concerns. Have you been to see Mark?"

"Yes. He's fine. David's sister is an absolute dear and loves having the baby there."

"I think you'd feel a lot better if you had him with you."

"I know I would. I just don't want to stay here – not one more night. Even now, I keep thinking that John's going to walk through that door. That frightens me, sometimes."

"Too many bad memories. But since David wants you to live with him, why don't you do that?"

"I've certainly considered it, but I still think it's too early. If I *do* decide to do it, I'd like to start afresh. I'd rather David wasn't involved in this bloody mess left by John. I don't want it hanging over us both to remind us of him. No, I'm afraid I'll have to sort my problems out first, and that might take a long time."

"I'm sure David would be willing to share the burden with you."

"I don't care. I won't let him."

The decision was a correct one, making Jennifer feel proud of her. "Well," she said, "I agree that you shouldn't stay here, but I still think you should get the baby back. Why not move in with me, at least temporarily? You'll be working most weekends, when I'll be at home, which means I can look after Mark during the day. In the evenings, when you'll be at home, I'll be at the club. What do you think?"

"Are you sure we wouldn't be a nuisance?"

"Of course you wouldn't."

"Just until I get myself sorted out?"

"It's a breathing space, Carol."

Carol nodded solemnly, thinking about it, still confused, but eventually broke into a grateful smile and spread her hands in the air.

"I accept," she said.

Chapter Seventeen

~

"Do you like it here?" Denholm asked, smiling brightly as he raised his glass of brandy and studied its golden depths.

"Mmmm," Maureen replied, still distracted and trying not to be. "A real old-fashioned English club, just like we see in the movies. By the way, isn't that – ?"

Denholm followed her gaze, then smiled over his brandy glass. "Yes," he said, lowering his voice. "Sir John Gielgud, no less."

"God, I *love* – !"

"He's the only actor I've seen in the place," Bill complained. "Most of the others are politicians or businessmen. I thought this was supposed to be a club for those involved in the *arts*!"

"Alas, those days have gone," Denholm explained. "The artists couldn't possibly afford it. Now it's filled with those who either *finance* the arts or ignore them completely."

"And he's not even joking," Maureen told Bill. "That's why God made the movies."

"You haven't changed, Denholm," Bill said. "If anything, being a wealthy man has just made you more cynical."

"And he got it so easily," Maureen said. "He didn't even work for it."

Denholm wasn't offended. "That's true enough, Maureen. I learned shortly after the war that money makes money, and since then I've simply sat on the telephone and played monopoly. I make nothing, invent nothing, contribute nothing tangible – yet simply by keeping money in circulation I *do* create wealth. A strange society, yes?"

"Yes," Maureen said firmly.

Denholm grinned wickedly and called for the bill. "Anyway, talking about the movies, I still can't understand why you want to take on the enormous, generally unsatisfying burden of producing *and* directing your film, instead of simply writing it as usual."

"I have my reasons," Bill replied. "For a start, the only way I can ensure that it isn't tampered with is to co-produce and direct it. I have to have complete control in order to do it the way I want, without compromises."

Denholm's smile was faintly mocking. "Well, dear boy, it's an admirable ambition, but I seriously doubt that you'll get the finance you need *without* compromising. Even Philistines don't finance movies for nothing: apart from money they want to *contribute* something – wives or mistresses, awful script ideas, company products, gigantic egos – and that makes them difficult."

Bill had often been frustrated by Denholm's refusal to stand on any principle and now, faced with his cynicism, he felt a trace of annoyance.

"Some things are worth fighting for," he said, a little testily, "though I don't expect *you* to believe that, Denholm."

"I'm glad you don't. I had quite enough fighting during the war and can now do without it. Peace and prosperity, my dear boy, are what I believe in."

"You and Anthony certainly had a lot of it. Too much, too soon."

"The horrors of war," Denholm replied with a melodramatic sigh. "The best years of our lives, in fact."

"Do you really think so?"

"Yes, Bill, of course. Nothing makes one enjoy life as much as the threat of death. You know as much about that as I do, since you also went to Europe. Even journalists get shot at, old son, and you too could have died. Yet you loved it, Bill. We *all* loved it and will never forget it."

Bill felt a little embarrassed and glanced sideways at Maureen. She was focusing intently on Denholm, intrigued by what he was saying. "Bill visited Anthony today," she said, "while I went for my interview. How *was* your old friend?"

Bill looked down at the table, recalling his lunch with Jennifer. "He's fine. No, dammit, he isn't. He's suffering from arthritis – a particularly crippling kind. He hasn't got a soul in the world and is just goddamned miserable. I'm going to get him out of there – believe me, Maureen, I have to – then I'll have Martin Brennan examine him. I just can't let him live that way."

"Martin Brennan's expensive," Denholm said.

"I don't give a damn." When he glanced at Maureen, she placed her hand on his arm and said, "Neither do I. It's OK, Bill. I understand."

Departures

"You always *were* a soft touch," Denholm said. "When *I'm* ill, I'll call you."

"I thought he was your friend."

"My friend, not my wife. If I tried to help every friend who's suffered since the war, I'd need to enlist the help of the Bank of England. So don't chastise me, old son."

"I'm sorry."

"No sweat, Bill."

"I just thought that you and Anthony would have kept in touch. You seemed such good friends."

"We were. We fought the war in the same aeroplane, shared the same dangers, and an awful lot of times were damned near killed – so, yes, we were friends. But then the war ended and we went our separate ways. Oh, we met on the odd occasion, had a drink, shared a laugh, but really, we had little in common and gradually drifted apart."

"So why did you and I stay in touch?"

"Business," Denholm replied.

The remark didn't sound like a joke and Bill felt a bit shocked, but Denholm grinned and smoothly changed the subject. "Poor Maureen. You weren't too enamoured of your director. Postman *can* be a pain."

"The TV business in London," Maureen said with some bitterness, "is obviously not very different from the movie business back home. It's definitely still run by the boys – and they relish their power."

"Come, dear, I'm sure he wasn't *that* bad."

"Disgusting. He deliberately kept me waiting – then not only interviewed me in front of his technicians, but also condescended horribly to me, when not being sarcastic."

"Anyway, Maureen, I take it that the audition – "

"It was *not* an audition. That ordeal comes Friday week."

"All right, your *meeting*. I take it that your meeting has only served to remind you of the horrors of the acting profession."

"It sure as hell has."

Their waiter arrived with the bill. Denholm didn't bother checking it. He simply threw a Gold Card on the plate and handed it back. "Anyway," he said as the waiter departed, "perhaps you're placing too much importance on having a come-back."

"It is not a *come-back*!"

"All right," Denholm said, unperturbed. "But perhaps you're worrying too much about not being at work. What's so grand about work, anyway? What's so hot about acting?"

Bill saw a flash of anger in Maureen's eyes and felt trepidation.

"God," she said to Denholm, "you're as chauvinistic as the other bastards!"

"Which you always knew!"

"Let me remind you, Denholm, that Bill and I don't have any children."

"So?"

"Well, if Bill can attempt to forget this loss by making his precious movies, I don't see why *I* should sit at home, darning his socks and looking after the house. *I* need distraction as well."

Bill felt that Maureen had just slapped his face, but when he glanced at her, she merely stared him down with bright-eyed, flushed defiance.

Departures

"My mistake," Denholm said. "I tried to get off one delicate subject and obviously fell on another."

"I'm sorry," Maureen said, instantly looking ashamed. "I shouldn't have said that to you, Denholm. And Bill, dear," she added, taking his hand and squeezing it affectionately. "I owe you even more of an apology. I didn't mean what I said, I promise. I just feel so angry, so *humiliated*, by that damned director. It's not you I should be insulting – it's Mr Postman. You just happen to be here. Forgive me?"

"Sure."

She kissed the back of his hand and gave a warm smile, but though it made him feel a lot better, he was not wildly happy. The outburst of frustrated anger, while certainly justified, had made him face the fact that Maureen, being childless, was wondering fearfully what she could do with the rest of her life.

"By the way," Denholm said, obviously trying to lighten the mood, "since neither of you has met my latest wife, I might as well tell you that I'm presently in the middle of my third divorce – which makes me, in this particular sense, more American than you two."

"Good God, Denholm," Maureen said, perking up at the smell of gossip. "What was it this time? Another case of adultery?"

Denholm spread his hands in a pleading manner. "I am innocent of all charges! She's accusing me of neglect and also claiming irreconcilable differences. By which she means I'm rarely at home."

"Which is true," Bill said.

Denholm chuckled at that. "A man's work is never done. I am simply misunderstood."

The waiter returned with the credit-card slip; Denholm signed it, added a tip in cash, then watched him departing. "So, pets," he said, turning back to them, "shall we depart?"

"Let's do that," Bill said, adding, as they stood up: "Three times married and three times divorced. You should get an award."

Denholm laughed and walked on, looking as dashing in his pinstripe suit and old-school tie as he had so many years ago in his RAF uniform.

"Who *was* this third wife of yours, anyway?" Maureen asked him.

Denholm sighed. "A high-powered PR lady. She was in charge of the publicity for a British movie I had financed, and I met her at the party after the preview and fell in love with her long legs. She was my Cyd Charisse fantasy – legs that seemed to never end. She was tall and elegant and had money, which made her highly seductive."

"And?" Maureen prodded him.

"She also had a volcanic temper and was very possessive. The type to *throw* things."

Bill nearly convulsed with laughter as they left the Garrick Club and stepped into the lamplit darkness near a busy, neon-coloured junction. "I'd love to see you trying to duck flying ornaments. Do you remain dignified?"

"I'm afraid not, old boy. I simply grab my coat and run for it – usually into the nearest bar! Now can I get you a nightcap?"

"No, thanks," Maureen said. "I'm still suffering from shock and we're both still jet-lagged, so I think we should get back to the Savoy and have a good sleep. Are we within walking distance?"

"Yes. The most pleasant route is that way." Denholm pointed towards some brightly lit theatres. "Straight down St Martin's Lane until you come to Trafalgar Square. Pass the church in the square, turn left into the Strand, keep walking and you'll come to the Savoy. As for me, I'll take a taxi to St John's Wood, where my lady awaits me."

"Your wife?" Maureen asked.

"Someone else's wife. I lay my weary head on her bosom while she lulls me to sleep."

Bill couldn't resist asking: "Do you ever see anything of your first wife – the one we knew during the war?"

"Lily Monaghan?"

"Yeah, right," Bill said, hoping he sounded casual. "What happened to her?"

"She's still alive and well," Denholm said, trying to wave down a taxi. "In fact, we're still in touch. She hasn't changed a bit – still good-natured and forthright. And like me, she's been married two or three times. Her present husband is a retired footballer, not too bright but decent, and they live in a modest villa with a swimming pool near Marbella, Southern Spain. She rings me up now and then – about once a year – and we occasionally meet. She hasn't changed in the least."

"Why did you get divorced?" Maureen asked.

"I can't remember," Denholm replied as a taxi pulled in to the pavement. "Of course, *you* would remember her," he said to Bill with a wicked grin, "since you had that entertaining romance with her best friend. Did he ever mention *her*, Maureen?"

"No, Denholm, he didn't."

"His dirty secret, dear. A typical wartime romance – but very intense!"

Maureen was amused and looked at Bill with mock sternness. "Just as well it was before my time," she said.

"A *long* time before your time." Bill felt a bit uneasy. "And I only knew her for a couple of months, before the war separated us."

"How sad!" Maureen sighed.

The taxi pulled into the kerb and Denholm opened the back door.

"I wonder what happened to her," Bill said, in a deliberately vague manner.

"She probably went back to Cornwall." Denholm slipped into the taxi. "To marry a farmer, have half-a-dozen kids, and grow fat on potatoes, sausage and strong country ale. We all return to our roots."

"I don't think she was that kind," Bill said without thinking.

"Common muck, dear boy," Denholm replied. "You just didn't see it." He closed the taxi door and looked out. "Good night and sleep tight, my dear friends. I will call you tomorrow."

He flashed his wicked grin as the taxi pulled away from the kerb and carried him into the night.

Maureen smiled at Bill. "So," she said, slipping her arm through his and walking them along the busy street of theatres. "Let's wander back to our warm bed and end the night gently."

Thinking of Denholm's "common muck", Bill nodded agreement.

Chapter Eighteen

The next morning, to ease the tension Maureen was obviously feeling over her forthcoming meeting with a Royal Shakespeare Company casting director, Bill took her on a trip by motor-launch, from Charing Cross pier to Greenwich.

As the boat moved along the great river, passing many historic buildings, as well as the old docks now being converted into luxury apartments, Bill pointed out what he remembered from the war years, showing her Cleopatra's Needle, the river view of their hotel, then the dome of St Paul's Cathedral, which, when last seen, had majestically dominated the surrounding ruins. Now it was practically obscured by the surrounding skyscrapers.

"I thought the English had more taste," Bill said. "I can't believe they'd allow that."

"Money talks," Maureen replied, "as Denholm will tell you."

"What a bitch!" Bill said, sadly.

The boat passed Billingsgate and the Tower of London, went under the great bridge to the modernised

St Katherine's Docks, then came to renovated docklands filled with more towering apartment blocks.

"During the war," Bill told Maureen, "those apartment blocks were great warehouses in which millions of tons of Allied munitions were stored. Since the German bombers had to fly over that area to reach London, the docks were bombed relentlessly; yet over 3,000 convoys sailed from there. I can't believe it's the same place."

"Denholm's invested heavily here," Maureen informed him. "That's why he's rich."

After disembarking at Greenwich, they visited the mandatory sights, then had lunch in a lovely old pub by the river. They had steak-and-kidney pie and two pints of English ale, and being seated close to an open fire, soon felt pleasantly drunk.

"Did you come here during the war?" Maureen asked him.

"Yes," he said, "as I recall. I'm pretty sure it looked a bit different then. I think it's been renovated."

"It's still lovely. I really like English pubs."

"They're warm and friendly," Bill said.

To revive themselves after the lunch, they wandered over the green expanse of Greenwich Park, which, as Bill informed Maureen, had been laid out for Charles II by the landscape-gardener of Louis XIV. They gazed down from the hill, beyond chestnuts, hawthorns and oaks, to a wonderful view of east London and the Docks, with Tower Bridge and St Paul's Cathedral still partially visible.

Bill looked dreamily at St Paul's, not aware that he was doing so until Maureen tugged gently at his hand and said, "Come, lover! Let's go! You can't dream here all day."

Departures

They took the boat back to London, standing together on the upper deck, taking pleasure from the beating of a cold wind, the waves splashing below them. It was a typical autumn afternoon, bitterly cold under low clouds, but Bill still felt drunk, pleasantly drowsy and at ease with himself. He also felt at ease with Maureen, safely distanced from their mutual problems, and was pleased when she leaned against him to hug him, sharing her warmth.

"I love you," she said. He glanced at her, surprised. "I know you know it, but I wanted to say it, because of last night."

"Last night?" he asked.

"My dumb remarks. Dumb, cruel and uncalled for – and they haunted me all night."

"I wasn't bothered, believe me."

"Thanks, Bill." She kissed him on the cheek, then looked up at the dome of St Paul's cathedral. "Was it true that you had a great love during the war? And was she really, as Denholm described her, no more than common muck?"

"I was young and in love," Bill replied. "And common muck, she was not."

Maureen merely smiled and nodded. She asked him no more questions. The boat was passing the steps that led up to the cathedral, and as Bill thoughtfully studied it, he remembered it as it had been – surrounded by blackened ruins and mountains of rubble, the great dome remaining magically untouched throughout that fierce devastation.

Up there, the girl described as "common muck" had affirmed her love for him . . .

Chapter Nineteen

~

One of the two most memorable days of Bill's life was May 7, 1944. He met Jenny in Trafalgar Square, by the base of Nelson's column, where he found her feeding the pigeons.

"Hi!" he said. "You look good down there."

She glanced up with a smile. "Aren't they wonderful?" she said, indicating the pigeons feeding around her. "I could spend all day here."

"I'd prefer it if you spent the day with me as we originally planned."

"Yes, sir!" And she stood up to kiss him. "I've missed you dreadfully, Bill."

"Since last night?"

"All *through* the night!"

"That makes me feel passionate, Jenny."

"And hearing that makes me feel good. So!" She waved her hand to indicate the stately buildings around them. "It's Saturday and the whole day is free. Where will we begin?"

"It's *lunchtime* on Saturday," he replied. "What about a pub lunch?"

Departures

She shook her head. "No, I don't want to drink yet. Let's go to a Lyon's Tea House for a teetotaller's lunch. Then I'll take you to the Royal Academy show and let you soak in some culture. And finally, when the pubs are open again, we can have a few drinks. Yes?"

"Yes," he said. "So where's the Lyon's Tea House?"

"Near Piccadilly Circus. That will make a nice walk. And from there it's only another short walk to the Royal Academy."

"OK, Jenny, let's go."

The walked across the great square, towards the National Gallery, which made Bill realise just how far from home he was.

Oklahoma was yellow wheat fields, sheer blue sky and wide-open spaces; whereas London, for all its beauty, was essentially grey and cramped – if this day, as it had been for many weeks, enlivened with sunshine.

"Are they keeping you busy?" Jenny asked him.

"Yes, Jenny, they are. But I've never had a better time in my life – I meet so many people, all of them keyed up about the invasion, wondering when it will happen."

"June," she said. "The tides are good then. It will happen in June. Then they'll all go to Europe and get killed and it won't seem so wonderful. What do you write about?"

"About their optimism and excitement, their belief that they'll win. Stuff to make the folks back home feel proud. A little flourish of trumpets."

"Propaganda."

"I suppose so. It's not exactly fearless journalism, but serves its purpose, I hope."

"And you'll be a proper, fearless writer after the war?"

"I like to think so."

"You will be."

He felt good about that, since she normally teased him. She did it nicely, without malice, but he knew what she meant – that his lofty principles had no relevance here.

Her parents had died in this war. His own country had not been touched. He was writing propaganda, turning brutal truths into dreams, while she, forced to live with the brutal truth, was clinging to real life.

"It's better than death," she had told him. "And that's *all* I know. In this world, in this particular city, what else *is* there to know?"

"Love?" he had dared to suggest.

"That's life," she had told him.

So now he walked beside her, wanting life more than art, aware that his love was an education that would not be repeated. They walked past the National Gallery, glancing up at those gazing down, and he felt the tender warmth of her fingers, held in his hand.

"How are things at the hotel?"

"Quieter for me," he said. "Denholm and Anthony are back in East Anglia, which means I don't see them during the week. I miss their nightly banter. On the other hand, I've more time alone with you, for which I am grateful."

"It's nice to be wanted."

"You are."

"I like the lads as well," she said, referring to Denholm and Anthony, "but seeing them at weekends is enough – I mean, they sometimes exhaust me. Still, I don't envy what they're doing – those bombing raids over Germany. It can't be too nice for them."

"No," Bill said. "Not nice at all."

They turned up the Haymarket, towards Piccadilly Circus. The road was busy with trucks filled with soldiers. D-Day was drawing close and changing the face of the country. Troop-trucks, jeeps and glossy staff cars jammed the roads, thousands of troops were pouring into coastal areas banned to civilians, and the enemy was being softened up with massive day and night bombing raids.

Denholm and Anthony took part in those, flying out from East Anglia, and at weekends looked more exhausted than ever, if determinedly jolly.

Yes, Bill admired them, though sometimes had doubts about them – particularly Denholm, whose wit could often be cruel and based, at least to Bill's foreign eye, on the unearned, inherited superiority of a privileged class.

It was a reservation that Jenny shared and often discussed with him – though thankfully, not this particular day.

"I want to hear all about you and your family," she said when they were seated in The Lyon's Tea House. "Yes, Bill, your family!"

"They're simple working folk," he told her. "The best people in the world. My Dad sells agricultural products, my mother runs the house, and we live in a place called Norman, the seat of the University of Oklahoma, which is where I obtained my higher education. I have a sister, one year younger than me, even nicer than I am, and if you want to know our relatives and friends, who are many, you'll have to visit us during Thanksgiving. It's a very big clan."

"You had a happy childhood, didn't you?"

"Yes, I did."

"That's why you're so sweet." She had a sip of tea, glanced around the crowded restaurant, put the cup back on its saucer and smiled brightly at him. "Oklahoma sounds so romantic," she said. "I love American names."

"It's a romantic territory," he told her. "It was really cowboys and Indians. The name's derived from two Choctaw Indian words – *okla*, meaning 'people', and *humma*, meaning red – and white people stole the land from the red people and then wrote songs about it. Hence – "

"*Oklahoma!*"

"Right." He took hold of her hand. "And your parents? Can you talk about them?"

"Yes, I can talk about them. At first I felt that I had killed them by inviting them to London. I don't blame myself now and can talk about it – at least to you, Bill."

"They were coming to visit you?"

"That's right. They took the train from Cornwall and got off at Paddington just as German bombs fell on the station. They died quickly, I think."

"Nice parents?"

"God, yes. My whole childhood was a dream. My father was an accountant, my mother ran his office, we lived in a lovely cottage in a village by the sea, and I had an older brother and younger sister and knew nothing but love. I wasn't spoilt – I was disciplined when I needed it – but I *was* given a feeling of self-esteem, which is very important. I think I'll always miss them terribly. They've left an emptiness that can never be filled. I – "

"Let me fill that emptiness, Jenny. I can . . . *and I will!*"

Squeezing her hand, he thought he could feel her heartbeat through it. The beating was coming out of her heart and all the way down her arm, to touch the palm of his hand.

He wanted to die for her.

Her smile was radiant, her green eyes like the sun. "You're making me feel embarrassed," she said, blushing, "so let's go for some culture."

He was warmed enough by that, moved by English understatement, and paid for the lunch and followed her outside, where the sun was still shining. They walked along Piccadilly to the Royal Academy, passed under its imposing archway, joined the tail-end of the queue that snaked across the quadrangle and up the steps to the entrance. The women were wearing wide hats and dressed in spring clothing, while the men, when not in uniform, were mostly in drab suits.

"It all feels rather festive," Jenny said. "You wouldn't know there's a war on."

"What war?" Bill asked.

The exhibition inside was not to Bill's taste: Dame Laura Knight's paintings of bombers and aircraft factories; Augustus John's unflattering portrait of General Montgomery; and other unappealing works showing various slices of life in deprived, wartime Britain.

"Art as propaganda," Jenny whispered, smiling. "Just like all that rubbish you write for the good folks back home."

Bill wasn't offended. On the contrary, he was amused. She was pricking his pretensions, mocking his writer's pride, and he saw it as a sign of her commonsense and loved her all the more for it.

"OK," he replied, "you win. I'm just an evil

propagandist. And since everywhere I look, I'm reminded of it, I want to get out of here."

"Yes, dear!" she whispered.

They left the building hand-in-hand, crossed the crowded quadrangle, and stopped indecisively on the pavement of Piccadilly along which, at that moment, a convoy of troop-trucks was rumbling, the soldiers packed like sardines under the flapping canvas, their weapons glinting in the sunlight, as they waved and wolf-whistled at female passers-by.

"It's hard to believe," Bill said, "that a lot of those healthy, good-humoured men are going to die soon."

The radiance left Jenny's face. "Oh, it's real enough," she said. "God knows, it's *too* real. It's certainly going to happen – and all for victory. For peace." She watched the trucks disappearing, then sighed, as if saddened. "And you'll be going as well, Bill. That's what you're here to report."

"Yes, that's right."

"You want to go, don't you?"

"Not if it means losing you."

"Even if it meant that, you'd still want to go. It's a once-in-a-lifetime opportunity, too important to miss."

"Yes, I suppose so."

"I don't want you to go," she said.

"What we want is irrelevant."

"I lie awake at nights worrying about it. I imagine the worst things."

"I can't imagine not coming back. I can't believe that anything could prevent me from returning to you. My love for you has made me invincible. Nothing can stop me now."

Departures

She smiled and turned into him, wrapping her arms around him, to let him feel the softness of her breasts and the heat of her body.

They had not yet made love.

"Can you feel my heart beating?" she asked him.

"Yes, I can."

"All for you," she said. Then she nibbled his ear, chuckled throatily, and pulled away from him, still holding onto his hand as she waved down a taxi. "Come on," she said. "I want to show you something. Then we'll go and get drunk."

She whispered instructions to the taxi driver, then opened the rear door of the vehicle and climbed in. Bill followed her in and sat beside her as the taxi moved off.

They were driven back to Trafalgar Square, along the Strand, past the Savoy, then along Fleet Street and on towards the City. The ruins began there, an appalling, widespread devastation, but out of them, miraculously, as if protected by God, rose the majestic dome of St Paul's cathedral, towards which they were heading.

Bill looked up at it, startled. Its survival seemed magical. Its eastern windows had been blown in, numerous incendiary bombs had scarred it, but its dome, the second largest in the world, still towered above the sea of black ruins and grey rubble that appeared to have flowed right up to the cathedral walls without actually touching them.

"Here we are," Jenny said.

Bill paid the driver as she got out, then she took his hand and led him up the broad steps, into the cathedral. Once inside, by the memorial to the Duke of Wellington, he looked in awe along the vast, gloomy length of the building, at its fonts, lecterns, statues and altars, its fine wrought-iron gates and choir stalls and wood carvings, and felt dwarfed and humbled by its grandeur, reduced to mortality. It rendered him breathless.

"This is the west end," Jenny whispered. "The High Altar is at the far end. Churches are usually built from east to west. Would you like to know why?"

"Yep."

"To ensure that the High Altar, being at the east end, would be as near as possible to Jerusalem. Now come on! Follow me!"

She didn't let him inspect the ground floor of the cathedral, but instead, with an enigmatic smile, led him upstairs. They climbed nearly 600 steps, steps 300 years old, and finally arrived, breathless, in an immense, circular gallery whose diameter, as Jenny explained to him, was almost exactly the same as its height from the pavement.

Below Bill, in that deep well, was the great floor of the cathedral; above him was the magnificent dome, created and raised by nameless men in the seventeenth century, and since enhanced with paintings of scenes from the life of St Paul.

It made him feel dizzy.

"Why did you bring me here?" he asked, as the choir, in the deeply shadowed depths, sent its hymn soaring up to him.

She smiled and turned away, then pressed her lips to the wall.

"It's called the Whispering Gallery," she explained. "Because what's spoken into this wall can be heard at the other side of the gallery. And now I'm saying, *'I love you!'*"

Departures

She whispered into the ancient stone, leaning against it with her forehead, and he imagined that he could hear her words of love rippling around the great dome. Then she kissed the stone and turned back to face him as he quietly approached her.

He stopped in front of her, trembling, choked up by overbrimming emotion and his heart's urgent beating.

"It's been said," she told him, her smile like light and song, "that the dome soaks up sound in a magical manner and retains it throughout the ages – a great heart given life by the beating of the hearts of we mortals."

He took another step towards her, but she stopped him with her hand. She spread her fingers and pressed her palm against his breast, as the choir below, united as a single voice, raised its hymn up around him.

"I can feel your heart beating," Jenny said. "Is it beating for me?"

"Yes," he replied.

"Then your heartbeat," she said, "which exists just for me, will be preserved in these ancient walls for as long as they stand. I love you, my sweet American boy, and now the walls know that also."

Bill took hold of her open hand and gently pressed it against his lips. Then, bereft of words, torn from his roots and released from childhood, he fled up the next flight of stone steps, not knowing why. He found himself in the Golden Gallery. From there he could look out from the dome of the cathedral – over that terrible sea of charred ruins and rubble.

He felt his heart beating, so breathed deeply of the air. When Jenny came up behind him to slide her arms around him, he lowered his head, heard that hymn to

God and life rising up from far below – ethereal, majestic, as if seeking to bless them – and was swept away by longing and grief.

He wept and felt blessed.

Chapter Twenty

While Maureen went with a friend to the theatre, Bill talked to his Harley Street buddy about Anthony Barker's situation, arranged for Anthony's immediate transfer to the hospital recommended, and visited Anthony to assure him that he would be seeing him the next day at the new hospital. Then, feeling as nervous as an adolescent, he took a taxi to Jennifer's club in Soho.

He was pleasantly surprised, when he arrived in Frith Street, to discover that the club had a respectable facade, with a tastefully designed sign above the door, announcing the establishment as *The De Quincey Club*. The door was open, leading into a small, gloomy hall, which led him through crimson-coloured curtains into the surprisingly large club itself. It had fake Dickensian decor, Victorian tables and chairs, some comfortable settees in crimson velours, and antiques and brown-tinted prints that looked genuinely old.

All in all, it was bigger and better than he had thought it would be.

There were only a few customers, mostly pin-striped

city gents, some sitting alone at the tables or on the settees, others accompanied by male friends or by ladies who seemed a bit gaudy, both in manner and dress.

A couple of ladies were sitting alone by the bar, talking to a barman who sported a blue-and-white striped shirt and polka-dot bow tie.

Jennifer, who was also behind the bar, was staring steadily at him.

He walked towards her, feeling embarrassed, not convinced that he should have come. She was wearing another wig, this one red and wild, and her surprisingly slim body was cleverly displayed in a tight black skirt and white-lace blouse.

"Oh, Bill!" she exclaimed grandly in greeting, "you actually came! I wasn't sure you would."

"I said I would, Jenny – "

"Jennifer!"

" – and so, here I am." He glanced left and right, at the gaudy ladies along the bar, then took in the predominantly crimson-coloured room, the men eating and drinking at the tables, or talking in low voices to the women who did not look like ladies. "It's a swell place," he said, turning back to Jennifer. "I didn't imagine something as grand as this. I was expecting a cubby-hole."

Jennifer beamed with pleasure. "It looks smaller from outside." Her face was too thin, its lines hidden by make-up, emphasising the intensity of the eyes above her luridly painted lips. For sure, it was not his Jenny Birken. This was *Jennifer* Birken. "Would you like a drink, Bill?"

"On the house?"

"Of course."

He smiled. "Scotch with water, thanks."

Departures

"James!" She glanced sideways at the barman. "One whiskey with water for my friend!"

"Yes, Madame!" James replied.

"He's as gay as they come," Jennifer said without malice, "and a cheeky, unprincipled sod to boot. But he's also a very good barman – and doesn't bother my girls."

"Your girls?"

Jennifer indicated the tartiy dressed ladies along the bar. "My hostesses. Hey, Marjorie! Barbara! Say hello to my American friend, Bill Eisler. He's here on a visit."

Marjorie, the blonde, and Barbara, the black-haired vamp, smiled and waved in an easy-going manner.

"Hi!" Marjorie called. "We've never seen *you* here before. You must be a *close* friend!"

"That's enough of that, Miss Mischief," Jennifer said. "Attend to your business."

"What business?" Barbara rejoindered. "It's as dead as a morgue in here."

"Just sit there and be a good girl. The night is young yet." Jennifer smiled and lit a cigarette.

"You never used to smoke," Bill pointed out.

"Forty years ago," she replied. "I've learned a lot since then, Bill."

He thought of St Paul's cathedral – her loving embrace, his tears – and could not match the woman before him with the girl he had known. "Why's it called the De Quincey Club?" he asked. "I mean, it sounds like a literary club – not a watering hole."

"De Quincey, when impoverished, lodged just up the road and I've always loved the sound of his name. A literary club? No, it's not – but it's strictly for *gentlemen*."

"Wearing a pinstripe suit doesn't make you a gentleman."

"It helps," Jennifer said.

Bill glanced at the women along the bar. "Friendly ladies, I note. Do they keep the customers satisfied by any means?"

James returned, placed Bill's drink in front of him, raised his eyebrows, flashed a seductive smile and hurried back to a customer.

"Your assumption," Jennifer said, "is commonplace, but not remotely accurate."

"No?"

"No. My hostesses aren't here to satisfy the customers by *any* means. They are here to keep them company while *in* the club. That's as far as it goes."

After pouring some water into his whiskey, Bill held up the glass. "The world's greatest drink," he said.

"You never used to drink whiskey," Jennifer responded, "but that also was forty years ago."

"*Touché!*"

"*Touché*, Bill."

Clearly, she hadn't lost her spirit. Bill sampled his whiskey, which was excellent. "And that's it?" he asked.

"Yes. This is a place where *gentlemen* can eat and drink and enjoy good conversation."

"With the ladies."

"Correct."

"And what happens if the gentlemen desire something more exotic with the ladies?"

"Are you suggesting that my hostesses are prostitutes?"

Bill drank some more whiskey. "I wouldn't dream of it, Jennifer. I'm merely trying to ascertain how far their duties go when it comes to keeping your customers satisfied."

He couldn't resist it. He needed her response. He had to find out what made Jennifer tick; and, by so doing, perhaps discover how the original Jenny had given birth to her.

He had to search for *his* Jenny.

"I find your remarks offensive," Jennifer said. "I would *not* countenance prostitutes, high-class or otherwise, and certainly don't encourage my girls to do anything other than converse with the clientele."

"I *still* think your description of this club, and the women who work in it, is a little less frank than it could be. Morally speaking, it's – "

"Morality," she said sarcastically. "You always *were* keen on that! You even preached the morality of writing as you wrote propaganda. Naturally, you could afford to do so – you were so *privileged*, after all! You had come from the land of milk and honey to a city at war. So you talked about morality and the need to have values, while we poor Brits, being bombed every night, could only think of survival."

"I don't think – "

"I'm just an elderly woman, struggling constantly to survive, and I can't afford to make fine distinctions between what's right and wrong. The question is: *Will you help me?*"

There it was again – and again he felt shocked. He studied Jennifer's "hostesses", whatever that meant, and concluded that they were a lot more than Jennifer claimed. As if to confirm the point, when a new customer entered, Marjorie and Barbara homed in on him, their painted lips pouting.

"This club of yours," Bill said, feeling light-headed and mean, "doesn't seem to require the financial assistance you *claim* it needs."

"What do you mean? It's half empty!"

"Early hours yet."

"It will look the same at midnight. We do get these pinstriped gentlemen, but in recent years it's been mostly tourists – *American* tourists." She sighed melodramatically. "As I told you, after a few threats from that buffoon, Colonel Qadaffi, the Americans are cancelling any trip that involves taking an aeroplane. And now my club is suffering badly. No Americans, no money."

She stared at him in a haughty manner and he felt like getting the hell out of there.

"While despising the Americans, you want me, another dumb American, to make up for your losses. It sounds like a bad deal."

"I'm not begging for money. I am asking for help in my hour of need – and who else can I ask?"

"I don't know, Jennifer. *Who* else? You live here, I don't. You must know other people. We haven't seen each other for forty years, so why the hell turn to *me*?"

"Because of what we meant to one another. That must count for something."

He was deeply hurt by that. She was using the love he had felt to emotionally blackmail him.

"OK," he said. "Twenty thousand pounds. What's in it for me?"

"If you're going to treat my request like a common

business transaction, I would rather you go and not return."

Shocked, Bill stared at her, not believing what he had heard. He thought of St Paul's cathedral, the Whispering Gallery, lips to cold stone, Jenny's utterance, *I love you*, resounding around the great dome.

No, this wasn't Jenny. He could not have loved this creature. This was someone called *Jennifer*, an old tart with a heart of steel; and he refused to be exploited by her knowledge of the depth of his love for her.

"I don't need this," he said. "I don't even know why I came. You and me, we have nothing in common. I'm surprised that we ever did. Goodnight, Jennifer. *Goodbye!*"

Then, feeling insulted and outraged, he spun on the ball of his foot and stomped out of the club.

"Goddamn her!" he muttered.

Chapter Twenty-One

∽

Later that evening, after closing her club, Jenny walked home alone, through the relatively quiet, lamplit streets, brooding darkly on how Bill had stormed out and convinced that she would never see him again.

Although told by her doctor that she must not smoke at all, she lit a cigarette, inhaled with defiant pleasure, and reasoned that if it did indeed hasten her death, her passing would be a blessing to everyone, especially Carol.

She felt guilty about dying, as if she was betraying Carol, giving her more to worry about, another loss to deal with – and this conviction, even more than the fear, kept her awake at nights.

Crossing Piccadilly Circus in the dead of night, she saw the derelicts, alcoholics and drug-addicts who had appeared in vastly greater numbers in recent years. They were sleeping on the steps around Eros, lolling in litter-filled doorways, and the sight of them, while deepening her depression, also made her realise how lucky she had been to have had the best years of her life in a much better world.

Departures

Yes, her best years...

Leaving the Circus and walking along Piccadilly, she thought again of Bill and welled up with the kind of emotion that now threatened to break her. She passed the Royal Academy, remembered visiting it with Bill, then recalled their few months together during the war, until, on June 6, 1944, he had taken part in the invasion of Europe and disappeared from her life.

The pain of losing him had been great, but knowing him had been worth it – and in understanding this, she tried to think of her illness as the bill to be paid for a life that had, all in all, been a good one.

Nothing in life was free, after all... And nothing lasted forever.

Walking along Piccadilly, she glanced across the lamplit road, saw the ribbons of lights on the Ritz hotel and nearly choked up.

Yes, tea at the Ritz. Her and Bill, so long ago. Just before he'd stepped out of her embrace, then out of her life.

It hurt to recall it.

She passed the hotel, walking towards Half Moon Street, wanting to get home as soon as possible and lay her head on a pillow. To sleep, perchance to dream, to take solace from the past, when she and Bill had been different creatures, much younger and finer.

She turned into Half Moon Street, glad to be nearing home – then heard a clicking sound, saw a glittering blade, and was stopped by the presence of a dishevelled adolescent who snarled, "Give me that handbag, you old cow, or I'll cut you up proper!"

Jennifer stopped, turning cold, then said without

thinking, "Don't be silly. You're just a child. Please don't – "

"Give me your handbag!"

His voice sounded inhuman, something wild, as he grabbed at her handbag.

"Bloody bitch!" he whispered. "Stupid – !" He tugged violently at her bag, making her fall into his body, and he jumped back, waving the knife over her, as she fell to the pavement. Pain shot through her knees, making her cry out, but she pulled her bag down and then pushed herself back up as the youth, in a panic, slapped her face, pushed and pulled, started sobbing, then threw her away from him.

She fell onto the pavement, still clutching at her bag, and the youth, his eyes wide with fear, cried, "You bitch! You stupid old whore!" and leaned forward to slash her with the knife.

She thought she was screaming, but it was all inside her head, and as the glittering blade missed her, slashing only thin-air, another man rushed out of the darkness, like another assailant. He jerked the mugger away and threw him into the wall, and as he stepped back, the young man dropped his knife and ran off down the narrow street.

Breathless, Jennifer stared at the man bending down to help her up.

"Are you OK?" Bill asked.

"Yes, I think so."

"Let's get you back on your feet," he said, helping her up.

She leaned against him, trying to get her breath back, then stepped away from him.

"What on earth are you doing here? Did you *know* I was going to need rescuing?"

"No. It was a lucky accident, believe me. After leaving your club, I felt goddamned stupid, so I went for a soothing drink, then returned to the club to apologise – just before closing time."

"You didn't need – "

"Yes, Jennifer, I did." He smiled and shrugged. "Anyway, I got back to the club just as James was closing the doors. He told me you'd just left, so I followed what I thought would be the route you'd take along Piccadilly. I saw you turning into this street, and then – "

"Came to my rescue."

"Right. That's the picture. And I *still* want to apologise for my behaviour in the club."

"Reunions aren't easy, are they, Bill?"

"No, I guess not. But we're even. OK?"

"Yes, Bill."

"So, can I walk you home, just like in the old days?"

"Please do," she said.

He took her by the arm and walked her up Half Moon Street, making her feel like the twenty-year-old she had been when in love with him.

She stopped at her apartment and turned her back to the door as his familiar, grave expression broke into a gentle smile.

"This is it?" he asked.

"Yes, Bill, this is home."

"If we were younger, I'd invite myself in."

"If we were younger," she echoed.

"I promise to come and see you again."

"Good. I'd like that."

She nodded, feeling flustered, then opened the door and started inside . . . but turned back to face him. He was taller than she was, looking down, his grey eyes gentle, then he leaned forward to kiss her on the cheek, his lips lingering uncertainly. She closed her eyes, seeking darkness; then, when her cheeks started burning, she looked at him once more.

He appeared to have the shyness of a schoolboy when he backed away from her.

Slowly, she closed the door in his face, saying only, "Goodnight, Bill."

He had no time to answer.

She pressed her forehead to the door and listened to his retreating footsteps, then thought she heard the sound of her own heartbeat.

"Death," she quoted, whispering into the closed door, *"where is thy sting?"*

Then the tears came.

Chapter Twenty-Two

∽

Bill couldn't sleep that night, being tormented by thoughts of his two meetings with Jennifer Birken, as well as vivid recollections of Jenny during the war. These made the darkness intolerable, and eventually, when the guilt became too great, he slipped out of bed, leaving Maureen to sleep alone.

He poured himself a glass of water, drank it and felt better, then sat at the small table by the window and looked over the Thames. The black water reflected moonlight and the lights strung on the bridges, giving the river a mysterious appearance in the morning's vast silence. Turning away, he glanced at Maureen, saw her red hair on the white sheet, then thought of Jennifer's red wig and felt strange again.

Jennifer and Maureen: his first love and his wife. In seeing the former, he was betraying the latter. Not much to be proud of.

Sighing, feeling even more guilty, he decided to go for a walk. After dressing, he kissed the back of Maureen's head, then left the room and made his way downstairs.

The lobby was brightly lit, with people still coming and going, but when he walked into the Strand it was eerily empty in the light of the street lamps.

"Morning, sir," the uniformed doorman said. "Can I fetch you a taxi?"

"No, thanks, I'm just going for a walk. Where do you recommend?"

"Down by the river, sir, It's the only place at this time of morning. You might encounter a few friendly ladies, but they won't bother you unless you insist. They're just making a living, sir. Turn left twice, then along the Embankment."

"Thanks."

"Not at all, sir."

He walked towards Trafalgar Square, but stopped just before he got there, looking up at Nelson's Column, which seemed to sway beneath the clouds, then at the magnificent gateway of the Mall that led to Buckingham Palace. Standing there in a trance, surveying that great square couched in darkness, he vaulted back in time, leaping over the decades, to see the same square in daylight, packed with thousands of people, all of them celebrating VE Day: the victory in Europe. Then he saw, in his mind's eye, as he had done all those years ago, a young lady who may, or may not, have been Jenny Birken.

He'd lost her in that crowd in 1945 – lost her forever.

Or what he'd thought was forever.

Now, forty years later, alone in the English night, he remembered that fateful day, the disappearance of that girl, and wondered if it had in fact been Jenny or someone else altogether.

Feeling too emotional, he hurriedly turned away and

walked down a narrow side-street to Charing Cross Underground station. He went through the station, past sleeping derelicts and winos, and eventually found himself on the Embankment, by the murmuring water.

While walking by the river, his recollections of Jenny made him think of the screenplay he had based on the time they had shared together. Unfortunately, his plans were not working out as planned. Denholm had warned him again that he was being too idealistic.

"The men with money these days are different. They don't believe in taking chances. You'll have to meet them halfway, at least, and make certain changes. This has to be faced, Bill."

Bill had agreed to meet Denholm's backers, but now, as he looked across the black, moonlit river, he felt even more depressed, faced, as he was, with the distinct possibility of having to amend his original version of his screenplay, in order to get his movie made at all.

"Goddammit!" he muttered, unable to bear the thought, then tugged his collar up around his ears and leaned into the cold wind . . . until his thoughts wound inexorably back to Jennifer.

Helplessly drawn to her, he was also puzzled by her. There was something odd about her – she was like an actress playing a role – and he'd also noticed, at certain times, a haunted light in her eyes, which was certainly at odds with her behaviour.

You couldn't help wondering . . .

"Good morning," a lady purred from the darkness. "Would the Sir like some company?"

The English were so well-mannered, even the prostitutes were polite. Bill smiled at the woman, who wore a tightly-belted black raincoat, high-heels and a headscarf. "No, thanks," he said. "Those days have gone. But thanks for the offer."

"You'd be surprised," the woman crooned.

"No, I wouldn't," Bill said.

The woman chuckled. "Ah, well, too bad!" Then she disappeared back into darkness, as if she had never been.

Bill walked on, feeling better, reminded once more that England was a land like no other.

Which is why he wanted to make a movie about what he had found here.

His past was like a movie, a ribbon of dreams, and he wanted the greatest moments of his life to become part of that ribbon.

He wanted to translate into art his becoming of age.

In that cottage in Cornwall . . .

Chapter Twenty-Three

∞

The intensity of the bombing raids over Germany had been increasing dramatically in recent weeks and now, in the first week of June, 1944, there was a fairly widespread acceptance that the invasion of Europe was imminent.

No longer on extended leave, Denholm and Anthony had gone back to the RAF base in East Anglia, from where they were flying nightly raids; but they had still managed to get to the hotel over the weekends when they drank more heavily, looked progressively more exhausted, and developed an increasingly cutting sense of humour.

"It's a defence mechanism," Bill suggested to Jenny when she complained about the worsening venom of their jokes. "They're bombing the oil refineries of the Ruhr about four nights a week, it's dangerous and exhausting, and the more they do it, the less are their chances of survival. They're both pretty near the end of their tether."

"I appreciate that," Jenny replied, "but it still doesn't excuse their cruelty. Particularly all those jokes they make about Lily. She deserves more than that."

He knew that Jenny felt close to Lily Monaghan and thought that her good nature, which extended to her sexual favours, was being exploited in a cynical manner by Denholm. She was not talking about the sex, which she considered to be their concern, but about the fact that Lily, while pretending to be carefree, was in fact in love with Denholm, desperately wanted his approval, and was constantly humiliated by him.

"She loves him and makes no bones about it," Jenny said. "And Denholm, while enjoying it and wanting it as much as she does, makes jokes about how much she likes the sex – as if that somehow cheapens her without tainting him. God, the hypocrisy! If you ever treated *me* that way, I'd spit in your face."

"So far, I haven't had the *chance* to treat you that way."

"Given how Denholm treats Lily, perhaps it's better this way."

He was hurt by the remark, and also reminded by it that he and Jenny had not yet made love. But he didn't respond, feeling it prudent not to do so, understanding that her anger was not directed against him, but against Denholm.

"Denholm's not like us," she said. "I mean, not like you and me. He was brought up in Windsor by aristocratic parents, educated at Eton, and went into the theatre, quite deliberately I'm convinced, as a way of causing a little outrage and gaining himself some attention. But he's definitely upper-class, doesn't know what struggle means, and will certainly end up doing what he was bred for – namely, wearing a pinstripe suit in the City and charming people who're impressed by his good breeding into giving him money. Lily may not be sophisticated, nor well educated, but she's more decent and loving than Denholm could even imagine. And *he* makes fun of *her*!"

The following evening, when a ragged Denholm and Anthony joined them and, getting drunk dangerously fast, started swopping sarcastic remarks about Lily, almost as if she wasn't there, Lily's big eyes brimmed over with tears.

"What I like about you, Lily," Denholm said finally, "is your perfect equanimity in the face of any verbal onslaught. You're so *agreeable*, dear heart!"

When Lily fled sobbing from the bar, Jenny glared at Denholm and said, "*That* was fairly piggish!"

"Being a country girl, you'd know."

"Don't be so bloody superior, Denholm!"

"You look lovely when you're angry."

"Don't condescend to me either. I'm not impressed with your inherited sophistication."

"I'm sorry I don't impress you."

"No, Denholm, you don't – I don't care for *you*. It's *Lily* who cares for you – and you treat her abominably. I don't like to see it."

"Then stop coming around," Denholm said.

"In future I won't."

"Goodnight, Jenny."

"Go to hell!" she spat, then turned away and hurried out of the bar while Denholm, grinning lopsidedly, raised his hands in mock innocence.

"I think you went too far there," Bill admonished him.

"You may be right, Bill. I know I tease Lily too much, but in truth I'm very fond of her, perhaps more than you realise."

Bill left the bar, hurrying through the busy lobby, went outside and found Jenny helping Lily into a taxi. She kissed Lily's cheek, closed the door and waved goodbye, then, when the taxi moved away, turned back and saw Bill.

"Very funny," she said.

"No, Jenny, it wasn't funny – and I had nothing to do with it."

She stared steadily at him, then broke into a warm smile, stepped forward and slid her arms about him and leaned her head on his shoulder.

"Let's get away for a while – from Denholm, Anthony, Lily, the whole city. Let's go away for the weekend."

His heart started racing. He wasn't sure what she meant. "What I'm hearing sounds too good to be true. You and me? Away *where*?"

"I want to show you where I come from – Golant, in Cornwall. We could leave tomorrow morning, spend a night there and come back on Sunday. What do you think?"

"I think I'm in heaven."

When she turned up the following morning, she was wearing her uniform and sitting proudly in the jeep she used for work.

"Today you're a VIP," she said. "Get in. Let's get going!"

Because of his work, Bill had gotten to know London and the air bases nearest to it; but now, for the first time, he was able to see the English countryside, lush, green, undulating, and, this particular day, enhanced by the sunlight.

Departures

Instead of taking the shortest route to Cornwall, Jenny stuck to the minor roads, thus enabling him to see the most attractive towns and villages inland. She stopped a few times en route, notably at Glastonbury, home of the first Christian church and legendary burial place of King Arthur, where they had a picnic on the summit of the ancient Tor, in the shadow of the remains of St Michael's chapel, overlooking the red-roofed town.

"I'm going to write about this some day," Bill solemnly informed her as they sat side by side on the grassy slope, drinking wine and gazing out over what might have been either the Land of the Dead or King Arthur's Avalon. "I'm going to write about England and you and what you both mean to me."

"What's that?" she asked him.

"You'll have to read it when I write it," he replied.

"We'll both be old and grey when you write that. So how can I read it?"

"We'll be married," he said.

She stared at him, startled, her pale face turning red, then she gathered the picnic things together with great concentration.

"We'd better get moving," she said. "We've still a long way to go."

He felt good then, relaxed, taking note of her smile, and helped her to clear up the picnic, before they drove off. She drove him into the Blackdown Hills, around Exeter, across Dartmoor, and seemed perfectly at ease when he placed his hand on her shoulder, ran it down her arm, and finally let it rest on her thigh as they crossed Bodmin Moor.

"It feels very nice here," he said.

"The Moor or my leg?"

"I meant the Moor, but your leg feels nice as well."

"So does your hand, Bill."

They arrived at St Austell in the afternoon, but Jenny didn't stop, instead driving through the town and out again, along a road flanked by tree-covered hills and tilled fields in which stately homes and thatched cottages were nestling.

As they headed towards the coast, they were waved down more than once by uniformed members of the Home Guard, who were protecting the beaches on which the troops were gathering. Once shown Jenny's pass, they always let her continue, and she drove deeper into green hills and tree-covered lanes, eventually braking to a halt in front of a stone-walled, thatched-roofed farmhouse, with chickens squawking noisily in the gardens and sheep grazing nearby.

The house looked picturesque and inviting in the afternoon's fading light.

"Is this your home?" Bill asked her.

"No," she replied. "It's the house of an aunt and uncle. They took my brother and sister in after my parents died. Would you like to meet them?"

"Yes, Jenny."

The door was opened by a heavily-built, grey-haired woman who smiled with delight at seeing Jenny, then warmly embraced her. After being introduced as Jenny's aunt Nora, she shook Bill's hand with shy formality, then nushered them into the house, which was dimly lit and cluttered, its log fire burning warmly in the hearth and casting flickering shadows.

"Take a seat," Nora said, indicating the benches on

Departures

either side of a long wooden table. "Joe's out on the farm at the moment – that's my husband," she explained to Bill. "And your brother and sister are both helping him. Here, have a cup of tea while I go and fetch them."

But she didn't have to fetch them – they'd obviously seen the jeep – and the three of them hurried into the house as Nora started pouring the tea from an old, blackened kettle. Shrieking with delight, the slim girl in a blouse and skirt threw herself into Jenny's arms, while the boy, who seemed distinctly uncomfortable, held back in the shadows. He was wearing short grey pants, a matching jacket and rolled-down socks; he was handsome in a dark-eyed, haunted way, his gaunt cheeks smeared with mud.

"We've been helping uncle around the farm," Jenny's younger sister said, stepping back and smiling up at her. "That's why we look filthy."

"You look lovely, Donna."

Jenny stroked the jet-black hair of the slim girl in her arms while glancing uneasily at her brother, who still hadn't moved.

"Don't I get a kiss from my little brother?"

"Don't be soft," the boy replied.

"You're too old for it now, Tom?"

"It's just stupid," Tom said.

Jenny looked hurt – just a little, but enough to show – then her uncle, who was silvery-haired and had healthily flushed cheeks, wearing dirt-smeared coveralls and muddied Wellington boots, stepped forward, embraced her and kissed her cheek.

"My," he said, "it's good to see you! You still look as pretty as a picture. So who's this you've brought?"

Releasing Donna, her younger sister, Jenny introduced

Bill. Her uncle shook his hand and Donna beamed flirtatiously; but Tom merely nodded solemnly and took a chair near the fire, where he started pulling off his muddy boots.

"What's that you're drinking?" Joe asked.

"Tea," Jenny replied.

"I'm sure Bill here, at least, would like something stronger than that."

"So would I!" Jenny said.

The next two hours were enchanting, made so by the good-humoured, affectionate conversation and the cider poured so generously by Joe. The flickering flames from the open fire webbed the room with light and shadow, lending the copper pots and pans hung on the walls a rich, golden hue. A shaggy dog snored near the hearth with a black cat curled against it, and a radio, turned low, offered music and war news, where it sat on a deeply varnished, oak sideboard piled high with old papers, magazines and pieces of bric-a-brac. It was a cosy place, lived in, filled with years of shared feelings, and the affection between Jenny and her relatives was clear to Bill's searching eye – a camaraderie marred only by her brother, Tom, who remained dour and distant.

Jenny was obviously enjoying herself, hugging Donna a lot, but she also glanced frequently at Tom, as if hoping to somehow draw him towards her, though she failed to do so. The boy remained in the corner, shadows flickering across his gaunt face, his dark eyes turning towards them, then away, as if frightened of being seen. He looked frail and his shoulders were slumped in a pose of defeat.

When eventually, Bill and Jenny prepared to leave,

everyone embraced emotionally . . . everyone but Tom. He simply waved from his chair near the fire, then turned away from them.

Night had fallen outside. The sky was filled with stars. The hills were silhouetted like black breasts against the sky and a light wind was moaning through the trees, which were shivering and rustling.

Jenny walked to the jeep, the smile removed from her face, and just stood there, looking back at the house, as if waiting for something.

Bill was just about to ask her what was wrong when the door of the house opened, letting light beam out, and Tom emerged and raced across the garden to fall into her arms.

"I'm sorry, Sis'!" he sobbed. "I'm so sorry! I didn't mean to be nasty. I just don't know what to say anymore! It's not the same anymore!"

"It's all right," she whispered, stroking his head. "I understand, Tom. I still love you. We all do."

The boy sobbed for a long time, clinging to her, his body shaking, and she hugged him and tenderly stroked his head until he had calmed down. When he had done so, he sniffed, wiped his eyes and stepped away from her.

"You're going to the house?" he asked her.

"Yes," she said. "I have to see it."

"I don't want to see it," he replied. "Not ever again. Goodnight, Jenny."

"Good night, Tom."

He gave a faltering smile, nodded solemnly at Bill, then returned to the house and went inside, leaving darkness and silence.

Jenny wiped the tears from her eyes and clambered

into the jeep. When Bill climbed up beside her, she started the engine and drove off, heading back in the direction they had come from, along a dark, tree-lined road.

When Jenny headed for the coast, the road became narrower, not much more than a track, twisting and coiling between high hedgerows and densely packed trees, past cottages and houses whose lights shone warmly into the darkness. Then the car climbed steeply and Bill caught a glimpse of water, a green cove beyond the trees – but Jenny turned away from it, drove along another narrow lane and came eventually to the driveway and gardens of a white-painted, unlit house.

She stopped the jeep in front of the house, turned off the ignition, but just sat there behind the steering wheel, staring into the darkness.

There was a very long silence, until Bill, no longer able to bear the tension, asked, "Can I help?"

Jenny took a deep breath.

"When my parents were killed," she said in a hushed, hesitant manner, "it hit us all badly, but Tom's the one who took it worst of all – he just couldn't accept it. He suffered frequent nightmares, fell into long silences, and eventually insisted that he couldn't remain in this house, since it only reminded him of our parents and made him hurt all the more. That's why he and my sister are living with my aunt and uncle."

She leaned forward, touched the steering-wheel with her forehead, then sat up again.

"Tom's not the person he was. He was once so happy, but now he's miserable. He's given up all his friends, gets embarrassed by affection, and is happiest when working on his own in the fields of my uncle's farm. He's frightened of his own emotions – and we think he's retreating into himself and may never come back to us."

She turned her head to stare steadily at him, moonlight making her eyes shine.

"I didn't just lose my parents," she explained. "I'm also losing my brother. Will you hurt me even more?"

"No, Jenny." He almost choked on the words. "I want to love you – not hurt you."

"That's all I want to hear."

She led him into the house, closing the door behind them, then turned the lights on and wandered about, pointing out this and that, like a distracted estate agent, touching him lightly with her fingers when not stroking the furniture, clearly torn between the love she had lost and what she wanted from him.

It was a cluttered, comfortable house and he felt at home in it, but said nothing until she led him up the stairs and into her bedroom. The bed was still made-up, the pillows crisp white on brown blankets, and she flipped the blankets back, exposing the sheets, before turning to face him.

"Do you *really* want to marry me?" she asked him.

"God, yes," he replied.

"Then I consider myself to be your wife from this moment on. I love you, Bill Eisler."

"And I love you . . . Jenny Eisler."

She was shy, but not embarrassed, letting him watch her as she undressed. Still dressed, he held her naked in his arms and explored her with wonder. Her smooth skin was a revelation, her softness overwhelming. He heard groaning and realised it was himself as she pushed him away. He watched her slipping into the bed, stretching out beneath the sheets, caught the glint in her green eyes, her impish smile, as she watched him undress. Then he slid down beside her, pulling the sheets around them both, shivered briefly with the shock of her body's warmth through his cold skin, then glowed with an ethereal heat when she melted against him. He became of age then, as he lay upon her and entered her, and came alive, resurrected as someone else, when he heard her soft cry.

They made love for a long time, or what seemed like such, and then slept in each other's arms, as one, indivisible, and awakened in the pearly light of dawn to greet the world with a smile.

"Man and wife!" Jenny whispered.

Chapter Twenty-Four

∽

Before going to Jennifer's club for the second time, Bill paid a visit to Anthony Barker in the private hospital in Bloomsbury, recommended by Bill's Harley Street friend. As he entered the hospital, he suffered a wave of guilt, since he had told Maureen he would be making this particular visit, but hadn't told her that his real purpose was to see his old flame.

He was particularly guilty about it because Maureen, already depressed by her experience with the pompous TV director and trying to psych herself up for her theatre audition, was becoming increasingly anxious and irritable.

To make matters worse, he had promised to take her to the Henley Regatta boat races, being held that day at Henley-on-Thames, but Denholm, not knowing this, had arranged an important lunch for him with one of the financial backers for the film. Since Denholm was not planning to attend the lunch, feeling that Bill and the financier would be better off left alone with "the delicate subject of compromise", Bill had begged him to take Maureen to the Regatta.

After checking at the hospital's reception desk, Bill took the lift to the second floor, then walked along a pleasant corridor and into a spotless room. Anthony was propped up on the bed, his nose in a book. He glanced at Bill when he entered, smiled cheerfully, then waved him in.

"Welcome to my new world," he said. "And a much better world it is, Bill, so please let me thank you."

"My pleasure," Bill replied, pulling up a chair and sitting beside the bed. Anthony, who had been holding the book in an awkward manner in his crippled hands, placed it on the bedside cabinet, then rested his hands on his lap.

"This hospital is heaven," he said, "compared to the last one. And your Harley Street friend, Martin Brennan, has put me through the hoops and come up with a different approach, involving less drugs and more physiotherapy. He's convinced, so he tells me, that my condition *can* be improved, and already, since moving here and going off the other drugs, I'm feeling a lot better, if not yet like Superman. What can I say, Bill?"

"You've already said it all."

Anthony smiled and settled back against his pillows. "So what have you and Maureen been up to for the past few days? And why haven't I met her yet?"

"She's at the Henley Regatta with Denholm. I was supposed to take her, but couldn't. I had an appointment with one of Denholm's financiers, so Denholm kindly stood in for me."

"I hope you realise that Denholm's still a lady's man, regardless of age."

Departures

Bill grinned at that one. "I place my trust in my wife. And truth to tell, I don't think that even Denholm would attempt that with Maureen."

"A few years ago he might have – but now, even if just as immoral, he's probably too short of breath."

"Let's hope so, Anthony."

"How did your meeting go with Denholm's financier?"

"It's the old story," Bill said. "I want to produce and direct it myself, to protect my own script, but naturally the fat-bellied bastard had some ideas to contribute – such as a little less romance, a lot more sex, and some battle scenes to up the ante with video buyers."

"And you said?"

"I said I'd have to think about it – but I'm just buying time."

"What's Denholm's attitude to all this?"

"Pragmatic, as always. He says that either I compromise and get some of what I want or I stand on my principles and sacrifice the whole goddamned movie. That may indeed be true, but I just wish he'd do a bit more to come down on my side."

"Denholm knows them. He deals with them every day. If he antagonises them, he'll lose more than you – and it isn't *his* movie."

Bill sighed. "Yeah, you're right." He glanced around the clean white room, then turned back to Anthony, who was showing a marked improvement in appearance and spirit.

It made Bill feel that he had done some good – and even compensated a little for the guilt he was feeling at not telling Maureen about Jennifer. In fact, he wanted to tell Anthony – or at least ask him if he knew that Jenny was living right here in London – but he couldn't do it without also explaining that he had been seeing her in secret.

"I'd like to tell you I have an urgent appointment," he said instead, "but the truth is, I just can't stand hospitals. This visit is going to be as short as the last one, but I'm sure you understand."

"At our age, dear Bill, that concern is understandable. You've done enough already, God knows, so please don't feel embarrassed."

"I'll drop in again tomorrow."

"You don't have to."

"I will. And when I do, I'll bring some grapes to eat while you slaver in hunger. How does that sound?"

"Sadistic. The sort of thing one would expect from those bastards in that hotel in Kensington."

"God bless 1944," Bill said, standing up.

"Those days won't come again, Bill."

"Is there anything else I can get you?"

"I think you've done enough already, Bill. Enjoy the city! Stay young!"

"*Adios.*"

"*Au revoir!*"

Leaving his much improved friend and feeling better for having helped him, he took a cab to Soho. It didn't take long to get there, and after paying the driver, he glanced nervously left and right along the narrow, cluttered, rubbish-strewn street, then entered the shadowy portals of Jennifer's club.

It was busier than the last time, with most of the tables full, and Jennifer was sitting at the end of the bar, smoking a cigarette, sipping what looked like water, and

Departures

glancing around her dimly lit, large room with the eye of an eagle.

"Hey, Jennifer!" a woman's voice rang out. "You've got yer Yankee boyfriend back! And 'e don't 'alf look 'andsome!"

Embarrassed, Bill waved at Marjorie as he hurried across the floor. Jennifer smiled, as if amused by his discomfort, then kissed his cheek.

"Hello, Bill." She wiped the lipstick from his cheek with a paper tissue. "What a pleasant surprise this is!"

"I told you I'd come."

"I *know* you did, dear, but I couldn't be sure."

"I'm not the kind to break my word, Jenny – "

"Jennifer!"

" – which I'm sure you already knew."

She beamed. "Yes, dear, of *course* I did! Now what would you like to drink?"

"I think a beer would be fine."

"Do you mean English ale or foreign lager?"

"English ale, thanks."

"A pint of best bitter, please, James!"

"Coming right up!" James sang.

James pumped the pint of beer into a large glass, then placed it on the counter in front of Bill. "A pint of the best!" he exclaimed in his theatrical manner. "For our American friend!"

He smiled seductively and departed, leaving Bill alone with Jennifer, who sat beside him, at no more than elbow's length, her steady gaze disconcerting.

"Darling Bill. You really mustn't take me too seriously. I mean, I *could* do with a loan, with a little injection of capital, but that isn't the only reason I wanted to see you. I also *wanted* to see you."

"That's nice," Bill said.

"You're right to be sarcastic, Bill. I've hurt your feelings terribly. I should never have asked you for that money – though I *do* need it desperately. But it's not your concern. I just asked, I suppose, without thinking, and now I feel really bad."

"But you *do* need the money?"

"I am not a *liar*, Bill."

"I just need some time to think about it."

"Of course," she said. "Naturally."

"I was thinking about you last night."

"Yes?"

"Yes. I was remembering you and me during the war. The dome of St Paul's cathedral, then Cornwall. That night in your house."

She actually blushed. He saw it beneath her make-up. She took a last drag on her cigarette, stubbed it out in the ashtray, then blew a cloud of smoke and waved it away from him.

"That was a long time ago. *Too* long. I think it best forgotten. It was not you and I, Bill."

"No?"

"No."

"I think it was – you and me as we were and *are*. We *looked* younger, and possibly knew less, but it was *us* – it was you and me."

"Please drink your beer, Bill."

"You're trying to change the subject."

"I do not wish to dwell on the past. I see little point to it."

"But you want me to lend you money."

"So?"

"And you based your request on our shared past – on what we'd meant to each other."

"I did not!"

"Yes, you did."

She lit another cigarette, looking petulant. "Well, maybe I did. I didn't *mean* to, but perhaps I did. I didn't plan it, but then I saw you on the telly. Then the shock . . . and then . . ."

"You needed money and knew what I'd felt for you and thought I'd feel a certain obligation and – "

"*No!*"

"Then what?"

"I . . ." Obviously confused, she glanced around the club. Hearing a customer swear loudly, she announced to the gallery: "I won't tolerate bad manners in my establishment! *Ralph!* Please ask that gentleman to leave!"

Ralph materialised out of nowhere, as broad as he was tall, and went straight to the table of the man who had sworn. He leaned down to whisper something into his ear, thus encouraging the blushing man to jump up and hurry out of the club.

"*So* sorry," Jennifer said, "but a woman's work is never done and I was just doing mine."

"Very efficiently," Bill said.

"Thank you," she responded. "And now I have to attend to my other customers, so please enjoy your drink and let me come back to you in ten minutes. All right?"

"OK, Jennifer."

She went behind the counter and walked along to the far end of the bar where, after patting James affectionately on the shoulder, she welcomed the woman who had just entered and taken a stool.

The woman was in her mid-thirties, had lustrous, jet-black hair, and was wearing a navy blue coat over a grey dress. She was very attractive.

Jennifer kissed her on the cheek with what Bill felt was uncommon intimacy. Maybe *too* intimate.

Watching them converse, he started feeling strange: on the one hand intrigued by the intimacy they seemed to share, on the other, feeling drawn inexplicably to the younger woman.

Jennifer and the younger woman talked freely, leaning close to one another, and Bill studied them in growing confusion. He felt oddly, undeniably resentful . . . and even suspicious.

They seemed more than close friends.

He wanted to get up and leave, but he simply couldn't move, and was relieved when Jennifer, obviously remembering that he was there, smiled at him, whispered something to her friend, then walked back to join him. She smiled and licked her thin, painted lips. Not the lips he had once kissed.

"Oh, Bill!" she exclaimed with theatrical insincerity. "I'm *so* sorry to have left you for so long! Another drink, darling?"

"No, I have to go."

"Really?"

"Yep. I just dropped in to check the place out again – and to see you again."

"No need for false compliments. I'm too old to benefit from them. Can we, instead, discuss this little matter of dollars and cents?"

Departures

"No. Not tonight. I'll come back tomorrow evening, I promise, but I really have to fly now."

"I understand, Bill."

In fact, he wanted to leave because the dark-haired woman was going and he was, to his surprise, determined to follow her and find out who she was. So, as she left, waving goodbye to Jennifer's ladies, Bill pushed his stool back and stood up.

"Who's your attractive friend?"

"Carol. Just an acquaintance."

"She doesn't work for you?"

"No."

Bill nodded, feeling criminal. "Well, it's been nice. I'm sorry I have to run. I'll think about your request and try to work something out."

"That's kind of you, Bill."

"Those old days were good days, weren't they, Jennifer?"

"Yes, Bill, they were."

"Tomorrow evening?"

"Yes, Bill."

He hurried out of the club, looked right and left, then saw Carol walking towards Old Compton Street. He followed her down, kept on her tail through Soho, and didn't let her out of his sight as she crossed Piccadilly Circus, neon-lit and chaotic, then along in the direction of Green Park.

His heart sank with every step. He had guessed her destination correctly. She passed Fortnum and Mason, the light-strewn facade of the Ritz, and eventually turned into Half Moon Street. Then she entered Shepherd Market, which at this time was lively, and walked straight to the door of Jennifer's apartment, beside the wine bar. He watched her open the door and enter. He was holding his breath. When she closed the door behind her, he glanced around the small square, took in the crowded pubs, restaurants and wine bars, the elegant whores and tourists, then leaned against the wall behind him and took a deep breath.

Did Jennifer and that woman live together?

It certainly seemed so.

He stood there a long time, enfolded in darkness, staring dazedly into the bright lights, disbelieving his wild thoughts.

Jennifer and the dark-haired woman, Carol, whom he was certain he recognised.

From somewhere.

Sometime.

Eventually, too confused to think properly, he headed back to his hotel – and, he hoped, Maureen.

Chapter Twenty-Five

༄

"It was a wonderful day," Maureen said across the table in the dining room of the Red Lion pub in Mayfair. "I feel tired, a little drunk and very mellow, which can't be a bad thing."

"It was *my* pleasure, I assure you," Denholm replied, exhaling cigar smoke. "When you're happy, Maureen, *I'm* happy – and tonight I am joyous."

"You were always a smooth-talker, Denholm."

"I simply say what I feel."

"No, you don't. You lie. And you're doing that right now. You didn't take me to Henley out of the good of your heart, but because Bill asked you to – to keep me from feeling depressed while he was having his meeting. That's what old buddies do for each other. You and Bill are old pals."

"*Too* old," Denholm said. "It makes me shudder to think about it. Did we really meet forty years ago? I don't want to believe it."

"Bill said you were handsome in your uniform. A real lady-killer."

"I like to think I was killing Germans," Denholm replied. "But Bill *is* a romantic."

"He told me some stories about you."

"I'm sure he did, Maureen."

"You, Anthony Barker, and all the WAAFs you preyed upon. I sometimes feel I missed something."

"You didn't miss much, really. We were seedy, rather than glamorous. We drank far too much, played our roles as daring pilots, and hoped to hell that no one would see just how frightened we were. As for the WAAFs, we certainly tried to impress them, though not always successfully."

"Bill would say otherwise."

"He's a writer, dear girl."

"And you did, after all, marry a WAAF – your first wife, Lily Monaghan."

"I was always a decent chap and couldn't resist her lovelorn gaze. I much preferred her girlfriend, Jenny Birken, but Bill had won *her* heart."

"Ah, ha! My husband's dark past at last! I want to hear all the details."

"If I had them, you'd get them. It was a short-lived romance, rather innocent, quite touching. Bill met Lily through me, then met Jenny through Lily. He had a solemn romance that lasted a couple of months, then he was shipped off to Normandy, to cover the invasion of Europe, and he never saw his sweet young thing again. That's all there was to it."

"And you fancied his girl even more than the one you married?"

Denholm grinned and nodded. "I certainly did. My Lily was big and buxom, good-natured, not too bright;

Departures

but sex was the only thing we had in common and that's never a good sign. Bill's girl was more my type, and I *did* want to get into her pants, though I never succeeded."

"Did Bill?"

"I don't know. He wasn't the type to talk about it. Anthony and I were fashionably cynical, but Bill took life more seriously."

"You described his girl as common muck."

Denholm chuckled and shook his head. "My little mischief," he said. "She was common only in the sense that she was obviously working-class, but she was also clear-eyed, sharp-tongued, and attractive. Certainly *not* common muck!"

His grin was sardonic, but his steady gaze was searching, and Maureen sensed, as she had done in the past, that he was trying to gauge what she felt about him. She had never surrendered to him, though had often thought about it, and even now she could only dwell on the difference between him and Bill.

Bill was a romantic who would fight for what he believed in, whereas Denholm, though charming and certainly bright, was the ultimate pragmatist, or cynic.

That he and Bill had remained friends for so long had never ceased to amaze her.

"So *did* Bill ask you to take care of me?" she enquired. "Was this wonderful, very English day your small act of mercy?"

"It is *not* my act of mercy. I love your company, as you know. But Bill is certainly worried about you – about you being worried. He's convinced that your next interview has made you unduly nervous, and he doesn't want you left alone to brood. *Are* you that worried?"

Maureen glanced at the other diners in this attractively old restaurant, realised how far from home she was, then turned back to Denholm.

"Yes, I guess I am. And I've certainly let it out on Bill. I haven't been interviewed for years, which is a problem in itself, and my meeting with that supercilious TV director didn't help me at all."

"You have to take the rough with the smooth, Maureen. It's part of the business."

"I know it is, and I should be able to take it, but I don't think I can anymore. I've been away too long, Denholm. I'm not used to humiliation. And now this interview at the Royal Shakespeare Company – damn it, my knees knock when I think about it! I'm not sure I can face it."

"The worst is over. The RSC isn't TV Land. I'm sure you'll find the people there more civilised and less prone to self-love. TV people think thespians are a nuisance, but the theatre still loves them."

"I hope so."

"Stop worrying."

He gazed steadily at her, an enigmatic smile on his lips, and she understood why he would always have problems with women. He still looked ten years younger than he was – about *her* age, in fact – and his cynical wit and mischievous charm certainly made him uncommon. Even she, who had always been wary of him, found him attractive – and she knew that he knew it and would play on it, if he thought it would help him.

He was amoral . . . and dangerous.

"You're a damned attractive woman," he said quietly, as if reading her thoughts. "Bill's lucky to have you."

"I sometimes wonder," she replied, quietly shocked to be responding to his compliment.

"Oh? Why?"

"He hasn't been all that happy lately. I mean . . ."

"Yes?"

"You're his friend, so can I speak to you in confidence?"

"Of course, Maureen. Naturally."

Still feeling mildly drunk, aware that she was being indiscreet, yet driven to release her secret fears, she could not stop herself. "As you know," she began, "I'm ten years younger than Bill – "

"Lucky him!"

She shook her head in disagreement. "I don't think he sees it that way. Frankly, his sexual potency isn't what it used to be – he can't make love too often – and his anxieties over this are made worse by the difference in our ages."

"We are none of us what we were, dear. As for Bill, if you stay as you are, he'll probably get over it."

"I'm not sure he will. I've told him it doesn't matter, that our love is more important, but I don't think he really believes me. What man would, after all?"

"Not me!"

"Bill's *not* you," she replied. "And the fact that even *he* can be bothered by this makes me lose sleep at nights."

"I'm sure that if you tell him all this, he'll feel a lot happier."

"I *have* tried telling him this, but I don't think it helped him. Maybe because we never had a child. I know he thinks *that's* his fault."

"Lots of people don't have children."

"But I'm ten years younger than Bill. I'm convinced that makes him feel he's deprived me of the best part of my life."

"What do *you* think?"

"I certainly missed having a child. I always will, I suppose. But if I'd had a child by a man I despised, that would have been worse. I don't think there's any black and white to it – it's just one of those things. As for Bill, he's the finest man I ever knew – and that means a lot to me. More than sex. More than children."

Something shifted in Denholm's face. She wasn't sure what it was. A shadow, a fine film of surprise, that passed across the sardonic glint in his blue eyes and briefly rendered them naked. Then he sighed, blew a cloud of cigar smoke, and returned to his normal self.

"I still think he'll get over it," he said. "Given your understanding of the situation, nothing else is conceivable. He'll recover. Believe me."

"God, I hope so – because his anxiety is starting to make him act strangely. In fact, I think his concern about our relationship has something to do with his disappearances over the past few evenings."

"His *disappearances*?"

"Yes. He's either visiting Anthony Barker or someone else he hasn't mentioned. Certainly, if he's seeing Anthony every evening, he's giving him lots of time."

"Well, I'm sure he's seeing Anthony. I mean, Anthony *is* in hospital. And I know from everything Bill's said that he couldn't be inventing those visits."

"I don't think he's inventing them. I'm convinced they're just his excuse to stay out at nights."

"To see someone else?"

"Yes, Denholm, that's it."

And she felt terrible having said it, convinced that even if it was true, she should not be discussing it.

"You think he might be seeing another woman?"

She nodded. "Yes, I do. Damn it, I've never thought this before. It makes me feel almost . . . *dirty*."

Denholm stubbed out his cigar. "I think you're wrong, Maureen. And I certainly doubt that another woman is involved."

"What makes you so sure?"

"My theory is that if Bill *is* worried about his sexual potency, he's probably even *more* worried about this movie we're trying to set up."

"His *movie?*"

"Yes. If he wants to get finance, he's going to have to make changes he's bitterly opposed to – and I'm sure he's lost a lot of sleep over that. So if, as you say, he's disappearing during the evenings, he may be doing so just to be alone and think this thing through."

"You really think so?"

"I do."

She felt better immediately, was grateful to Denholm for that, and made no objection when he reached across the table to take her hand and squeeze it affectionately.

"No matter what happens between us," he said in a deliberate, actorish manner, "I'm still a friend to both of you."

"What could happen between us?"

He gazed steadily, intently at her, still holding her hand. "Oh," he said, slowly, as if considering each word, holding her with his gaze and trying to draw her towards him, "for a start, this movie could cause problems, and then . . ." He hesitated, shrugging. "No, Maureen, it's nothing."

But she knew that it wasn't all . . . He had been thinking about her and himself and what could happen between them.

Feeling his fingers around her hand, she recalled the many times he had stayed with them in California – those lazy days by the pool, the evenings enlivened with food and drink, the weekends filled with touring and socialising and friendships's intimate pleasures. She realised, with hindsight, that he had always found her attractive and that she, if not exactly encouraging him any further, had certainly appreciated the attention and not tried to hide the fact.

Now, reassured, but still not entirely happy, she found herself responding, even against her better judgement, to his charm and emotional support.

She saw the danger-line clearly drawn.

"Well," she said, trying to make light of her feelings, "now that I know Bill will probably get over his anxieties, the only thing I have to fear is my RSC interview."

"Don't worry about that either," Denholm replied. "I'm going to bring some influence to bear where it counts with the RSC. It's not much, but it may help – and will certainly make your next interview more pleasant, even if not successful."

Without thinking, she placed her free hand on his, and said, "You don't have to."

He stared thoughtfully at her, then smiled slightly, perhaps cynically, and she knew, in her insincerity and shameless need to pass the audition, that in letting her hand remain where it was, she was offering herself to him.

"It's my pleasure," he said.

Chapter Twenty-Six

The estate agent had already fixed the "For Sale" sign to the gate of Carol's house in Highgate.

Feeling oddly remote from herself, Carol walked up the garden path, opened the front door and entered the house. She stopped for a moment, reluctant to go farther, but eventually forced herself to close the door and walk into the lounge.

The furniture had been covered with white dust sheets and the oak-panelled room seemed eerily cold in the grey light.

Carol switched the lights on.

The estate agent had thoughtfully left her mail on the *secretaire*, along with his company's brochure for the house.

Lighting a cigarette, Carol read the sales pitch, hardly recognising the house as her own.

Amused, she placed the brochure back on the *secretaire*. She was selling up, moving out, and felt no regret at all – only the urge to get it done and turn her back on the past.

She examined the mail as she smoked. It consisted mostly of window-envelopes, a pile of bills and formal papers, most of which she threw back on the *secretaire* without bothering to open them. When she had glanced through the ones that seemed important, she gathered them together, put a rubber band around them and put them into her shoulder-bag.

There were more debts than the sale of the house would cover.

Feeling crushed, she stubbed her cigarette out, glanced around her former prison, switched off the lights and left the house.

"To hell with it," she murmured to herself as she closed and locked the front door.

She would not go back until the house was sold and she had to sell off the furniture.

It was behind her for good.

Driving away from the village, she headed for Chelsea, distracted throughout the journey, set upon by all her problems, torn between the situation created by John's death and her awareness that her mother had terminal cancer, with all that implied.

Yet her mother was so courageous, refusing to accept defeat, still running her business and not displaying the slightest self-pity.

She had always been like that, of course, having struggled to survive, an unmarried mother in a time when that was scandalous, fighting humiliation and lack of cash to bring up her daughter. There had been men in her life, the odd lover now and then, but her lasting love had been reserved for Carol's father, shot down so long ago.

Departures

"He was the best man I ever knew," she had often told Carol, "and I'd rather stay married to his memory than end up with a lesser man."

Carol had thought about that often, intrigued by that kind of loyalty, and was glad that her mother liked David and thought him a good man.

As she drove along the King's Road, towards David's shop, she faced the fact that whether or not she was wearing rose-coloured spectacles, she loved David as she had loved no one else, finding with him the emotional security she had formerly lacked.

Parking the car in a side street, she walked back to the King's Road, then turned into David's shop. The door was closed, but she let herself in with her key and walked up the stairs to the flat. David was in the lounge, which was cluttered and homely; he was leaning over the cot and playfully shaking a rattle in Mark's face.

"Cha! Cha! Cha!" he was singing.

"Cha, cha, indeed!" Carol exclaimed.

David stopped shaking the rattle, glanced around, then gave a wide, unembarrassed grin. "Ah! You're back! You've come to collect our child. He is, as you will note, fat and sassy – and well entertained! Here," he said, pressing the rattle into the baby's hand, "let's see *you* do something!" Straightening up as Carol approached, he took her into his arms and kissed her, then stepped back to let her lean over the cot. When she saw her son's face, she felt whole again.

"He's so lovely," she said, lifting him out of the cot and hugging him. "God, I love you." Rubbing her face against his soft cheek. "I do! I adore you."

David chuckled and shook his head. "One would think you'd been parted for a year rather than a few days."

"It *seems* like a year!"

"Yes, I'm sure it does. And now that I've gotten used to him, this place won't seem the same without him. Would you like a drink?"

"A glass of white wine would be nice."

"Fine. Coming up."

She reluctantly placed Mark back in his cot, then took the nearest chair.

"So," David said as he poured their drinks, "you're moving into your mother's flat this evening."

"Yes."

"I still think you should move in here with me."

"I'd really love to – you know that – but I can't. I still think it's too early."

He handed her a glass. "I miss *you* badly enough," he said. "Now I'm going to miss both of you."

"Just give me some time," she said.

He nodded gravely, kissed her on the forehead, then took the chair facing her.

"I really want you to marry me."

"I want that as well, David. I just feel that I've got to sort myself out first."

"I can help you do that. You've always had a bad time with men, not least of all your husband, and now you're frightened to commit yourself again, which I think I can understand. But I'm not like the others, Carol. I don't want to dominate you. I want to love you and share life with you. I want nothing in the world but you and Mark – to make you both happy."

"Yes, David, I know."

Departures

She rocked the cot with her free hand, torn between love and lack of confidence, not knowing her own mind.

"It's not just me. Not *only* my personal feelings. I have to sort out this dreadful financial mess left by John and I don't want you dragged into that."

"You've been to the house, I take it."

"Yes. They've put the 'For Sale' sign up. The market's buoyant at the moment, so selling it should be no problem; but even if I get a high offer, it still leaves me short. That's why I want to start my own business. I can't depend on a normal wage."

"You need a lot of money, Carol."

"God, don't I know it?"

David puffed out his cheeks, exhaled air. "I just wish I could help you there."

"I wouldn't take it if I could get it. I don't think that's fair to you. I'm not going to have you involved with debts created by my late husband."

"So where will you get the money?"

"I don't know. And right now, I can't think about it. It's just part of the whole mess: John's death, all the debts, my mother's illness . . ."

"How *is* your mother?"

"As good as can be expected. Though how on earth she can still run that club, I just can't imagine."

"It probably keeps her distracted."

"Yes, I suppose so. But it hurts me to look at her."

"You can't stay with her," David said. "It wouldn't be fair to the baby. Your mother can deal with it right now, but she's going to get worse, and when she does, you shouldn't be there with Mark. Babies need a lot of attention and make a lot of noise. Your mother's nerves will be bad enough with her illness; the baby's presence will make them worse. And besides, I know she *wants* you here with me. She's told both of us that."

"I can't carry this alone, can I, David?"

"No," he told her, "you can't."

She sighed and stood up, placed her glass on the mantlepiece, then looked down through the window at King's Road. The traffic was dense, the pavements crowded with punks and tourists, and she thought of how lively it all looked, divorced from death's silence.

Then Mark shook his rattle, gurgled happily, and stared up with a radiant smile. No, it wasn't fair – neither to Jennifer nor Mark. Nor was it fair to Mark's father, David, who was now quietly watching her. Carol smiled, loving him, wondering how she had ever found him, then walked up to him and knelt by his feet to place her hands on his knees.

"I can't think about marriage yet, David, but I will move in with you."

"Hallelujah!" he said.

Chapter Twenty-Seven

"Hi!" a familiar voice whispered, close to Jennifer's ear. "Here I am again. I just can't keep away." Looking up, she saw Bill grinning at her. "Don't stare at me as if I'm a ghost," he said. "A small beer would be helpful."

Taken by surprise, but secretly pleased and relieved to see him, she placed her newspaper on the counter and called to James for a half-pint of bitter.

"You took me by surprise," she said to Bill.

"A nice surprise?"

"Yes, but don't be so vain."

"That sounds like the girl I used to know. It makes me feel right at home."

They made small talk until James brought the bitter, smiled seductively at Bill, whispered, "Enjoy!" and hurried away again.

"I've been thinking about your situation," Bill said, "and I want to discuss it."

"We *have* discussed it, Bill."

"OK. We *have* discussed it, in a sense. But I've had a good think about it and reached a kind of decision."

"A *kind* of decision?"

He sipped some beer and placed the glass back on the counter. "I've another week here and I promise to make a decision before I fly back. This is *not* an idle promise – I won't run away from this. Whichever way I decide, yes or no, I'll tell you straight to your face. OK?"

"Yes, Bill."

He glanced over her shoulder, as if searching for someone. Looking disappointed, he sipped some more beer.

"I'm sure you can appreciate that I can't give you what you want without serious consideration – and that my money also belongs to my wife."

"I understand, Bill."

Again, he was obviously scanning the long bar.

"Part of my reluctance to come to a decision," he said in a distracted manner, "is based on the fact that I'm certain – and please forgive me if I'm wrong – that you're not levelling with me."

"Pardon?"

"You're hiding something from me – "

"I'm not!"

" – and since you're asking for a sizeable sum, I need to know the real facts. There's something odd about you, Jennifer, something hidden, and that makes me nervous."

Shocked that he should have noticed the anxiety she had tried to hide, she covered her confusion by lighting a cigarette.

"Rubbish! There's nothing odd about me at all. I'm simply not the girl you remember, but you can't quite accept the fact."

"I'm not the Bill *I* remember," he said, "but I accept

that sad fact. No, Jennifer, it isn't that you're older; it's something other than that. You're hiding something. I just don't know what it is. But I feel I've a *right* to know."

"I don't know what you mean, Bill."

He sighed. "OK, Jennifer." After staring around the club, again with that special interest, but failing to find who he was looking for, he tried to sound casual. "I noticed this other lady last night. Not one of your hostesses. Dark-haired and pretty attractive. You were talking to her at the far end of the bar." Jennifer's heart started racing. "The first woman I've seen in here," Bill continued, "who didn't actually work here. That's what took my attention." Jennifer felt breathless. "You and her seemed pretty intimate," Bill said. "She sure seemed like a good friend."

Jennifer felt a bubble of panic expanding inside her. He was discussing his own daughter, though he didn't know that fact. And the irony was that the money she wanted, she wanted for Carol.

Why couldn't she tell them both the truth? She had lied to Carol all her life and to Bill for the past few days; and in both cases had placed herself in a trap from which she might not escape.

"Carol's a friend," she lied again. "Runs a car-hire service. Specialising in chauffeuse-driven limousines. Of course, she drives as well."

"She's pretty attractive. And even from this distance she looked like a really nice lady."

"That's why we're such good friends."

"Despite the difference in your ages."

"That reminder is ungentlemanly, Bill."

"I retract my foolish remark. A mere slip of the tongue."

"I forgive you this once."

At that moment, to Jennifer's horror, Carol entered the club, waved at her, then walked across the floor, stopping to talk to Barbara, Marjorie and Doreen, where they sat at different tables with male customers. She took the same seat on the high-stool at the other end of the bar.

Jennifer's mind nearly went blank with panic, but she rallied her senses.

"Talk of the devil, there's Carol herself! Excuse me, Bill, I have to discuss something with her. I'll be back in a moment."

Before he could reply, she hurried along the bar to kiss Carol on the cheek and sit beside her. Carol looked at the cigarette in her hand and said, "For God's sake, Mother, you shouldn't – !"

"Keep your voice down!" Jennifer hissed. "And don't call me 'mother'!"

"What . . .?"

"Don't look now, but there's a gentleman sitting at the other end of the bar – an old friend, an American – and I don't want him to know you're my daughter."

"Why ever not?" Carol removed the cigarette from Jennifer's fingers and stubbed it out in the nearest ashtray.

"It's to do with business," Jennifer lied. "A possible investment in the club. We're negotiating at the moment and if he knows you're my daughter, he might start discussing my finances, which could make for embarrassment."

"You've been *lying* about your finances?"

"Naturally. This is *business*!"

Carol shook her head, bemused. "I don't *believe* this!" She glanced along the bar, at Bill. "Mmmm, quite a handsome specimen! Silvery-haired, suntanned and well-dressed. Just the type you could do with."

"Don't be funny, Carol."

"He's staring right at us."

"Oh, God!"

"He's smiling and nodding at me."

"Take no notice!"

"Too late," Carol said, amused. "He's coming to join us."

Jennifer glanced back over her shoulder and saw Bill advancing, carrying his glass of beer and smiling like a mischievous schoolboy. He stopped right in front of her.

"I'm sorry," he said, "but I couldn't resist joining you. I feel alone and unprotected down there – and your friend seems so nice."

Carol returned his smile.

"Carol, this is Bill Eisler, an old friend. Bill, dear, this is – "

"Carol." He held out his free hand. "I know your name. Nice to meet you."

He was being flirtatious and Carol was clearly amused. Jennifer felt shaky and could hardly bear to look at them. "Bill saw you yesterday, Carol, and was rather intrigued by you."

"Intrigued?"

"Yes. He had the impression we were very close friends, which of course is the truth."

"Ah, yes," Carol said, even more amused, "we're certainly old friends. I suppose you thought I worked here, Bill?"

"Yes, I did. But Jennifer soon corrected me on that point."

"So when did you and Jennifer first meet?"

"During the war."

Jennifer's heart almost missed a beat.

"Bill was a journalist," she said in a panic. "We met through mutual friends. Since then, he's become successful writing books, as well as scripts for the movies. That's why he's so suntanned."

"I live in California," Bill explained.

"My!" Carol responded, being as mischievous as Bill. "This all sounds so terribly glamorous! Books and movies! *Hollywood!* Why have you never mentioned Bill before? I'm really *surprised* at you!"

"We've been out of touch for some time. And Bill's just here for a visit."

"Business or pleasure?" Carol asked him.

"Mainly business," Bill replied. "And it really isn't as glamorous as you think. It's mostly hard work and hustling."

"More glamorous than *my* work!"

"You drive, I believe."

"Yes."

"Isn't that funny? Jennifer used to drive during the war, when we – "

"I taught her to drive." Jennifer felt very strange. "That's why she's such a good driver."

"And now you're a chauffeuse with a private car-hire service?"

"That's right," Carol replied. "We'll drive you in style anywhere, anytime – *if* you're loaded with money!"

"Anywhere? Even outside the city?"

"We'll drive you across the whole damned country if you like. So long as you pay."

Departures

Bill gazed thoughtfully at her. "Could you take me, my wife and a friend for a drive as far as Devon or Cornwall? I'd like to show my wife Stonehenge and a few other sights, so it would obviously have to be a weekend trip, including an overnight stay. Would that be possible, Carol?"

"Certainly," she replied, clearly delighted, as Jennifer burned hot and cold. "It sounds fine to me."

"I'd like to surprise my wife, so could we make it this weekend, starting early tomorrow?"

"Where are you staying?"

"The Savoy."

"*Very* posh, Bill! What if I pick you up there at nine?"

"Terrific," Bill said.

He finished his beer and grinned wickedly at Jennifer. "You sure have some lovely friends, Jennifer. This has been a real treat." He kissed her on the cheek. "I'll see you next week . . . And I'll see *you* tomorrow, Carol. Till then, *adios*!" Then he waved goodbye and left the club.

Jennifer gave a sigh of relief, then saw Carol's pleased smile.

"What a delightful man! And what a good job to be offered! I'm *glad* I came to see you today – though *you* don't look too happy."

"I'm fine," Jennifer said as Carol slid off her stool. "I was just surprised by his request. And, I must confess, I'm *still* concerned that if he finds out you're my daughter, he's going to ask you awkward questions about the club and my financial situation."

"I think you're being paranoid, but I'll enjoy the play-acting. I won't mention that I'm your daughter – and if he *does* grill me about you or the club, I'll profess complete ignorance."

"You promise?"

"Yes. Now I have to leave. Since I'm going away for the weekend, I'd better let David know. By the way, I've decided to move in with him – maybe some time next week."

"I'm delighted. I'll feel much better when you do that. I've a lot of faith in David and think he's just what you need – and it will certainly be better for little Mark. Now give me a kiss, dear."

Carol kissed her, then walked out, waving at the girls as she went. When she had gone, Jennifer had a cigarette, inhaling deeply, with relief, and watched the smoke spiralling around her before drifting away.

She calmed down eventually, but still felt uneasy, hardly able to believe that Carol and Bill were going to travel together over the weekend. She was frightened of what might happen if they learnt the truth about each other; and was convinced that either they would recognise one another or that Bill, if Carol mentioned her mother, would sense the truth of the matter.

Thinking about it made her heart race again.

After nearly forty years a father and daughter had met for the first time . . . and neither knew who the other was.

Feeling guilty and confused, Jennifer burned hot and cold, thinking of how, almost forty years ago, today's events had begun.

The last time she saw Bill . . .

Chapter Twenty-Eight

∼

From the moment she first made love with Bill, Jenny felt married to him. After two nights in that bed in her home in Cornwall, she had made herself part of him.

"I still feel you inside me," she told him on the Monday, as she drove him in the Jeep back to London. "And now you'll always belong to me. Man and wife, though not married."

"So marry me," Bill replied. "Let's make it real."

"I want to – God knows, I do – but not while this war's on. Ask me again when you come back from Europe. I'll be waiting. I promise."

"I'm not sure I can wait that long," he said. "Why not now, Jenny?"

"It's too complicated," she lied. "Too much paperwork. And you'll be going off soon. When you return, Bill. I promise."

She dropped him off at the hotel in Kensington, distraught to be parted from him, gazing into his gentle eyes and wanting to touch him.

"Come up to my room!" he whispered urgently, his knuckles white where they gripped the side of the jeep.

"I can't," she replied, leaning out to kiss him. "I have to report back by midnight. Tomorrow evening, as usual, in the bar. Goodnight, husband. Sleep tight."

"I love you, Jenny. *I do!*"

She blew him a kiss, waved goodbye and drove off quickly.

She could hardly bear the thought of being parted from him, even for one night.

Driving back to the barracks, she felt alive in the midst of death. As she drove towards the City, she saw the dome of St Paul's cathedral, towering miraculously over the dreadful ruins spread out all around it. The broken walls were bathed in moonlight, casting their shadows on the mounds of rubble, but she saw charred wooden beams, scorched furniture and toys, twisted bicycles and prams, a glittering sea of smashed glass in pulverised stone. She was driving through a great graveyard, the land of the dead, yet she would never feel more alive than she was at that moment, buoyed up on the tidal waves of her love, exalted and rapturous.

She arrived back at her dormitory in the gloomy Victorian building to find Lily sitting on her bed, wearing a nightdress, her long blonde hair pinned up, her large blue eyes moist.

"What's wrong?" Jenny asked her.

"That bastard, Denholm," Lily replied. "I was supposed to meet him in the hotel on Saturday night, but he didn't show up. Not on Sunday either."

"And Anthony?"

"He was missing as well."

Jenny glanced around the large room, which had once been a dining hall, and saw the many other WAAFs preparing for bed. Then she sat on the side of Lily's bed and placed her hand on her shoulder.

"They were probably flying missions," she said. "Why didn't you ring him?"

"They don't fly on weekends," Lily replied. "Denholm *said* they wouldn't be flying. I rang the base in East Anglia, but the bitch there wouldn't put my call through. She said only official calls were being taken. So I've spent the whole weekend on my own, getting drunk alone both nights in that bar, feeling like a real fool. God, Jenny, I'm in love with Denholm Wilding, but he *can* be a bastard!"

"I'm sure there's an explanation."

"Yes. Another woman."

"You've always known that Denholm had other women. You always closed your eyes to it."

"I'd have lost him if I hadn't. But he's never actually stood me up before – and two nights running, the swine! I hate him! *I hate him!*"

She turned away and leaned over to sob into her pillow, so Jenny stroked the back of her head and said, "I don't think that even Denholm would arrange for a switchboard operator to say the base wasn't receiving social calls. I think something is up."

Lily rolled over and stared up with tearful eyes. "You think so?"

"Yes, I do. Since Denholm and Anthony were *both* absent this weekend, it can't be because of Denholm's women. It must have been something else."

Lily's eyes widened as she contemplated the possibility that most women normally tried to ignore . . . a loved one shot down over Europe. "You don't think . . . ?"

Jenny stroked her friend's cheek. "I'm sure it's not

that. If something like that had happened, someone would have got a message to you by now. No, I think the invasion might be imminent and their base has been sealed off."

"Oh, my God!"

"Yes, Lily. Now it's going to be lights-out in a minute and I've got to get ready for bed – so why don't you just relax, have a good sleep, and I'll see what I can find out at headquarters, tomorrow. All right?"

"Right." Lily climbed under the blankets, tugged them up to her chin, started curling into a foetal position, then looked back and smiled. "Hey, Jenny, do you remember when you first came to London?"

"Yes."

"I thought you were so naive, so sweet and inexperienced, and I took you in hand and looked after you. Now it's *you* who's looking after *me*! Isn't life funny?"

Jenny smiled. "Very funny. Now please go to sleep."

"Goodnight, Jenny."

"Goodnight."

Jenny managed to undress just before the lights went out. Then in the darkness, on her uncomfortable, steel-framed bed, she realised what she had actually said to Lily.

The invasion was imminent.

She tossed and turned a long time, wanting Bill, worried about him, aware that he would soon be leaving, with thousands of others, to take part in the invasion of Europe.

He might not return. She had to accept that fact. When she finally dropped off to sleep, her dreams were filled with love and terror – and she awakened to a muffled, relentless rumbling passing over the city.

Departures

A great armada of aircraft.

Lily was sitting upright, staring at her with wide eyes, and beyond her the other WAAFs were doing the same in the dawn's pearly light.

"The sixth of June, 1944," Lily said. "We'll both remember this day, I'm sure. Has it really begun?"

"I think so," Jenny said.

As if breaking free from a trance, most of the WAAFs in the room were suddenly galvanised into action, all rushing to stare out the windows. Joining them, Jenny looked up to see the sky filled with aircraft – a vast fleet of heavy bombers and their fighter escorts – all heading towards the English Channel and the battle for Europe.

The WAAFs cheered and applauded wildly, then some started dancing, while others eagerly switched on their radios to learn what was happening.

The invasion of Europe had indeed begun that morning, with the biggest combined land, sea and air operation of all time. Landings had already been made along a hundred miles of coast, from west of Cherbourg to Le Havre, heavy fighting was raging, and the town of Calais was under attack.

The WAAFs squealed, applauded, and shed tears of delight or loss, while Lily hugged Jenny, almost in tears herself, and said, "God, you were right! It's the invasion! That's where Denholm and Anthony are!" Then she took a step back, her eyes widening in panic. "Oh, my God! Of course! That's where they are! *They're over Europe right now!*"

"And maybe Bill!" Jenny whispered.

At that moment, in the midst of exultation, a spasm of terror lanced through her at the possibility of losing him.

She felt herself shaking . . .

Dressing hastily like the others, she was still buttoning her tunic when she rushed out to the telephone in the corridor, to ring Bill's hotel.

There was no answer from his room, she was informed.

He had obviously left.

Feeling dry-throated, Jenny left a message for him to ring her if possible, then reported to the motoring pool to start work.

"You're in for a busy day," the WAAF sergeant told her. "They're already frantic out there."

The day was indeed hectic, though surprisingly normal otherwise. Jenny raced through it in a dream composed mostly of thoughts of Bill, whom she feared had already left for Europe, to cover the invasion. The 'phone never stopped ringing, she hardly had time for lunch, and as she drove excited officers to and fro across the city, she was swept by alternating waves of exhilaration and dread.

Yet the city itself was quiet (she had expected celebrating crowds), with the people going about their normal business as calmly as ever.

By afternoon the streets were almost empty. Jenny bought a Red Cross Flag and pinned it to her uniform; and later, as she drove back to the barracks in Whitechapel, she noted that the city seemed deserted.

There was no message from Bill.

And Lily hadn't heard from Denholm either.

After the King's broadcast, Jenny and Lily took a taxi to the hotel in Kensington and found an unusually quiet bar. The pianist wasn't playing, most of the servicemen had disappeared, and the ladies, including those in civilian clothes, seemed at a loose end.

"Jesus," Lily said, downing her drink and gradually getting her spirits back, "I can hardly recognise the place! This is the first time I've seen the walls and floor. It seems so big and . . . *empty!*"

"It *is* practically empty. And we've never stood alone at this bar before. I feel so strange, Lily."

"You think Bill's gone as well?"

"I think so."

"Then let's get drunk alone."

Which they did. And learned from the radio bulletins that RAF bombers had been pounding the French coast throughout the previous night; that at daybreak more than 1,300 heavy bombers of the US Army 8th Air Force (to which Bill belonged, Jenny thought with woe) had taken over the attack; that several thousand ships, brought together from widely scattered ports in Britain, had converged on the invasion coast soon after dawn; and that by evening Allied troops, with tanks and artillery, had penetrated several miles inland on a broad front.

The liberation of Europe was under way, with much fighting and bloodshed.

So Jenny got drunk with Lily, trying to dim the pain of loss, choking back her tears when she thought of Bill on the beachheads (not a soldier, but still in the line of fire) and was distraught that they hadn't had time to say goodbye, or even make love one last time.

She and Lily took turns crying, but also laughed at themselves.

And Jenny was just about to cry again when the barman called out to her.

"The telephone, Jenny!"

It was Bill. "No," he said, "I'm not in France. Damn it, Jenny, I missed it! I didn't even know it had started – and I wasn't invited. I'm down here in East Anglia. I was called to Denholm's air base. He and Anthony were among the first to go and they're about to go back. But I'm leaving the day after tomorrow, destination unknown. I have to stay here all night – I'm sending reports out by the hour – but I'm going to be free tomorrow afternoon. What about you?"

"I'll make it," Jenny said, feeling breathless. "I don't know how, but I'll do it."

"How about tea at the Ritz?"

"We'll have to dress up."

"Let's do that," Bill said. "Let's at least say goodbye with style. I want no morbid memories."

"Four o'clock in the lobby?"

"See you then."

"Do you love me?"

"God, yes!" he said.

This time, when she burst into tears, it was a sign of relief.

The following morning she cajoled the WAAF sergeant in charge of the motoring pool to give her the afternoon off. During lunch break, an excited Lily helped her to take in an elegant evening dress borrowed from a larger girlfriend, then kissed her goodbye as she hurried out of the barracks to catch a taxi. And eventually, at four o'clock in that dry afternoon, she met Bill in the intimidating luxury of the Ritz hotel's lobby.

Departures

Bill was wearing a brand-new, dark suit, with striped shirt and tie.

"You look terribly English," she told him.

"You look wonderful," he replied.

"It's a borrowed dress, Bill. It's not me."

"It *is* you. The real you. Now let's go in for tea."

It was their first tea at the Ritz, in the splendour of the Palm Court, and she felt glamorous and deeply in love. They neither kissed nor held hands – the Ritz was not the place for that – but his gaze told her all there was to know, his sad smile made her glow.

"Is it true that clothes make the man?" he asked. "I certainly feel very English here."

"Clothes *don't* make the man, but you do look terribly English. You also look handsome and distinguished. My kind of man."

"*That's* good to hear."

She smiled, wanting to give herself to him and thus be taken by him. "So what were you doing in East Anglia?" she asked, sipping tea like a lady.

"I was driving around, describing D-Day for the folks back home. It wasn't happening here in London – it was all in the country: the farmers watching the bombers and fighters passing overhead; trucks filled with troops clogging the country lanes; the jeeps and half-tracks being taken by train to the embarkation points; then the first wounded being brought back on the very same trains. Suddenly, instead of pastoral peace, there was nothing but constant noise and movement. The last great battle has started."

"Do you think it will be the last?"

"It has to be. At least the last of *this* war."

Jenny stared at her cup, feeling dangerously emotional, but controlled herself by taking a deep breath before looking up again. "Lily's worried about Denholm," she said. "Do you know if he's all right?"

"Yes, he's fine. He and Anthony are exhausted, but they're also enjoying it. They'll be flying missions every day, so they'll be gone for a bit."

"And you're leaving tonight?"

"Tomorrow morning."

"I can't bear the thought of that."

He reached out to touch her, changed his mind, withdrew his hand. "I can't bear the thought of it either, but I'm booked on the plane." He stared steadily at her, his eyes filled with love and pain, then leaned across the table and clenched his fist. "I need you, Jenny. I *want* you!"

Moved by his intensity, she had to look away, instead taking in the ladies and gentlemen and blank-faced, polite waiters.

"I'm frightened for you," she said.

"I'm just a journalist, Jenny."

"Journalists also get killed in wars. And I know you – you're too brave."

"You have no proof of that."

"I don't need proof, Bill. You're a brave man who hasn't had the chance to prove it – and that could be dangerous."

"I won't try to prove it."

"Please don't. Think of me and survive instead."

"I'll think of you. I'll come back."

Her heart was breaking at that moment. The pain was greater than grief. She had not felt so devastated since the pain of her parents' death, and she wanted to fall to her knees and cling to him.

"You want me, Bill?"

"Yes."

"And you need me?"

"Of course, Jenny!"

"We're man and wife already, aren't we, Bill?"

"Yes, Jenny, we are."

They didn't speak after that. At least not in the Ritz. They sipped their tea in silence, ate their sandwiches and cream cakes, then paid the bill and left the hotel to walk along Piccadilly. It was a bright summer's evening. The barrage balloons swayed in blue sky. There were troops around the big guns in Green Park, looking bored and lethargic.

Jenny held Bill's hand, wanting to cling to him. She could not imagine London without him, nor dwell on her future.

Without him, she was nothing.

They went to his hotel, had a final drink in the bar, then he took her to his room for the first time, where they made love in his narrow bed.

The aircraft rumbled overhead. The battle of Europe continued. There were no German air raids that evening, but the dead multiplied.

In the midst of death, he gave her life. She had no doubts when it happened. When he came, she came too, convulsing, crying out, and felt him touching her deep inside where that life would be given shape.

"I'll always love you," she whispered.

He didn't reply, but kissed her fingers, one by one,

and she knew, in the silence of that moment, that she would willingly die for him.

"I'll come back," he said. "Nothing can kill me now. I have too much to live for."

"Please don't leave."

"I'll never leave you, Jenny. It's impossible. I'm part of you now."

"I know it's true, Bill. I can feel it. Now I have to go back."

He wanted to walk her down, but she made him stay in bed, then dressed without washing herself, wanting to keep his smell on her. When she was ready, he sat up and started slipping out of bed, but she pushed him back down, wagging her finger, saying, "No, please don't move."

"But I want – "

"I won't leave if you touch me, I swear it. I love you. Goodbye."

"Husband and wife," he reminded her.

"Oh, I know *that*!" she whispered.

Then she left, closing the door quietly behind her. In the corridor, she leaned her head against the wall, closed her eyes and wept silently.

When she had recovered, she took the stairs down to the lobby and walked into the street, without looking back.

Then she walked away from the hotel, from the best weeks of her life, aware that she might never see him again.

"Come back to me," she whispered.

Chapter Twenty-Nine

~

Early in the morning, before the drive to Cornwall, Bill met Carol in the lobby of the Savoy.

"Please don't mention that we met through Jennifer," he told her, feeling guilty and stupid. "In fact, don't mention Jennifer at all. As far as they're concerned, you were booked routinely through the hotel. OK?"

"Of course," Carol replied, clearly intrigued. "Whatever you say."

"It's nothing to do with me or Jennifer. I just can't explain it."

"Then don't try," Carol said.

He loved her for that. It made her seem so understanding. And when Maureen arrived in the lobby, followed shortly by Denholm, who had come from St John's Wood, he was able to introduce them to their driver without feeling demented.

"A beautiful chauffeuse!" Denholm proclaimed grandly. "This is something I never expected. Bill's surprised me again!"

"Thank you for the compliment," Carol responded. "Can we leave now?"

"Yes," Bill said.

His stated reason for the trip was to show Maureen the "real England", but in truth he had been compelled, by the recent onrush of old memories encouraged by his reunion with Jennifer, to retrace the footsteps of their old affair and go back to where he and Jenny had first made love.

Since the presumed purpose of the trip was sightseeing, he asked Carol to go the slow way, by the A30, thus reliving the journey he had made with Jenny forty years ago, through the pretty towns and villages of Wiltshire, Somerset, Devon, and finally Cornwall itself – even stopping at Glastonbury.

They did not climb the Tor, but Carol drove them around it; and Bill remembered how he had sat on its grassy slopes with Jenny, vowing that some day he would write about what she and England had meant to him. So far, he hadn't done that – he had only written about his homeland – but he hoped to make amends by producing his film, secretly based on those same two young people during the war.

When Carol eventually drove away from the Tor, he had to compose himself.

"Damn," he said, "it's so beautiful."

"And so mysterious," Carol replied.

"Right. It's sure as hell that as well. You've obviously been here before."

"I *am* English, Mr Eisler!"

"I didn't mean to offend you. I just thought you might have come from here, since you obviously know the place."

"I came here in the Seventies. They had rock concerts

here. Rock 'n' roll, mysticism and drugs. It was part of my time."

"It *was*?"

"I'm older now. I'm forty years old. You don't go to such concerts at my age, so those days are gone for good."

"You don't look forty, Carol."

"I don't believe you, but thanks."

"Where are we now?"

"By-passing Exeter."

"It sure is pretty," he said.

During the rest of the journey, which took them through green countryside, Bill found it increasingly difficult to disguise his growing fascination with Carol.

He was therefore embarrassed when it finally dawned on him that Maureen and the perceptive, cynical Denholm were aware of his interest.

"A very *attractive* young lady," Denholm said after lunch, when Carol, having been invited to join them, took herself to the Ladies. "And she certainly seems to have taken *your* eye, Bill – or is that just my evil mind?"

"It's your evil mind, Denholm."

"I don't think so," Maureen said, not looking amused at all. "You've been talking to that woman in a really strange way – obliquely asking her all sorts of personal questions – and you haven't been able to take your eyes off her. Or is that just *my* evil mind?"

Denholm coughed. "I didn't mean to imply – "

"You're both talking goddamned nonsense," Bill interjected. "I'm just being polite to her."

"Polite!" Maureen exclaimed.

"What's wrong with *that*?" Bill enquired.

"I think we should drop this conversation," Denholm suggested, "since the lady's returning."

Bill raised his eyes to take her in, felt strange just looking at her, and realised that he *did* think her attractive and somehow... *approachable?*

It was a form of recognition, an inexplicable rapport, and it made him feel as guilty as he had been when planning the trip.

When Carol saw the three of them staring at her, she blushed with embarrassment.

"What – ?" she began.

"So!" Denholm interjected in a falsely jocular mood. "Let's hit the road and go to Land's End!"

"Not *that* far," Bill said, "but let's get moving or we won't find a hotel."

"Such adventures!" Denholm exclaimed.

As Carol drove them on to Cornwall, in the deepening light of evening, Bill felt only the shame of his deceptions and was relieved when Maureen, perhaps only to break the uncomfortable silence, said as she glanced at the lush green fields and hills, "This is a lovely part of the country. Is it going to be one of your locations, Bill? Is that why we're here?"

"Yes, it is. I made the same trip during the war. And though I wanted to see it again, I also wanted *you* to see it, just because it's so beautiful."

"It's beautiful and... *empty*," Denholm said. "All these wide, open spaces!"

The remark got a smile from Maureen. "The urban man speaks! And since we've actually brought up the subject of Bill's movie, how's it going, Denholm?"

"You mean the finance?"

"What else?"

"I think I can say with certainty that eighty percent of the budget is in hand."

"And the other twenty percent?"

Denholm sighed.

"What does *that* mean?" Maureen asked, glancing at the back of Carol's head as if wanting to spear it.

"Anyone mind if I smoke?" Denholm asked.

"Roll the window down," Bill said.

Denholm rolled the window down, then lit his cigarette.

"What it means," he said, "is that the other twenty percent is being withheld because of doubts regarding aspects of the screenplay."

"*My* screenplay."

"Quite."

"What doubts?" Maureen asked.

"Well, to be blunt – "

"Please be blunt," Bill interjected.

" – the backers withholding that vital twenty percent have expressed their belief that while the film, as scripted, would make a nice, small-budget, essentially *British* movie, it wouldn't get international distribution – which means that it wouldn't recoup its costs."

"An art-house movie," Maureen said, as if uttering a four-letter word.

"Yes, Maureen. Precisely."

"So why don't you change your screenplay, Bill?"

He sighed with frustration. "If I've said it once, I've said it a thousand times: the screenplay is based on the love affair between two young people during World War Two – an English girl and an American GI. The war's merely the background. It's never actually seen. It's a story about love, not sex; about war, not battle – and I don't see how adding sex and violence could make it better box-office."

"You can worry about the box-office when the movie's *made*," Maureen said grimly. "What matters is getting *the finance* to make it – so why not make some changes?"

"Because what you call some changes can make an awful lot of difference to a project like this."

"It's better to have the movie made with some changes than not have it made at all."

"I won't compromise, Maureen!"

"Do you think *I* enjoy being humiliated by directors and their cronies? Dammit, Bill, we *all* compromise!"

Deeply wounded that Maureen, who had previously always defended his insistence on artistic integrity, now seemed to be turning against him, Bill looked nervously at Carol, beside whom he was sitting in the front seat, then glanced back over his shoulder and said with too much anger, "Listen, damn it! I wanted to make a simple, honest movie about the love of an American serviceman, a GI, for an English girl during a war that deserved to be fought, but should not be glamorised. What you call *some changes* would in fact change tender love scenes into scenes of irrelevant nudity and sex, as well converting my antiwar stance into a paean to the American war machine. I do *not* need sex, nudity and bloodshed to convey what I mean! It's not *that* kind of movie! Right?"

"Right," Denholm said on Maureen's behalf, when she refused to reply.

They were crossing Dartmoor, which had a barren, russet grandeur, and Bill knew that they would soon

Departures

reach St Austell and its wealth of old memories. This disturbed him even more, making him regret having come.

He looked to Carol for comfort.

"OK," Maureen said, as if determined to punish him for that. "We *are* aware, Bill, that you're concerned with *human* issues, that you've managed to avoid the more commercial aspects of Hollywood, and that you've also managed to make a good living without compromising your integrity."

"Gee, thanks."

"But I'm afraid," Maureen continued, glancing at the silent Carol, "that in this particular instance, you're taking integrity too far. You're in cloud-cuckoo land!"

Bill was shocked into silence. He had never heard Maureen speak this way before and so could hardly believe she was doing it now.

Feeling betrayed, he glanced again at Carol, wondering why she fascinated him, then looked straight ahead as the moors gave way to villages, and tried to see through the back of his head what Maureen and Denholm were thinking.

He couldn't even imagine it.

His heart fluttered for a second, then settled down again, and he sank into his seat, determined to say no more, luxuriating in old memories as Carol by-passed St Austell and eventually drove along the narrow, winding road to Golant.

It was an unspoilt village perched above the Fowey Estuary, and there, in the Comorant Hotel, they would stay for the night.

"Here we are," Carol said.

Chapter Thirty

∽

Opening sleepy eyes, Carol glanced around the unfamiliar bedroom, remembered where she was, licked dry lips and thought of last night.

She had drunk far too much. All of them had. They'd had dinner in the candlelit dining room of the hotel, washing the food down with beer, then gone on to red wine and finally brandy. There had been a lot of conversation, some of it quite heated, and Carol was certain that she had been the cause of it, for mysterious reasons.

As she now remembered it, they had argued mostly about Bill's movie, but she sensed that Maureen's antagonism, her odd outbursts of anger, had not really been caused by that, but by Bill's embarrassing, obvious interest in her. Certainly, Bill had given her a lot of close attention – of the kind that had caused Denholm amusement and made Maureen mad.

Eventually, feeling herself to be the centre of a growing storm, Carol had pleaded a headache and left them all to it.

Departures

Now she *did* have a headache. She was also hungover and nervous. She sat up in bed, rubbed the sleep from her eyes, then slipped out and went to the window to look over the estuary. The water was silvery, glittering around the many boats, and the seagulls were flying overhead, under clouds streaked with sunlight.

It looked like the day would be fine and that made her feel better.

After bathing, dressing and putting on her make-up, she went downstairs, not knowing what to expect. She was aware of Bill's interest in her, sensed that it wasn't sexual, and felt inexplicably drawn to *him*, which only made matters worse. He was intensely curious about her – that much she knew – and she was curious about why he wanted his friendship with her mother kept secret.

It was all quite a mystery.

Entering the dining room, which was cluttered with antiques, she found the three of them already at the table. Bill and Maureen were visibly hungover and suffering, though Denholm, who had drunk more than anyone, looked the picture of health.

"No, thank you, old sport," he was saying to Bill. "I feel safer walking the streets of London – so no cliff walks for me!"

"It'll do you good." Bill said.

"I'd rather suffer, dear boy."

"I don't want to go either," Maureen said. "I'm too ill even to think about it. I'll just stay here and rest."

"Good morning," Carol said.

They all looked up, surprised.

"Morning, Carol," Bill said.

"Sleep well?" Denholm asked her.

"Yes," she said, "I slept like a log. I'm glad I went to bed early."

She sat down beside Denholm, who offered her tea. When she nodded, he filled up her cup and even put in the milk. It was all she wanted for breakfast.

"We drove all this way and you won't even explore the place," Bill accused.

"I hate seaside towns," Denholm said.

"I just feel ill," Maureen explained. "It's your own fault for letting me get drunk, so stop complaining about it."

Grinning uneasily, Bill turned to Carol. "Any excuse. I want them to come for a walk, but they're both begging off."

"Go alone," Maureen said. "You *like* being alone. You spend hours all alone on the beach at home, so you can do the same here. As for me, I'll take a rest in the lounge and let my racing heart settle down."

"And you, Denholm? Are you sure you won't come?"

"Definitely not, Bill. I'll probably walk around the town, have a read of the morning paper, then revive myself with a Bloody Mary. You're all alone out there, dear boy."

"So be it. What about you, Carol?"

She hurriedly finished her tea. "I'm ready right now, Mr Eisler."

"Good," Bill said. "Let's go."

After kissing Maureen's cheek, he followed Carol out of the hotel, clearly not too unhappy at being rejected – in fact, looking surprisingly pleased.

"Do you know this area?" Carol asked him.

"No," he said. "Just the one place."

"The cliff you want to walk?"

"No – a house. I just hope I can find it."

"You're *not* going for a walk along the cliffs?"

"No, Carol, I'm not."

She drove him out of Golant, back towards St Austell, then turned off the main road at his instructions and headed inland. Although she was intrigued, she also started feeling strange. She glanced left and right, across the hedgerows, to the green fields, and realised that they were in the area where her mother had once lived and which she, as a child, had visited once or twice.

It was quite a coincidence.

"Is there any particular reason for driving this way, Mr Eisler?"

"I owe you an apology," he replied, not answering her question. "I asked you a lot of questions yesterday – some of them pretty personal – but I didn't mean to be so inquisitive. It was just . . ."

"I think it seemed odd to your wife and friend."

He nodded. "Yes, naturally they'd have thought I was acting funny . . . And I guess you did, too."

"I don't have any secrets to hide, but you *were* so intense. And though none of the questions were that personal, I couldn't help wondering about your motives."

He didn't reply immediately, being too busy examining the scenery with unnatural interest.

"Damn it," he finally said, "it looks exactly the same! This is the place, all right!" Then before she could ask him what he meant, he looked intently at her, as if trying to recall her, and said, "I'm just convinced that I know you. I have the *feeling* that I know you, a sort of *rapport*, and it's left me confused. I'm an old man. Forgive me."

"Don't be silly. You're not old and there's nothing to forgive. I just wondered, that's all."

Which wasn't quite true, since she began to feel even stranger, filling up with inexplicable emotions and unformed intuitions...

She kept glancing at him, saw a gentle, distracted face, and was drawn to him like a moth to the flame, without knowing why.

"What are you looking for?" she asked him, breaking the silence.

"I told you: a house. One I knew long ago."

"During the war?"

"That's right. I stayed in it for a weekend. I was very much in love at the time and the girl brought me here – to the house we're approaching."

Carol was startled, beginning to grasp what she had missed. She was driving along a narrow, dangerously winding, familiar lane... and it suddenly opened out into a driveway in front of a building.

A crumbling, white-walled farmhouse that had been boarded up.

Her grandparents' old home.

Too shocked to speak, she braked to a halt and watched Bill climb out to stand in the driveway. She followed him out, stood beside him and felt the wind. His eyes were moist as he scanned the crumbling white walls and clinging green vines.

"I'm sorry." He wiped his eyes with a handkerchief. "Please excuse the emotions of an old man with an elephant's memory... It was during the war. I was a US Air Force journalist. I was very much in love with an

English girl, a WAAF driver. We made love for the first time in this house and I've never forgotten it."

"She brought you . . . *here*? To *this* house?"

"Yes. We had our last weekend here. We spent Saturday and Sunday here, drove back to London on the Monday, shared our last hours together on the evening of D-Day, then didn't see each other again . . . At least not until recently."

The mid-morning sun was shining in Carol's eyes. The ground seemed to shift under her.

"You met . . . *recently*?"

"Yes," Bill said, his voice breaking. "And after forty years I had to come back to make sure it was real – what we had, what we'd shared when we were younger and life seemed much simpler."

Carol took a step back. Her tears started flowing. She heard her own voice, the voice of a stranger, coming from what seemed like far away, exploding magically around her.

"Oh, my God . . . *you're my father!*"

Chapter Thirty-One

∽

Maureen went for a walk with Denholm. They wandered along the waterfront and through the unspoilt village, then back down, in the gathering heat of noon, to a pub near the water.

"Mmmm," Maureen said, drinking her Bloody Mary, "I sure as hell need this!"

Denholm grinned. "The morning after the night before. Thank God our driver left when she did, otherwise . . ." He just shrugged.

"You think I'd have exploded?"

"You were certainly getting close."

She felt a little embarrassed. "Yes, I suppose I was – because of Bill's embarrassing interest in that damned woman. I mean, at *his* age. Dear God . . ."

Denholm's grin was suitably cynical. "He certainly seems to be intrigued by her. Yet it's an odd kind of obsession. Neither romantic nor sexual. In fact, almost . . . *paternal?*"

"God help me, he wants a child! A forty-year old daughter! I never thought it would come to this."

Shocked, she had more of her Bloody Mary.

"Anyway," Denholm said, obviously trying to be helpful, "you're probably imagining more than you're actually seeing."

"I don't know what you mean."

"I think that Bill's fascination for our attractive driver, Carol, is simply a manifestation of his anxieties concerning his movie – a form of distraction."

Grateful for what she felt was a deliberate, kind deception, Maureen placed her hand on Denholm's wrist. "Do you really think so?"

"I think it's a fair bet."

"And do you think Bill will get to keep his screenplay intact and make his own movie?"

Denholm sighed and shook his head. "No, Maureen, I don't. I think it's damned near impossible. Without those changes, the people holding the remaining money will refuse to invest."

"I know my husband. He's a man of deep convictions. And he's likely to give up his movie, rather than let it be compromised."

"I think you're right, Maureen."

Uneasy, she finished her drink, then said, "Let's go back."

"As you wish, dear."

Walking along the waterfront and back up to the hotel, Maureen found herself wondering why Denholm had gone to such lengths to set up a movie which he seemed to believe would never be made. The only possible explanation would be the desire to break Bill's heart – and dwelling on this possibility, which she could not ignore, she realised that she had never really known Denholm at all.

That he and Bill were old friends didn't necessarily mean they were good friends.

Still, she was attracted to him, perhaps drawn by his boyish wickedness, and now, slightly intoxicated and emotionally overwrought, she was feeling dangerously close to him, and even dependent upon him.

Despite her nagging doubts, she took his hand and squeezed it. "You've always been a mystery to me, Denholm. I've never managed to scratch more than your surface. What do you want from life?"

Surprisingly, he took the question seriously.

"I don't know," he said, as they reached the top of the steep path and entered the gardens of the hotel. "I've been haunted all my life – or at least since my university days – by the knowledge that I seem to be incapable of believing in *anything*. I suppose that's why I opted for being a success in the material world, even while admiring the morality of people like Bill. In fact, the only thing I ever believed in – and *you* won't believe this of me – was the love I felt for a certain woman long ago. I lost her, of course – we always lose the things we love – and her loss simply increased my desire for material success. It also deepened my cynicism – my refusal to value anything other then the price tag on objects."

"Has it made you any happier?"

"What's happiness?" They were approaching the front door of the hotel. "Is Bill happy? Are you? No, you're not, neither of you. Because happiness is too elusive and ephemeral – here today, gone tomorrow."

He opened the front door and she stepped into the

Departures

hotel, saddened by what she believed was his old, romantic, secret loss. When he followed her in, she turned to face him, gazing up at his impossibly youthful face, which for once seemed quite thoughtful.

He seemed to loom over her.

"I gather that Bill and his bright young thing will be having lunch somewhere after their walk, so I might as well have a lie-down before we depart."

"A good idea," Denholm said.

He stepped aside and waved his hand, indicating the stairs, and she brushed past him and started the short climb. He followed her up, stopping behind her at her room, and when she turned around, leaning against the door, he moved closer to her.

He stopped just before his body touched her, gazing down at her, smiling.

She felt emotionally overwrought, lightheaded and confused, but understood that a heart beating quickly has a will of its own. So she turned away from Denholm, opened the door and stepped inside. Then she faced him once more, aware even in her shame and the anguish of betrayal, that she was silently, helplessly inviting him into her bed.

He walked in and she closed the door behind him as the silence embalmed them.

Chapter Thirty-Two

～

Dazed but exhilarated, Bill held Carol's hand across the table in a pub in Pentewan Sands. "I'm still not sure I understand. You thought I was an RAF officer killed during the war? How did you – ?"

"All I know," Carol said, "is what my mother told me: that my father had been a pilot shot down over Germany. She met him when she was still a WAAF driver. It was in a hotel in Kensington, when she was with her best friend and two RAF officers."

"That was Denholm, Anthony Barker and Lily Monaghan, who became Denholm's first wife."

"I see." Carol's smile was soft and sweet. "Anyway, she also told me that she and her RAF lover spent a bit of time in her old home in Cornwall, and that they'd married just before D-Day and spent their honeymoon in the same hotel in Kensington."

"I was the so-called RAF officer, we certainly didn't get married, but she *did* consider us to be man and wife, and we spent our final night in that hotel. The story's essentially correct – she just changed a few things."

Departures

"Doubtless to protect me. In those days, illegitimate children weren't treated too kindly." She suddenly looked troubled. "Did you say that Denholm was one of your two best friends during the war? And that later he married Lily Monaghan?"

"Yes. Why?"

"Well . . ." She slipped her hand out of his and flexed her fingers distractedly. "Mother always insisted that she'd become pregnant during the evening of D-Day; that the following day her RAF husband – obviously you – had gone off to Europe; and that a few weeks later, his best friend had come to see her, to tell her that her husband had been killed in France."

Bill could hardly believing what he was hearing. "If we'd really been married, she would have received an official notification. In the event, since we weren't married, she wouldn't have been notified if I'd been killed, so conceivably . . ."

"Yes." Carol shrugged and looked embarrassed. "The person who told her you'd died in Europe was your friend . . . Denholm Wilding."

"Denholm told her I'd been *killed* in Europe?"

"Who else could it have been?"

"Maybe my other friend, Anthony Barker?"

"No," Carol said. "I know it wasn't him. Mother insisted that the friend who gave her the news was her husband's *best* friend. That could only be Denholm."

Bill sat back in his chair, feeling shocked and bewildered, but also uplifted to be in the presence of the daughter he had not known about.

"This is a day of pleasant surprises and nasty shocks. I don't think I can handle it."

Carol smiled. "You'll manage."

"I'm not so sure about that. I'm so angry... Why the hell would Denholm...?"

Carol shrugged and reached out for his hand. "It's all in the past."

"No, it's not. It's here and now. We're all still alive, Carol." However, wanting to change the subject he asked, "Where were you born? In that house we've just been to?"

"Yes, Father." When she said that word, his heart sang. "Apparently, when it became clear that Mother was pregnant, she was discharged from the Women's Auxiliary Air Force and went back to have her baby in Cornwall. I spent my first two years there. Then, before I became old enough to hear village gossip about illegitimacy, Mother sold the house and returned to London, where we've lived ever since. She looked after me well."

"Always in London from then on?"

"Right. I think she had a hard time of it as an unmarried mother, but she did at least have one stroke of luck. An unknown benefactor left her that property in Frith Street. It wasn't you, was it?"

"God, no!"

Carol shrugged. "Anyway, that particular blessing came along at the right time – just when Mother was running out of money and, because of me, was having a hard time getting a job. At first, she was going to sell the property, but then, canny woman, she realised how valuable it was and so decided to keep it. For the first couple of years, we lived in the top floor flat, renting out the other rooms, which is how she made the money to convert the ground floor into that club. It was successful

Departures

for a long time, but then, with rising rates and the recent disastrous fall in tourism, it began losing money."

"Do you know why Jennifer never married?"

"She told me she'd been traumatised – first by the loss of her parents, then, so soon after their death, by losing her husband – actually you. She was chronically depressed for months after my birth and had to have psychiatric treatment. Then, though recovering, she simply couldn't accept that another man could ever replace you . . . *Very* romantic, yes? Anyway, by the time she did start seeing other men, she'd decided not to marry and had made my welfare her prime concern. See what you did, Dad?"

Warmed by that remark, and temporarily forgetting the shocking trick played by Denholm, Bill again took hold of his daughter's hand, regaining faith in her presence.

Then he told her of that fateful day, in 1945, when his relationship with Jenny had ended for what he had thought was forever . . .

Chapter Thirty-Three

∽

As a budding writer, Bill had dreamed of seeing Paris, but it wasn't to be.

He regained consciousness in a bed in a hospital in Caen, facing a window that framed the ruins of that once-beautiful city. He soon learned that the city had been captured by Allied troops and that he had been picked up unconscious in other ruins, those of Cherbourg, hospitalised, practically catatonic, then moved on to here.

He could study the ruins all day.

He had been wounded in the left leg, not badly, but enough to hurt, and had already had two operations to get rid of the shrapnel. He could hardly bear to examine it. His leg looked like butcher's meat. He couldn't imagine ever walking again, though they told him he would.

He breathed easier after that.

At first he couldn't think straight. His thoughts collided and scattered. He remembered Omaha Beach, the bloody dead of the US 5th Corps, the scorched corpses of German soldiers in their shattered concrete fortifications, the thunder of explosions, clouds of smoke, bloody chaos in swirling sand.

He had scribbled in his notebook. Stones had drummed against his helmet. The naval forts and arsenal of Cherbourg were captured, the Tricolour was raised once more over the Hotel de Ville, and two weeks later, somewhere else, feeling exhausted and dazed, he was watching his fellow Americans blasting the steel doors of pillboxes and throwing in phosphorous grenades to flush out the Krauts. He followed the troops farther inland, recording death and victory. They threw themselves against the Panzers, were crushed under their tracks; were blown apart, stitched and scorched, and generally butchered.

The Battle of Normandy became the Battle of France – and exhausted, Bill fell.

He would never recall it clearly, just a dream of noise and motion. The collapsing walls of a chateau, American infantrymen climbing the rubble, ricocheting rifle-fire, machine-guns, a lot of screaming. Explosions all around, coming closer, then the world turning inside-out.

A sudden bellowing in fierce heat, the air sucked from his lungs, sheets of white flame that dissolved into darkness and a terrible silence, then bad dreams and eternity.

He was wrapped up in pain.

"Jesus, Jenny," he groaned.

And recovered in due course, passing in and out of consciousness, gradually returning to his body in a bed that gave a good view of blackened ruins.

The ruins of Caen.

His leg hurt like a bitch.

He never got to the streets of Paris. Ernest Hemingway did. *"Vive Paris!"* de Gaulle said in August, 1944, as Bill painfully forced himself to sit upright and stare at those ghastly ruins. A few weeks later, as General Bradley led the Allies onto German soil, Bill used a cane to hobble to the nearest table and write a letter to Jenny.

She didn't write back.

Bill kept writing. Jenny never replied. He wrote to Denholm in East Anglia, but he didn't reply either, so he wrote again to Jenny, then to Lily, and still received no reply.

His nights became sleepless.

He was shipped back to England and driven around London the same evening the lights were switched on in Piccadilly, the Strand and Fleet Street after five years of blackout. He still couldn't walk, but he could hobble on a cane, and by doing so managed to use a telephone and ring a few friends.

Denholm and Anthony Barker had been shot down over France. Nobody in the hotel bar had seen Jenny or Lily for months.

Bill broke up inside.

He read the newspapers. The world had changed forever. Allied bombing had made millions homeless in Germany; the city of Dresden had been devastated; Churchill, Roosevelt and Stalin had carved up the postwar world; Mussolini's corpse had been hung upside-down in Milan; and two days later Adolf Hitler had killed himself in the ruins of Berlin.

Bill read this like a man in a trance.

He was pining for Jenny.

In April, 1945, still limping, but mobile, he was

released from the hospital in Kent and allowed to go back to London.

He had been given three days rehabilitation leave before being shipped home.

He didn't want to go home.

He just wanted Jenny.

His first stop was Whitechapel. He was horrified by what he found there. The WAAF barracks had been bombed and the building was a ruin, merging perfectly into the ruins around it, its charred rubble dust-covered.

Worse . . . His enquiries about what had happened to the women living there produced the information that many of them had died, some had not yet been identified, and the records had been burned in the flames.

"Jenny Birken?" the ARP man said. "No way of knowing, mate."

Bill was heartbroken.

He managed to get a room in his old hotel in Kensington (most of the journalists and servicemen were still following the war in Europe) and spent his first evening in the bar, reliving old memories. He became drunk and maudlin, was tempted to take a whore, resisted the temptation and went to bed and slept like a log. The next day he walked the city, searching for Jenny, finding nothing, then he read about the Nazi death camps and so decided to get drunk again.

He went back to the hotel bar, which was practically empty, and ordered a large whiskey with water and started to drink it. The pianist was playing, but there was no one singing around him, and when the melody reached *"We'll Meet Again"* tears came to Bill's eyes.

"Mr William Eisler, I presume?"

Jerking his head around, Bill saw a familiar, wicked grin.

"Denholm!"

"It is I – not a ghost. Now buy me a drink, old son."

"I don't believe – "

"Anthony and I were shot down . . . Yes, I know. I've heard all the stories."

"They weren't true?"

"Of *course* they were! That's why you never heard from me. We were shot down, but baled out over France and were picked up by Allied troops. Of course I have a gamey hip." He waved his walking-stick in the air. "Not enough to do me permanent damage, but enough to get me a discharge. I'm on my way out, old boy. Now where's that damned drink?"

"Coming up. Gin and tonic?"

"It's so medicinal, dear boy."

Bill ordered more drinks. When they came, he and Denholm touched glasses and each took a good swig.

"Ah!" Denholm exclaimed, licking his lips. "Just what I needed!"

"And Anthony?" Bill asked. "He's OK, too?"

"Perfectly fine. A battered head, but otherwise quite chipper. He's going to be right as rain in a month or so."

"Apart from that limp, Denholm, you look remarkably fit."

"Never been better, Bill. I feel as fresh as a daisy. I'll be given a medical discharge a few weeks from now, and already I'm planning my lucrative future, calling up my old school chums."

"What *are* you planning?"

Departures

"There'll be a post-war boom, Bill. An awful lot of rebuilding. There's going to be money in property and I'll be in on the ground floor. First property, then the stock market, then the higher realms of finance. The next time we meet, if we ever do, you will find me a rich man. And you, dear boy? What are *you* doing, still here? Why aren't you back in Oklahoma, enjoying the good life?"

"I'm looking for Jenny."

"Ah, yes." Denholm abruptly turned sombre. "Jenny," he said.

Bill noticed, when he picked up his glass, that his hand was visibly shaking. He had a stiff drink, then asked, "What have you heard?"

"You saw what happened at Whitechapel?"

"Yes, Denholm. And I know that a lot of the WAAFs were killed. Was Jenny one of them?"

"No," Denholm said. "But she *is* missing, Bill. I haven't seen her since returning from France, though I'm still seeing the buxom Lily Monaghan. Luckily she was *not* in the barracks when it was bombed, since she was on temporary transfer in Norfolk."

"I wrote to her as well, but she didn't reply either."

"She probably didn't receive your letters. They were doubtless being held at the barracks in Whitechapel and went up in smoke with the whole damned building. Anyway, Jenny certainly wasn't among either the wounded or those who managed to escape entirely. She hasn't yet been officially listed as dead, but she's vanished. Lily hasn't seen or heard from her since – nor has anyone else."

"But her death hasn't been confirmed," Bill said with pitiful desperation.

"No, Bill. But I don't think you're going to find her. No one else has."

"Jesus Christ!" Bill said softly.

Denholm squeezed his shoulder. "You're going home in two days time, Bill. It's finished for you here. You'll find a girl in Oklahoma, fall in love again, get married and have a lot of kids and grow fat and sassy. Go home. It's all over."

"It's not over until I get that plane."

Denholm sighed. "Two days, Bill." He nodded at the barman, indicated their empty glasses, then said, "Tell you what. I'm going to keep you as busy as possible. I'm not free tomorrow, so you can visit Anthony; then you, Lily and I will share your last day together. What do you think?"

"It sounds great."

Denholm took the fresh drinks off the barman and held one out to Bill. "Cheers," he said.

"Cheers," Bill replied, feeling disconsolate, but appreciating Denholm's consideration and kindness. "Let's go out with a bang."

Which they did, in the end.

The next day, Bill did his last-minute shopping, then saw Anthony Barker in hospital, where he found him with his head wrapped in bandages. Otherwise, as Denholm had remarked, Anthony *was* in good shape.

"My head was filled with broken glass," he said. "Now it's just filled with tiny holes."

"You were lucky."

"Denholm's luck. All villains get off clean in the end, so I was in the right company. I believe you also got wounded, Bill."

"Yes, in my left leg. It wasn't much really."

"Kept you in hospital for months, I hear."

"I was just resting up."

"And now you're going back to America – to a hero's welcome, no doubt."

"They're *like* that in American small-towns."

"I hope so. You deserve it."

"I only *reported* the war, Anthony."

"And thus made us immortal."

They laughed a lot together, as if the war had never touched them, but eventually, when the visiting hour was up, Bill took his leave.

"It was nice knowing you, Bill."

"Let's shake hands and call it a day."

"Good-day, Bill."

"Goodbye, Anthony."

He walked out near to tears, feeling as if he'd left his family, blinked against the afternoon's pearly light and then commenced walking.

He was searching for Jenny. He would *always* search for Jenny. And so he walked the streets for hours, searching for Jenny, saying goodbye, and ended up in the bar in the hotel, where he got drunk alone.

He awakened to the day he would not forget as long as he lived.

VE Day.

Victory in Europe . . .

Bill hurried out to join the thousands already thronging

the streets of London. Fireworks were exploding, hundreds of flags were fluttering, and the normally staid English were marching arm-in-arm, hugging and kissing, dancing and singing, on the roads and pavements, in the shops, with uninhibited joy.

By mid-day Bill was standing with the thousands lining the Mall as Winston Churchill, in his siren suit and homburg hat, drove past on his way to Buckingham Palace.

Shortly after, in a jam-packed Lyon's Tea House, Bill met Denholm and Lily, both of whom, though sipping only tea, were unusually flushed. Lily shrieked when she saw him, jumped up and embraced him, and told him how much Jenny had loved him and how tragic his loss was. Denholm had a hip-flask filled with whiskey, which is why they were both so flushed, and he poured some into Bill's tea and said, "Drink up, you poor sod!"

Which Bill did. Then the three of them went outside and were swept up in the euphoria of the crowds, before going quiet with them.

It was three o'clock in the afternoon. The sudden silence was startling. Then the Prime Minister's voice was broadcast over loud-speakers, announcing that the war in Europe would end at midnight.

"Long live the cause of freedom!" he proclaimed. "God save the King!"

The massed people went mad again and Bill found himself holding Lily, who in turn was holding Denholm, as they took part in a massive "hokey-cokey" that snaked around Queen Victoria's statue while more fireworks exploded. They ended up at Buckingham Palace. The crowd was shouting, "We want the King!" Eventually, the

Departures

Royal Family stepped out onto the Palace balcony, with the King, Queen and Princess holding hands before waving at an ever-growing throng of jubilant subjects.

Thousands roared their approval.

Lily was in tears. "Oh, they're lovely!" she sobbed. Denholm laughed and uncorked his hip-flask and made them both drink some more. Then they moved off arm-in-arm, swept away in a human tide, back along the Mall, around Trafalgar Square, then along Whitehall in a sea of bobbing heads that lapped around the Ministry of Health.

Winston Churchill appeared again. He had returned from lunch in the Palace. The Guards Band struck up *"For He's a Jolly Good Fellow"* and the crowd cheered and joined in the song until it had ended. Then Churchill, still wearing his siren suit and homburg hat, sang and conducted the joyous throng in the deeply moving *"Land of Hope and Glory."*

Lily's tears flowed again, but many others were also weeping. Churchill waved and the crowd roared, then Churchill disappeared, and Bill found himself, still with Denholm and Lily, being swept back up Whitehall, towards Nelson's Column.

He wanted Jenny here, to share this great moment with him, and remembered the full extent of the tragedy that was about to befall him.

He was leaving at midnight.

That evening, from all corners of the city, Londoners streamed into Piccadilly. Bill kissed and hugged strangers and was kissed and hugged in turn. Because they were still in uniform, he and Denholm were picked up and carried shoulder-high through the revellers. Then with

Lily they went through many pubs in a river of drunken flesh.

Bill wanted Jenny with him. He confided this truth to Lily. She burst into tears, hugged him and kissed him, then was pulled off by Denholm.

"She's not really bad, is she?" Denholm said. "I think I'm going to marry her."

"Do it!" Bill said. "God, do it!"

And Denholm proposed there and then, like an actor, on his knees; and Lily accepted and sobbed as the crowd around them cheered wildly, then placed them high on strong, willing shoulders to carry them off.

Bill waved at them, then lost them. They were swept away on the tide. He was then swept away also, and eventually found himself in Trafalgar Square. Darkness had fallen, but more fireworks were exploding. There was cheering, applauding and singing as the crowd pushed him onward.

Then he thought he saw Jenny.

It was near Charing Cross. He saw her heading towards the station. He caught a glimpse of her face and the back of her head, then she moved across a gap in the dense throng and he saw her more clearly.

Not long enough, but enough to make his heart leap. She was wearing a grey overcoat and black hat and carrying a suitcase. Then the crowd poured into the gap and he saw only the back of her head again.

"Jenny!" he bawled.

It was her. He was certain. He couldn't be sure, but was convinced. *"Jenny!"* he bawled again, his heart racing, and then tried to get to her.

The crowd hemmed him in on all sides, swirled

Departures

around him, forced him back, pummelled him this way and that as the woman moved away from him.

He broke free and ran. He was calling her name and waving frantically. He managed to get to the pavement as she reached the station entrance – then his wounded leg betrayed him, a spasm of pain made him wrench, and he cried out, fell and rolled over as Jenny went inside.

"Here, mate, let me help you up!"

Someone helped him to his feet. He couldn't see them through his tears. He said his thanks and raced into the station and ran back and forth, muttering, "God! Oh, please God!"

He didn't see her again.

It may not even have been her.

There was no way of knowing. He knew only that soon he would be on a plane back to the States . . . and that Jenny, the girl he loved so deeply, would become a mere memory.

He shook and sobbed silently.

Two hours later, at midnight, as fireworks exploded over London, the provinces, the whole country, as thousands cheered and got drunk, he was flown away from that green land with some fellow Americans – away from love and war, from the best days of his life – unaware that forty years would pass before he returned . . .

Chapter Thirty-Four

∽

As the limousine carried him from London to Elstree, Bill recalled how he had taken his leave from Maureen – and felt very uneasy.

Since Denholm had only phoned that morning to insist that he take this unexpected opportunity to meet his potential backers in the Elstree Film Studios, Bill had been compelled to cancel his promised visit to the Tower of London, thus leaving Maureen with most of the day to fill.

Already angry with him, she had vented her frustrations by telling him that she was sick of being left alone and no longer trusted him. Nor had it escaped her notice that he had given undue attention to their driver, Carol, during their trip to Cornwall.

Bill had been mortified. Yet unable to tell Maureen exactly who Carol was, which would have explained his affection for her, he had only been able to say that he had no designs on her or anyone else, and that everything would be explained in due course, when he felt that the time was ripe.

Departures

"Go to hell!" Maureen had replied.

Now he sighed, torn between conflicting loyalties, and was glad when the limousine turned into Elstree Film Studios and pulled up at the open door of a large hangar.

Stepping inside, he saw the usual chaos of moviemaking. Denholm and two elegantly-dressed men were deep in conversation beside a house that lacked exterior walls and roof and was bathed in the white glare of spotlights and reflector-umbrellas.

"Hi, Denholm," Bill said, stifling his rage and trying to appear as civilised as possible.

"Bill! Good to see you!" Denholm shook his hand, then introduced him to the financiers, a sleek Italian, Salvatore Renati, and a more portly Greek, Alexander Pangalos.

"So pleased to meet you," Salvatore said, shifting his fine grey coat on his shoulders and extending a heavily ringed hand. "I have heard so much about you."

Bill shook his hand.

"And I, too, am delighted to meet you," Alexander said, wiping beads of sweat from his forehead and squinting up at the spotlights. "I very greatly admire your work."

He did not extend his hand.

"I was just about to show Salvatore and Alexander around the studio," Denholm said to him, "so you might as well come along and discuss these few little changes."

"OK," Bill said.

Since Denholm was babbling like a tour-guide as he showed his guests around the large complex, Bill didn't have to make small-talk, for which he was grateful. However, as they were making their way back to

Denholm's office in the main building, Salvatore adjusted his coat and said, "Your screenplay I love very much, Mister Eisler, but is too tame, I think."

"Too . . . *tame*?" Bill asked.

"Too *polite*," Alexander clarified, still wiping sweat from his brow, though they were out in the open. "Your screenplay is subtle, very literate, but does not *show* enough."

"It shows what it needs to show."

"For English audiences," Salvatore said. "But for the international market, not English-speaking, such subtleties are worthless."

"Can you be more specific?"

"More sex," Alexander said. "Your love affair is mostly one of words. We want to see more bare skin."

Salvatore nodded obediently. "That is so," he said. "More bare skin. We must give the audience something to *watch*, not something to think about."

"A little boom-boom," Salvatore explained.

"Lots of fucking," Alexander clarified.

"I'm not into pornography," Bill said, "and that's what you want."

"We have our rights," Alexander said. "It's our money, Mister Eisler. Just a little skin and sex is all we ask. This also helps with the videos."

"I'm not interested – " Bill began.

"And more action," Salvatore continued. "In your script, all the fighting is off-screen, which would frustrate the audiences. We need more action sequences."

"Sex and violence," Bill said.

"I think – " Denholm began.

"I'd planned a small-budget movie. Perhaps even a TV

feature. I don't really believe that the inclusion of sex and violence will broaden this particular kind of film in the way you anticipate."

"We change the title," Alexander said.

"It is sex and war," Salvatore added. "We can sell it if we think of these aspects when the advertising is being done. Boom-boom and bang-bang, my friend. We can package it anywhere."

Bill stopped walking, thus making them all stop with him. He glared at Denholm, then turned to the financiers and said, "Since you're only putting up twenty percent, you're asking a lot for a little."

Salvatore stopped smiling. "A little?" he said sarcastically.

"What I think Bill means," Denholm said, "is that – "

"I know what I mean. And *they* know what I mean. They're only putting up twenty percent and they want the whole show. They don't even want *my* story at all; they just want the basics."

"When we pay, we expect returns." Alexander was solemn. "And without our crucial twenty percent your movie will not be made."

"We'll get it elsewhere."

"I don't think so," Salvatore said. "Mister Wilding is a very bright man, but he has come to a dead end. Had he not, he would not have come to us. He comes to us when he's desperate."

Denholm shrugged and raised his hands. "I'm sorry, Bill, but what he says is the truth. I have no other resources."

Bill studied Denholm at length. His old friend's face was closed. When he looked at Salvatore and Alexander, he knew he was beaten.

"Let's have a script conference," he said, "and see what we come up with. Can we make it next week?"

Denholm glanced at the financiers. They both nodded solemnly. Denholm said, "Fine, Bill, next week. Let's all check our diaries tomorrow and then get in touch."

Salvatore and Alexander agreed.

"Excellent," Denholm said, then placed his hand on Bill's shoulder. "Why not meet me in the bar, Bill? We'll have a drink to celebrate. Let me escort Salvatore and Alexander to their car, then I'll come back to you."

"OK," Bill said.

He shook hands with the financiers, feeling too grim to smile, then walked in the direction indicated by Denholm and entered the bar. He was halfway through his beer when Denholm returned, smiling uneasily.

"This is a celebration," he said. "I think that drink should be champagne."

"Why should we be celebrating?" Bill asked him.

"The money, Bill! *We're in business!*"

"*You're* in business." Bill let his anger rise to the surface. "You'll make money out of money, as usual, but you'll do it while my movie's being destroyed. Is that what you wanted?"

Denholm stared at him, startled, then cocked his finger at the barman. "A large gin and tonic," he said. "No champagne today." He stayed silent until his drink came. "OK, Bill, just say it."

"You knew I'd have to sell out, didn't you?"

"I would call it compromise."

"I didn't want to compromise, Denholm, and you damned well knew it."

"Compromise is unavoidable in history's most

expensive art form. You, Bill, coming from Hollywood, should surely know *that*."

"I compromise in Hollywood – it's a different world altogether – but this was *my* screenplay, my most personal work, and you knew that from the start. This wasn't an ordinary movie, Denholm; it didn't *have* to be box-office. I thought you were trying to get me backing because you also believed in it."

"I did."

"No, you didn't. You just played your dirty game. You wanted me to get egg on my face."

"You're imagining things!"

"No, I'm not." Then he exploded, letting it all hang out, telling Denholm about Carol and what he had learned from her, his bitterness and rage boiling over with each word he spoke. "*Why*, Denholm?" he asked again, when he had finished. "Why did you tell Jenny I'd been killed? What the hell made you do that?"

Denholm had a good sip of his gin, then studied his glass.

"Because I loved her. Yes, Bill, it's the truth. I loved her from the minute I laid eyes on her – then *you* came along. That's all there was to it."

Bill turned cold. "I don't understand. You went with Lily. You even married her . . ."

"Oh, Lily was fun. A good-natured, simple girl. She was good to be with, but I only stayed with her because she was my excuse to see Jenny. Of course, I treated Lily badly. I did so because I loved Jenny, who had fallen in love with you." He met Bill's accusing gaze with a shrug and sad smile. "I never forgave you for making Jenny love you – and that, Bill, probably explains it all. I'm not proud of it. *Honestly!*"

"And that's also why you told her I'd been killed?"

"God help me, yes." Denholm shook his head in shame. "I thought it was my last chance. Since you were hospitalised in France and due to be shipped back home, I assumed you would never return to London – so I imagined that if I told her you were dead, I'd get her eventually."

"But you miscalculated."

"Yes. Instead of falling to pieces and into my helpful arms, Jenny told me she was pregnant with your child, about to be discharged, and intended returning to Cornwall to give birth in her own home."

Hearing this, even though outraged at Denholm, Bill swelled with pride. "When was that?"

"October, 1944. Four months after D-Day."

"And then?"

Denholm shook his head, as if perplexed. "I only know that the baby was born in Cornwall in February, 1945, and that Jenny visited London the following year, to see some old friends – though not me or Lily. I only heard about that visit later, when you'd returned to America."

"Do you know exactly *when* she visited London?"

"How could I forget? It was May 7, 1945 – VE Day! The day you spent with Lily and me, before flying home."

Bill closed his eyes, looking inward, at his past, and saw Jenny entering Charing Cross Station while the city went wild. She would have taken the Underground to Paddington, then the night train to Cornwall – where Carol, her daughter, *his* child, had already been born.

"You bastard," he said, opening his eyes again.

Denholm had another drink. "I wasn't quite sane," he explained. "I wasn't myself at all. I was literally mad with love for Jenny and couldn't bear losing her. But once she made it clear that she was going back to Cornwall – that she would rather have no one than live without you – I got my senses back and realised exactly what I'd done."

"And then?" Bill asked, offering no mercy.

"I thought it best to live with my ghastly lie, rather than cause even more damage by confessing too late. I was ashamed of myself, yes – and lost sleep because of it – which is why, when you turned up unexpectedly in London, on your way back to the States, I proposed to Lily in your presence . . . To convince myself, I suppose, that it was Lily I wanted, not Jenny. Then, about a year later, I heard that Jenny had moved back to London for good and wasn't doing too well. But I didn't even try to get in touch with her. I just couldn't face her."

"Dear God," Bill said softly.

He shook his head despairingly from side to side and turned around to walk out.

"We're friends, Bill," Denholm said. "We always were. And we always will be."

"Yes, I suppose so."

They left the bar together, side by side, in fraught silence, and once outside, where the limousine was still waiting, stopped to face one another.

"She was a woman to love, Bill. You *know* that. And that's my only excuse."

But Bill, feeling only contempt, walked back to the limousine. When it moved off, he glanced out and saw Denholm receding, windblown and forlorn in the grey light, growing smaller each second.

Chapter Thirty-Five

∽

Jennifer was in bed when the pain, worse than any she had known, clawed her from sleep. She cried out instinctively, then covered her mouth with her hand, still not too sure of where she was and frightened that someone might hear her. Eventually, realising she was at home, she slid out of bed.

"Dear God," she gasped, "kill me!"

But He wasn't ready for her yet. She must suffer to come to Him. She did so as she doubled up, breathless with pain, before swallowing some capsules.

Shortly after, she knew what heaven was.

A place without pain.

Temporarily in heaven, she had a bath and dressed herself. It was just before noon when she carefully applied make-up to her face and put on a dark wig.

With the wig on, she looked like someone else, which helped her a lot.

She needed the help. She was starting to lose weight. The day before, she had seen her doctor, complaining about the pain, and he had booked her in for the radium treatment she had tried to avoid. She knew nothing about it other than the rumours, but those were enough.

She was brooding fearfully about this, wishing God would strike her dead, when the front door of the apartment was opened and Carol walked in. She hung her coat up. "Is that tea you're making?"

"Yes."

"Good," Carol said. "I could do with it."

"So how did the weekend go?" Jennifer asked while pouring the tea.

"Very good. I've just dropped them all off. I learned things I could hardly believe, and my mind is still reeling."

She took the chair by the window and accepted the cup of tea offered to her. "Thanks, Jenny."

"*Pardon?*" Jennifer said, stepping back. "*What* did you just say?"

"I said, 'Thanks, Jenny.'"

"Jenny? You've never called me *that* before. Why – ?"

"You know why."

Jennifer had to sit down again.

Carol sipped some tea, then placed the cup back on the saucer. "I know who my father is, Mother. Why didn't you tell me?"

"Oh, God." Jennifer reached for her cup, noticed her hand was trembling, so changed her mind and lit a cigarette instead.

"Mother!" Carol admonished her.

"I'm sorry, dear, I just need one."

"You're killing yourself, you know that?"

"I really doubt it, my dear."

Carol's face was grim, then it softened as she leaned foward.

"Why didn't you tell me, Mother?"

"Do you like him?"

"Yes, I do. In fact, I adore him – and I've missed him badly all these years, so why didn't you tell me?"

"This isn't easy, dear." She could hardly recognise her own voice. She distracted herself by inhaling on the cigarette in defiance of commonsense. "But I really am so pleased that you like him. Does he also like you?"

"If he doesn't tell his wife who I am, I think she'll divorce him. Yes, he likes me. Now why didn't you tell me?"

Jennifer felt confused, caught between the past and present, hardly remembering her original motives. "You were illegitimate. It was just after the war. People weren't very liberal in those days."

"I know," Carol said. *"Bastards."*

Jennifer winced, feeling wounded. "Yes, Carol, that was it. I invented my marriage to an RAF pilot to save you from that kind of humiliation and give you some pride."

"My childhood . . . You protected me well . . . But why on earth didn't you tell me he'd come back? Why, when I actually met him, didn't you say who he was?"

"I didn't realise he was alive until . . . "

"I know that – he told me. But then, when you wrote to him, you didn't mention me to him or vice versa."

"I didn't know how you'd react to the discovery that your father was alive, was someone other than I'd described; and perhaps more troubling, was rich and famous, married to another woman, and living in the

United States. Honestly, those were my reasons – and I think they were sound."

"Why on earth didn't you tell him about me?"

"As I hadn't seen him for forty years, I couldn't judge him too clearly. And as he's married, his wife had to be considered, also. I mean, how would *she* react? My vanity made me assume that if she's married to Bill, she must be nice; so I didn't want to hurt her – and knowing about you could have done that. Do you understand, dear?"

Carol stared thoughtfully at her, as if judging her merits, then eventually, after taking a deep breath, she smiled with love and deep pleasure.

"I think my father's wonderful," she said. "But then, so are you. I love you. I truly do."

Jennifer felt enormous relief and was on the verge of crying when Carol walked up to her and leaned down to warmly embrace her.

"Hello, Jenny," Carol said.

Chapter Thirty-Six

"I'm sorry, Maureen, but it isn't so. I was neither having, nor planning to have, an affair with our driver, Carol. I just liked her, that's all!"

Bill glanced across the river, at the South Bank, then turned back to face Maureen.

"Rubbish!" she snapped. "Your attentions were so blatant! Your questions were so personal! You made a goddamned fool out of yourself and – "

"Dammit, Maureen – "

"Damn *you*!"

She turned away from him, walked across to the bed, studied the dresses spread upon it, then covered her face with her hands.

"Maureen – "

"Shut up!"

"This is getting us nowhere."

She removed her hands from her face and stared down at the dresses. "I can't bear it. I can't face this goddamned interview. I've been worrying about it all week – and now I've got *you* to worry about! You and your – "

"Don't say it, Maureen!"

"Say what? I'm saying nothing! I'm just saying that this interview's upsetting me and you've just made it worse. God damn it!" she added, sitting on the bed. "To hell with it! I don't have to do it! Let the RSC screw itself!"

"You've got to go, Maureen."

"I don't have to do anything."

"You know you'll regret it if you don't, so please put on a dress."

She pouted like a child, then picked up a dress. "Damn!" she snapped and threw the dress back on the bed. "No! I'm not going!"

"You are!"

"No, I'm not!" She glared at him with. "Damn you, Bill, you were *obsessed* with that girl! Weren't you! *Admit it!*"

The telephone rang.

They both stared at it, but it refused to stop ringing. Maureen flopped down onto the bed while Bill, his nerves quivering like bow-strings, picked up the phone.

"Mr Eisler?" the desk clerk asked.

"Yes, this is Eisler."

"We have someone down here to see you, sir. A Mrs – sorry, *Miss* Jenny Birken. She wants to come up, sir."

"Oh," Bill said. "I see."

He was shocked into silence, hardly believing she had come here, and wondered, in a whirlpool of panic, why she had done so. He glanced at Maureen, saw her flushed face and felt even more confused.

"Can I send her up?"

"Yes," Bill said, automatically, in a trance, not knowing what else to say. "Of course. Send her up."

"Thank you, sir."

Bill heard the buzzing of a dead line, stared dumbly at the telephone, nervously placed it back on its cradle and turned to face Maureen.

"You better put on *one* of those dresses," he said. "Someone's coming up right now."

Maureen sat up straight. "Someone's coming to see us?"

"Yes."

"Who?"

"An old friend. Jennifer Birken. I'll tell you about her later. But she's going to be at the door any second, so please put on a dress."

Maureen glanced at the door, as if expecting it to burst open, then swept all the dresses off the bed and rushed into the bathroom.

The silence, which lasted about a minute, seemed to go on forever.

Then Jenny knocked on the door.

Hardly able to think straight, wondering what Jennifer was here for, Bill managed to pull himself together and greet his unexpected visitor.

Jennifer was wearing a simple, black dress and a string of pearls, with a dark wig instead of the more garish kind. She looked quietly elegant.

"Can I come in or can't I?" she asked, smiling.

"Oh, sure!" Bill said, stepping aside to let her walk through. "Come right in!"

When she had passed him, he closed the door and turned to face her. He was just about to speak when Maureen emerged from the bathroom, seductive in a white blouse and black skirt, her long hair hanging loose.

"Oh, hi!" she said, extending her hand to Jennifer and offering a glacial smile. "You're – ?"

"Jennifer Birken," Bill said quickly.

"Jenny!" he was corrected.

"An old friend," he continued, feeling more confused. "We met during the – "

"My friends all call me 'Jenny'. And you're Maureen, of course – Bill's wife. He's told me so much about you."

"He has? When was that?"

"Over the past two weeks," Jenny said, and Bill felt his heart sinking.

"Listen, Jennifer, I – "

"Jenny!" she corrected him again.

"You and Bill have been meeting over the past two weeks?" Maureen asked, looking grim. "He didn't mention the fact."

"I'm not feeling too well," Jenny replied. "Do you mind if I sit down?"

"No," Maureen said, "of course not."

Jenny started to sit on the edge of the bed, but changed her mind and took a chair instead, then smiled sweetly at Maureen.

"I know he didn't," she said. "He had reason to be concerned." She glanced searchingly at Bill, then back to Maureen. "Have you two just had a fight?" she asked.

"Yes," Bill confessed.

"Was it about Carol?"

"How did *you* know?" Maureen asked.

"Carol's my daughter and we were talking this morning."

"About us?"

"Yes, Maureen, about you. She said that during the

weekend, when she drove you to Cornwall, you developed the notion that Bill was obsessed with her, perhaps even romantically."

"Which he was."

"He was obsessed with her, certainly, but not romantically. Clearly, he still hasn't told you about it, which shows concern for your feelings. He's frightened of hurting you."

Maureen glanced at Bill, no longer grim-faced, but puzzled, then returned her attention to Jenny, who was impressively calm.

"I think *I'd* better sit down," Maureen said, taking the chair facing Jenny. "Please continue, Miss Birken."

Jenny folded her hands in her lap and leaned forward a little.

"Bill kept this secret from you because he didn't want to hurt you, but I don't think you've reason to be concerned. You see, Bill and I were lovers during the war – forty years ago, Maureen, when you were just a child – and after our brief affair we got separated and lost touch with each other. I was, however, pregnant and had a daughter – your driver, Carol."

Maureen straightened up, looking stunned, while Bill sighed and sat on the bed.

"Please go on," Maureen said.

Bill covered his face with his hands as Jennifer, speaking with studied care, recounted all that had happened in the past, including the fact that Carol was his daughter. He only removed his hands from his face when Jennifer stopped speaking.

"Oh, God," Maureen murmured, then she stood up, walked to the window, and looked out at the river.

Departures

The silence was terrible and Bill was shaking slightly. Maureen remained at the window, her back turned to the room.

"So what happens now?" she asked.

"Nothing," Jenny said. "Carol's forty years old and delighted to find her father, but she also has her own child and a very good man, so you needn't fear any unwanted involvement. As for me, I have no claims on Bill, emotionally or otherwise. I'm simply throwing myself on his mercy regarding the money."

"*Our* money," Maureen said bitterly. "So what do you need it for?"

"That's not your concern."

Maureen turned away from the window to stare at Jenny, astounded. Bill, still sitting on the bed, felt his heart sinking farther.

"It's not my concern? You want me to consider the loan of all that money, but I'm not to know what it's for? What damned impertinence!"

Jenny smiled sweetly. "I apologise, Maureen. I don't mean to be insulting. It's just that it's a very personal matter and I can't talk about it."

"I think I'm going crazy," Maureen said. "I can't take this in."

Jenny stood up, small and frail beside Maureen. "I'm glad I told you the truth. It may hurt you at the moment, but you'll both feel better later. Now I have to be going. I hope to see you again."

She started towards the door, but Maureen stopped her with: "Wait!" When Jenny turned back, Maureen stared flatly at Bill, making him feel even worse, then she gazed again out the window, surveying the river. "I'm in a state of shock. I need time to take this in. Bill, why don't you take Jenny home and leave me alone for now?"

"Maureen – " he began, standing up.

"Don't say anything. Just go."

Jenny smiled and nodded, silently indicating that he should do as Maureen wanted.

"OK, Maureen," Bill said.

He put on his coat, opened the door, and led Jenny out.

Chapter Thirty-Seven

Maureen turned to face the room when Bill and Jenny were gone. Heaving a sigh of relief, she tried to compose herself, which wasn't that easy.

Though angry at Bill because of his subterfuge, and shocked to discover that he had a forty-year-old daughter, she also felt increasingly ashamed of herself because of her adultery with Denholm.

Deciding that she couldn't bear the silence of the room, she resolved to distract herself by keeping her appointment with the director of the Royal Shakespeare Company. After checking her clothes and make-up, she left the hotel. In the back of the cab, she felt only growing panic and looked out at the people in the streets without really seeing them. She felt unreal and a little deranged, throat dry, heart racing, tugged constantly between her anger at Bill and her fear of the interview.

Arriving at her destination, she had some time to spare and, like a frightened schoolgirl, wandered about the magnificent lobbies of the Barbican Centre. Finally, when her time was up, she took a deep breath, let it out slowly, then entered the RSC Theatre.

It was an unusually large theatre with an impressive stage, upon which, at this moment, auditioning actresses were trying to emote against the noise of carpenters, painters, prop-men and scene-shifters.

Maureen felt lost.

In a row near the front of the stalls, the director, casting-director and some others involved in the production were whispering amongst themselves, even as they studied those auditioning. Seeing them, Maureen felt even more nervous, but managed to walk down and introduce herself.

"Maureen Kennedy!" It was Maureen's professional name and the young man was smiling in welcome. "I'm so pleased you could come!" He stood up and shook her hand. "I'm Maurice Williams-Ellis, the casting-director. And this is our director, Joseph Eperon, and our producer, Harold Gasgoyne. So, how do you feel?"

"Scared to death," she confessed.

"But you've done *so much* work, Maureen! You should be used to all this."

"This is England. The RSC. I haven't worked for some time and I've certainly never worked for a company like *this* – so believe me, I'm scared."

Williams-Ellis raised his hands in a reassuring gesture. "The best talent is always nervous. It's a very good sign." He glanced at the stage, where another actress was auditioning, then turned back and said encouragingly, "I saw you doing Blanche in New York. I thought you were wonderful."

"I bet you say that to all the girls."

He chuckled softly. "Maybe, but you *were* good. Is it a play you have a particular fondness for?"

"Very much so."

"Of course, we'll do it a little differently here – the rest of the cast will be English. Do you think that will give you any problems?"

"I don't know. I really can't answer that."

"That's a *good* answer, Maureen . . . Now what's going on up there?" He glanced back at the stage, where the actress, wearing a chequered shirt and denims, had stopped her reading and was walking off. He observed the way she moved across the stage, then turned back to Maureen. "Would it help if you just sat down for a while and watched a few of the others? It might give you time to relax, get used to the theatre, and generally put you in the right frame of mind."

"That sounds like a great idea," she said.

"Excellent. Sit right here."

"Do you mind if I sit farther back? I think it'll give me a better feel of the theatre."

"Good thinking, Maureen. I'll give you a wave about ten minutes before we need you. How's that?"

"That's fine, Maurice."

Gratefully, she walked towards the back of the theatre and took a seat about halfway down. A new actress was walking across to centre stage, also young and dressed casually, and Maureen looked on with care when she started her reading. She fumbled, lost her lines, lost her voice, regained control, then glided into a more careful reading, though without too much passion.

The director asked her to stop. He walked up to the stage, spoke urgently to her, then took a seat in the front row, directly under her, and told her to start reading again. She had hardly started when he lost his patience and snapped something at her, cutting her off in mid-sentence.

So it went on.

It was soon clear to Maureen that even though the younger casting-director had been nice to her, the actual director, who was older, was being relentless in his demands for different interpretations of the short scene being read by the hapless girl, who in turn was becoming more agitated and distracted.

Maureen started sinking into her seat.

It went on and on, with the director interrupting the young actress more frequently, shouting louder each time he did so, until eventually the girl became hysterical and rushed off the stage.

The director turned to his buddies in the stalls and raised his hands to the heavens in mock entreaty.

Maureen heard them all laughing.

She realised, then, that she didn't want this, that she was now too old for it, and that her maturity had placed her beyond the point where she could accept the unavoidable humiliation of auditions, not to mention the anguish of rehearsals, first nights and reviews.

No, her desire to make a come-back had merely been a means of escaping the fears and frustrations of her age. It had also been a distraction from her childless marriage and problems with Bill.

What problems? They didn't have any *real* problems. Bill had wanted a child and now he had found one, which knowledge could only make him happier and ease all his other hurts. As for his former love, Jenny, she was a figure from the distant past, too far removed from his present to be a threat to their marriage.

And her own feelings?

She still loved Bill and respected him more than most men, regardless of his recent, minor deceptions. And those, she now realised, had stemmed from his desire not to hurt her or even cause her embarrassment.

He had behaved like a gentleman.

There weren't many of those left.

Maureen looked at the distant stage. Another actress was walking out. She was carrying a script in her hand and gazing distractedly around the theatre, revealing by her walk and the stoop to her shoulders all the fears she would soon have to conquer.

Maureen wanted no part of it.

She now knew without doubt that her desire to be an actress was well behind her.

Accepting this, she stood up and left the theatre without looking back.

Chapter Thirty-Eight

∽

As Jenny walked with Bill along the Strand, across Trafalgar Square and on to Mayfair, Bill expressed his concern about Maureen's reaction to what she had just learned.

"It was forty years ago," Jenny responded. "She's a sensible woman. She's not the type to worry about an affair that's been over that long, particularly when you and she are clearly such a good team."

"You think we are?"

"It's so obvious."

She meant it and could consider it without resentment. She still loved him, but not the same way, since they were both so much older now. She loved the memory of what they had shared, which could never be changed.

"You were a terrific girl, Jenny. It was impossible to forget you. I love Maureen, but not the same way. Maybe as deeply and as truly as I loved you. I'm not sure. It confuses me."

"Both of you were older and more experienced when

you met, and that makes all the difference, Bill. One can never repeat the intensity of youthful passion, but one *can* improve on it."

He took her hand to squeeze it. They were passing the Ritz hotel and stopped to have a good look at it.

"Remember?" he asked her. "Our last day together? We dressed up and had tea at the Ritz, then went back to my room in the hotel and – "

"Yes, Bill, I remember."

"Tea at the Ritz," he murmured dreamily. "Just like in the movies."

"Let's go, Bill. I have things to do."

They continued along Piccadilly, heading for Mayfair, and it felt good, the way he held her hand, like a youth with his first girl.

"Why did you refuse to tell Maureen why you needed the money? Why did you say it was a personal matter, when in fact it's to cover your club's losses?"

"I don't know. The words just popped out. Perhaps I just wanted to make her angry."

"I don't think so, Jenny. I think your words *did* just slip out. And I believe they confirm what I've suspected all along – that you don't want the money for your club, but for something else altogether."

"What does it matter? I've told you I badly need that money. So if you care for me at all, or ever did, you won't ask any questions."

He jerked his head around to glare at her in sudden anger, and she knew, with a sinking feeling, that she had said the wrong thing again.

"Are you exploiting our old relationship?" he asked sarcastically.

"Is that what you think I'm doing?"

"I think you're an unprincipled woman in more ways than one."

"I can't afford principles, Bill. Only rich folk like you can."

"Your attitude still seems mercenary to me. And since your sad excuse for a brothel seems to be doing OK, I really don't know why you need the money."

"*What* did you just say? Did you say . . . *brothel?*"

"I didn't really mean – "

But now angry herself, she wrenched her hand out of his and hurried ahead.

"Jenny!"

"Goodbye!"

"Damn it, Jenny, stop this acting!"

She turned back to face him. "My club is *not* a brothel and damned well you know it – but even if it were, what gives *you* the right to cast stones? Indeed, according to what Carol learned during that trip to Cornwall, you're betraying your own lofty principles concerning the movie you want to make. There are many forms of whoredom, Mr Eisler, and you've not been immune to them!"

Bill froze where he was standing, as if she had slapped his face, then distractedly ran his hand over his mouth and took a step back, his shock turning to rage.

"All right, damn it," he snapped, "you win! You can *have* your damned money! On the condition that you never get in touch with me again. Is that agreed?"

"It's agreed."

"Good-day, Jenny."

"*Goodbye!*"

Then he spun around and marched away from her.

She wanted to call him back, but couldn't bring herself to do it. She just watched him leave, her heart breaking with each step he took, and only when he had gone did she understand what she was doing.

She realised that she still possessed the need for the *proof* of love – and that she wanted him to give her the money because of their shared past.

Not just because he had found a lost daughter.

And not out of guilt.

Even nearing death, she needed proof that their love, which certainly could have no future, had a past that could never be denied.

Yet she let him walk away, not knowing what else to do. Then she walked in the opposite direction, towards her home in Shepherd Market, thinking of death's implacable darkness and love's healing light.

Chapter Thirty-Nine

∽

Furious, Bill had just turned into Piccadilly and was heading for the Savoy, when he decided he needed a drink. Turning back into Mayfair, he went straight to the Red Lion pub, which he remembered visiting often with Denholm during the war.

It was an old-fashioned pub, quite beautiful, packed with people, and he ordered a pint of best bitter, hoping it would soothe his bad temper. He couldn't get to grips with Jenny, was repeatedly confused by her, torn between his affection for her and the outbursts of frustration which she now seemed, with perverse deliberation, to make him endure.

When his beer came, he drank greedily, not concerned with sobriety. Then he put the jug down, wiped his lips and glanced into the restaurant.

Maureen was facing Denholm over a table and holding his hand.

They were engrossed with each other.

Bill picked up his jug, tried to drink, but felt ill, so put the jug down and instead stared with disbelief and horror at his wife and best friend.

Departures

They were definitely holding hands. Denholm was stroking Maureen's wrist. Maureen was smiling at Denholm with a good deal of warmth.

She was supposed to be at the RSC, sweating blood for her new career. But she wasn't. She was here. Holding hands with Denholm. She was letting the bastard stroke her wrist, smiling warmly at him.

Bill couldn't believe it.

He started towards them, thought of Jenny and felt guilty, went back to the bar, studied his beer and felt ill again. Shaking, his heart racing, he hurried out of the pub, then caught a taxi and returned to his hotel. Once in his room, he poured himself a whiskey and drank it while waiting.

When Maureen walked in, an hour later, he was ready to tackle her.

"You got Jenny home?" she asked him in a neutral manner.

"Yes. Then I went for a drink."

"After this morning, Bill, that's understandable."

"And you? How do you feel now?"

"Still a bit shocked," she replied, taking her coat off and hanging it up in the wardrobe, "but I'm coming around. My husband has a forty-year-old daughter! It takes some getting used to."

"It was long before your time, Maureen."

"Yes." She faced him again. "I'm trying to keep that firmly in mind. I accept it. It's OK. I just wish you'd told me about Jenny. I don't like secrets, Bill."

"You don't?"

"No, I don't." She sat on the edge of the bed. "So where did you go for your drink?"

"The Red Lion," he said.

She had the courage to meet his gaze, but her cheeks turned bright red, then she clasped her hands, placed them on her lap and studied them thoughtfully.

"You mean the Red Lion in Mayfair?"

"It's where Jenny lives, Maureen."

"Oh," she murmured, almost to herself. "I didn't know that."

"Obviously not, Maureen."

Her cheeks were still burning, but she raised her eyes again. "And what did you see in the Red Lion?"

"You and Denholm," he said, his rage returning. "You both looked very cosy. You were holding hands across the table. Denholm was stroking your wrist and receiving your warmest smile. I always knew that Denholm found you attractive, but I didn't realise that *you* – "

"Stop it, Bill. Right there."

"You've slept with him, haven't you?"

"Just because we were holding hands in – "

"Have the decency not to lie to me. Did you sleep with him, Maureen?"

She sighed and studied her hands again. "Just once," she whispered.

He was shocked to realise that he wanted to strike her – even though she looked so defenceless, gazing down at her clasped hands.

There were tears on her cheeks.

"Just once," Bill said. "Christ!"

He still wanted to hit her and was ashamed of himself for that. The shame made him want to get down on his knees and rest his head where her hands were.

Instead, he asked as calmly as possible, "When and where did it happen?"

"In Cornwall. It happened when you went for the drive with Carol. It was all over quickly."

"*That* helps!" he said.

She wiped the tears from her cheeks and reluctantly raised her head. Her face, which was framed by her long hair, was a beautiful mask.

"It's been coming for years," she said. "I should have known, but I ignored the signs. Denholm's always been attracted to me and was never shy of showing it – usually in California; all those days he spent with us – and naturally I found him entertaining and enjoyed the flirtations. I don't love him, Bill, and he doesn't love me; but he wanted me, as he wants a lot of women, and in the end I surrendered. I was upset over Carol, thinking you had the hots for her. I even thought she was the reason you were disappearing so often, after giving me vague reasons or excuses. So in Cornwall, when I saw how fascinated you were by her, I assumed you'd been seeing her in London and felt deeply wounded."

"And of course," Bill said, "Denholm let you cry on his shoulder and you went to bed with him."

"Yes, Bill, that's it. But don't put the blame on Denholm. I'm not a child and I wasn't seduced. I knew what I was doing."

She took another breath, wiped more tears from her cheeks, but managed to keep her gaze fixed upon him with an odd, wounded pride.

"You were hurting me," she said. "Making me suspicious. I thought I was being betrayed and neglected – and I wanted revenge."

"I didn't betray you, Maureen."

"I know that now, Bill."

"So you went to bed with Denholm because of my *physical* neglect?"

"Not your physical neglect – that's male vanity talking. It was because of your *emotional* neglect: your obsession with your movie; all the evenings you disappeared; the ease with which you handed me over to Denholm while you did other things. You failed me . . . and yourself."

Bill put his face in his hands, sinking into the silent darkness. He used the silence for thinking, to examine his own feelings, and realised that his love for Jenny wasn't likely to fade away, but his love for Maureen, wrenched back from his anger, was as true for the present. Neither could ever fully replace the other, but for now, and in the foreseeable future, his love for Maureen would stand.

In a sudden rush of emotion, he placed his arms around her, resting his cheek against her stomach.

"I love you, Maureen."

She pressed him tighter to her, then kissed him on the head.

"I went to the RSC," she said, "but I didn't wait for the audition. I decided that there are more important things in life than acting, that I'm past the stage of needing it, and that I'd rather have the life we've shared together than go back to that madness. That's also why I phoned Denholm. You weren't around and I had to talk. And when you saw us in that restaurant, Denholm was actually trying to help both of us."

"How?"

"By agreeing that I didn't need acting anymore; and

by reminding me of the good life that you and I had found with each other. He said that we'd found what he had lost and should not give it up. He's still your friend, Bill."

She dropped to her knees, sliding down through his arms, then took his face in her hands and kissed his forehead.

"Let's go home early," she suggested. "Let's return to our own world. You have to attend the Academy Award ceremony tomorrow, but after that, we'll both be as free as birds, so let's take wing and fly away."

"Yes, let's do that," he said.

She kissed him on the lips. "We're both too old to be trying to prove things, Bill. We've done all we can do here."

"There's so much I want to say, Maureen, but I'm finally lost for words."

She leaned away from him, smiling tenderly. "Keep your words for your work," she told him. "I don't need the proof of words. Now come and lie beside me on the bed and don't try to prove anything – because I certainly won't."

Bill did as he was told, lying beside her on the bed, and there, in a natural manner, without thinking, not talking, they made love.

Eventually, they fell asleep in each other's arms and awoke, satisfied.

More than that . . .

Reunited.

Chapter Forty

The following evening, Bill attended the British Academy Award ceremony with Maureen. Denholm's chair was vacant. When Bill's name was called out, he hurried up to the stage, waving at old friends, shaking hands as he went, aware only of the sound of applause and the flashing light bulbs. He received his award from two old friends, both famous screen personalities, made a brief speech, which he would never remember, then hurried back to his table and Maureen's tremulous smile. He attended the party after the ceremony, shook more hands than he could count, drank more alcohol than was good for him, and eventually, exhausted, made his escape with Maureen back to the Savoy.

The next morning, he visited Carol at the address she had given him.

The door of the apartment in Chelsea was answered by a pleasant-faced, attractively dishevelled man in his mid-thirties. He was wearing corduroy trousers, white shirt and hush-puppies. His eyes, which were as brown as his tangled hair, were warm and good-humoured.

"Are you David?"

"Yes."

"I don't know if Carol's mentioned me, but . . . " He shrugged and grinned, feeling foolish. "I'm her father. Is she in?"

"Mr Eisler! Carol's told me all about you. Yes, of course. Welcome!"

They shook hands as Bill stepped in. Carol was stretched out on the sofa, reading a newspaper, but she looked up and broke into a smile when he entered the room.

"Wow!" she said, swinging her feet down to the floor. "It's my famous father! The award-winning screenwriter! I've just been reading about you in this paper and I'm swollen with pride!" She embraced him and kissed his cheek. "Take a seat and let me get you a drink. Wine, coffee or tea?"

"It's OK, Carol. I don't want anything to drink. I had enough to drink at that damned ceremony, so I'll stay pure today."

"They'll be showing it on TV," Carol said, "and I can't wait to see you. Did you make a nice speech?"

"Brief, precise and to the point. 'Thank you and goodbye.'"

"That's my Dad!" Carol sat on the sofa, inviting David to join her, but he hesitated, glancing searchingly at Bill.

"I came to see you because Maureen and I are leaving early tomorrow – and I wanted to say you're welcome to visit anytime."

"We accept," Carol said.

"Jenny thinks you two should get married."

"So do I," David said.

"Well, why don't you do it?"

"I'm thinking about it," Carol said, "but I've had too many bad experiences in my life and I don't want to spoil this."

"You won't spoil it. I can see that. You'll simply be able to share your problems and face life that much easier. I recommend it. Please do it."

Carol nodded. "We probably will, Dad."

There was a moment's silence, only broken when David said diplomatically, "I'm going to buy a bottle of wine. I'll be back in a short while."

"You're very understanding," Bill said.

David nodded and grinned, then grabbed his jacket and walked out.

"I came to see you," Bill said, "for the obvious reason – to say goodbye before I leave – but also to tell you I had a fight with your mother and won't be seeing her again."

"Oh? Why?"

"We fought about certain principles. I'm not sure I can explain them, since they're pretty damned subjective, but we certainly had conflicting views about points of morality."

Carol chuckled at that. "Oh, mein papa, give me one example, at least!"

"We were arguing about something pretty personal, and it led me into comparing her club to a brothel – which I know was wrong – and accusing her of being a woman without principles, which I think may be right."

"What on earth makes you think you can criticise my mother when *her* life, compared to yours, has been hell on earth?"

"I just don't understand how – "

Departures

"No, you *don't* understand! You've lived a privileged life, have no financial problems, and therefore can't see that some people can't afford your lofty principles."

"I don't think – "

"Have you *any* idea of what Jenny's been through? No, of course not! You fell in love with her, got her pregnant and went to war; then returned to America, where you became rich and famous while *she* struggled to survive and look after me, which she did against all odds. It was sink or swim for me and she kept me afloat – and she did it through the club you despise from your privileged heights! So how *dare* you criticise her for that! It was *me* she was thinking of!"

Bill sank into his chair, mortified by her attack. Recalling his argument with Jenny in the shadowed side of Half Moon Street, he took a cheque from his wallet.

"OK, I was wrong. But I came to England to find Jenny, the woman I'd once loved, and all I got was this mercenary creature, trying to screw money out of me. It was the proof of our love, she told me. In other words, emotional blackmail. To refuse to give her the money, which she claimed was only a loan, was tantamount to admitting that I'd never really loved her in the first place. It all came down to that."

"You mean the money?"

"What else?"

"Love," Carol replied. "The need to know that it had been real. The need to know that money was unimportant where the heart was concerned. Don't you understand that?"

"No. I'm not that bright."

"Apparently not."

He was hurt to the quick, but also ashamed of himself, so felt compelled to challenge the fury that his love had evoked.

He placed his cheque for £20,000 on the table between them.

"I don't know why she needs it," he said, "and I don't *want* to know. This is for Jenny. Not Jennifer. Not the one I've just fought with."

Carol stared at the cheque, clearly shocked, even outraged. "Is that the exact sum my mother asked for?"

"Yeah," Bill said. "Right."

Carol picked up the cheque, stared at it and smiled cynically, then let it fall back to the table.

"My mother," she said, "*your* Jenny, is dying of cancer."

"*What?*"

"Dear God, please help me. Is there a kind way of saying this?"

Though shocked rigid, Bill managed to say it for her: "*Terminal* cancer?"

Carol nodded. "And as she doesn't have much time left, she's desperate to set *me* up in business before the end comes. When she goes, there won't be anything left. The club's debts will eat up her inheritance, which is only more debts."

"I'm sorry, Carol. I – "

"My husband left me only *his* debts," Carol continued doggedly, "and they'll eat up every asset I have. Most jobs I could get wouldn't pay off even the interest, so I decided to form my own business, with a fleet of leased cars – and for that I'll need twenty thousand pounds, which is what my mother is after. Do you understand now, Dad?"

Departures

Bill wanted to sink through the floor. Instead, since that wasn't possible, he stood up, preparing to leave.

"I owe someone an apology," he said.

Then he heard a baby crying. It was obviously in the room next door. He looked at Carol and she smiled and took his hand and led him into the bedroom.

In the cot was her baby – his grandson, Mark. Carol picked him up and placed him in Bill's arms, where he cried and kicked happily.

Bill was reborn.

Chapter Forty-One

∽

"To hell with it," Jenny said, lighting a cigarette, shortly after receiving a phone call from Carol, who had informed her of Bill's imminent return to the United States.

Doreen, Marjorie and Barbara were also smoking as they played cards around a table; James, in his striped shirt and polka-dot bow tie, was preparing his bar for the evening; and a couple of the other girls were applying make-up before the doors opened.

Such sights were a comfort.

Still, she was upset. Bill would be returning to Los Angeles tomorrow night and after their parting words would almost certainly not return to see her, let alone give her the money she wanted for Carol.

These days she could often feel death gnawing at her, draining her of strength and will, but surprisingly she no longer dreaded it and, as she also realised, hadn't done so for some time. Yet what she did fear was the possibility that her life had been meaningless; that the

Departures

love she had felt for Bill, which had briefly ennobled her and changed her forever, had in truth been a hollow thing, a shadow-play, a young girl's self deception. It that was true, then even Carol, the child of that love, could neither lend meaning to her existence nor redeem her in darkness.

She heard the front door creaking open . . . then saw Bill walking in. He stopped in the doorway, as if frightened of coming farther, but eventually crossed the wide floor and stopped directly in front of her. He seemed very nervous.

"Hi, Jenny."

"Hello, Bill. I wasn't expecting to see you."

"I wasn't expecting to come."

"Why did you?"

"To apologise."

"Oh?"

"For what I said. For my behaviour."

"I was just as much to blame as you were. I apologise, also."

He smiled. "Two idiots. Two old fools."

"We don't necessarily learn from experience, Bill. Can I get you a drink?"

"No, thanks. I won't be staying that long. Carol told me about your situation. She also mentioned your illness."

"Please don't let it influence you, one way or the other."

"I didn't and won't. But apart from the apology, I also came to tell you that I left the cheque with Carol. And I want to make it clear that since I did this *before* I knew about your illness, the offer certainly wasn't influenced by it."

"Thank you," she said, trying to sound neutral, but welling up with gratitude, relief and a good deal of love.

She couldn't help herself. She had to take out her handkerchief and wipe her wet eyes.

He looked away while she did so.

"I have one burning question I'd like to ask," he said, turning back to her.

"Please do, Bill."

"Two questions, in fact. Why didn't you tell me you were suffering from cancer? And, more important, what was the real reason for not telling me about Carol?"

Jenny stubbed her cigarette out and sipped some of the Perrier water she had been drinking to wet her dry throat.

"Carol," she said eventually, "was the child of our love, and what I wanted for her and our grandchild had to come from that love – not from your pity. I had to know if our love was real – if it still existed in some form – and I could never have gauged that if I'd told you about Carol or my illness. I had to have your true feelings – not emotions influenced by sympathy or your love for our daughter. In other words, I'm a woman of principle. Please remember that, Bill."

And she took pride from saying it, being released from her previous doubts, and was rewarded when Bill's thoughtful expression turned into a tender smile.

"Can I ask you for a final favour, Jenny?"

"Yes, Bill, of course."

Departures

"Can we say goodbye, tomorrow, the way we did forty years ago? With tea at the Ritz?"

"That sounds lovely, Bill."

"It'll have to be the 3.15 sitting."

"I'll be in the lobby."

"Good," he said. "See you then."

He nodded affirmatively and walked out while she dabbed at her wet eyes.

Chapter Forty-Two

∾

The following morning Jenny had coffee in Hampstead with an old friend who had flown in from where she lived, in Marbella, Southern Spain. Her friend, Jenny's age, had put on a lot of weight, was lined and deeply suntanned, and had kept her hair youthfully blonde by dying it.

"Hello, Lily Monaghan," Jenny said. "You look as brown as a berry."

Lily shrieked with joy, embraced Jenny emotionally, then faced her across the table in the darkly attractive Victorian coffee lounge.

"You don't look bad yourself," she said, "if a bit on the pale side. You should sell that ridiculous club of yours and come join us in Spain. Lots of sunshine, cheap booze and bronzed men. It would do you the power of good!"

"How's Jack?" Jenny asked, referring to Lily's fourth, former footballer, husband.

Lily lit a cigarette, pouted her lips and blew smoke rings. "Oh," she said with a wicked smile, "the same as always. Dumb as they come, but kind and generous – and, God bless 'im, dotes on me like a love-sick schoolboy."

"What brought you back this time?"

"Just my annual jaunt. A bit of shopping at Harrod's and Fortnum 'n' Mason, tea and biscuits and diplomacy with the relatives, then a few days alone. To be truthful, you can get *tired* of daily sunshine, so this grey weather suits me fine."

"A regular English August."

"Right. And I *do* miss that sometimes. A cup of coffee, Jenny?"

"No, thanks. You drink up and then we'll go for a walk, which should do us both good."

"I'm finished, luv. Let's get going." There was a young man at the cash-register and Lily flirted with him as she paid the bill, then winked at Jenny and led her out, into the grey light. "Let's go up to Mount Vernon," she said. "I've always liked that little walk. I love the graveyard where all the show-biz folk are buried. I like to tramp on the famous."

Aware that Lily didn't know of her condition, Jenny nodded agreement. "That's fine. Not too near and not too far. We'll just about make it."

Lily laughed at that, then took Jenny's arm and led her along the High Street. They made small talk as they crossed the main road and walked up a narrow lane, then took the steep, steel-railed Holly Hill, which curved up under overhanging trees to the pastoral Mount Vernon.

"It's still as pretty as a picture," Lily said. "I keep forgetting how lovely it is. It's a pleasant surprise to come back to it." They turned the corner at Abernethy House, where Robert Louis Stevenson had lived, then wandered lazily down the picturesque Holly Walk, past a small church and other pretty cottages, towards the tower and spire of the larger parish church, which soared in solemn splendour above the trees.

"Anyway," Lily said, "I'm still enjoying myself in Spain. I love the long days of sunshine, I play tennis, Jack plays golf, and we do an awful lot of entertaining with very nice friends. It's not as dreary as England."

"I always thought you were a real Londoner."

"I was," Lily replied, "but it isn't *my* London anymore. I mean, apart from the odd area like this, the bloody city's a tip-heap."

"You think so?"

"I do. It's filthy, damp and cold, increasingly squalid, and run by property speculators and other sanctified robbers. By and large, given a few exceptions, I can't stand the bloody place. Anyway, what about you, Jenny? Has anything changed in *your* life?"

"Not really," Jenny said carefully. "Not much at all."

"Happy and healthy, are we, luv?"

"Yes, Lily, of course."

"Talking about property speculators and other slick reptiles, do you ever hear from that charming snake, Denholm?"

"We're not actually in touch," Jenny said as casually as possible, when they had turned into the rustic graveyard and were walking along a path between tombstones and overgrown grass, "but I pick up bits of news about him. With Denholm, as you can imagine, there's rarely a shortage of gossip."

"Yes," Lily chuckled, "I can imagine! And what's the old rogue been up to lately?"

"As a matter of fact, he's been trying to raise the finance for a movie to be co-produced with our old

Departures

American friend, Bill Eisler, who has, as it were, returned from the dead as a successful Hollywood screenwriter. You *remember* Bill Eisler?"

Lily stopped walking. "Did I hear right? Did you say *Bill Eisler*? The one we knew during the war?"

"Yes, Lily. He returned from Europe to London, tried to find me and failed, was told by Denholm that I was missing and flew back to America, thinking I'd probably died in the air raid that destroyed our barracks in Whitechapel."

"I remember. Denholm and I were with him on VE Day. But at that time, Jenny, even I thought you were missing – then Bill went back to America and that was the last I heard of him."

"Apparently Denholm kept in touch."

"Not while *I* was married to him. As I recall, he only received one letter from Bill during our marriage – written about a month after Bill had returned to Oklahoma, thanking us for our friendship and congratulating us on the marriage. After replying, Denholm received a final letter, informing us that Bill was going off to find work in Hollywood – and that, as far as *I* know, was the last word we received from Bill Eisler. Two years later, Denholm and I separated and I lost touch completely."

"Did you know Denholm had told me that Bill had been killed in Europe?"

Lily looked embarrassed. "Oh, Lord!" she said softly.

"So you knew?" Jenny persisted.

"Not at the time – but I *did* find out later." She shook her head sadly from side to side. "He really loved you, that man of mine."

"Pardon?"

"Yes, my innocent darling! Denholm was always in love with you. Of course, I'd always suspected it, but I wanted him so much, and then, when we were married, I found out – which certainly helped the divorce along!"

"Denholm loved *me*? I don't believe it!"

Lily stopped by one of the tombstones, lit a cigarette, blew smoke rings, watched them dissolving in the air and then smiled again.

"How did you get your club, Jenny, so quickly after returning to London?"

"An unnamed benefactor. Over the years, I tried to find out who it was, but never succeeded."

"Which of your old friends got rich on property just after the war? Yes, luv, it was Denholm. He'd found out you were back in London and struggling, and that's how he rescued you."

Jenny felt as if the ground had just shifted beneath her. "I think I need a cigarette. I can't take this in."

"Here, have one of mine." Lily gave Jenny a cigarette, lit it for her, then said, "Come on, luv, let's walk again."

Jenny let herself be led around the far end of the cemetery while listening carefully to what Lily was telling her.

"At first I didn't know who your benefactor was, either. But towards the end of that first year, when it was becoming clear that Denholm didn't really love me and was playing the field, I became wildly jealous and rummaged through his papers, hoping to find the names of his women. I didn't. What I found were the deeds to a property in Soho – and I saw that the property had been assigned to you and had the same address as your club.

Yes, Jenny, Denholm gave you that property – and did so out of guilt."

"Because of what he'd told Bill?"

"Correct," Lily replied with amused satisfaction. "When I confronted Denholm with the documents, wanting to know why he'd been so generous, he responded with a categorical denial that he'd ever laid hands on you – "

"It was true!"

"But he admitted that he'd always secretly loved you. He also confessed to telling you that Bill had been killed in Europe, thereby hoping to make you dependent upon him and then fall in love with him. Then, when that backfired, he tried to make amends by secretly giving you that valuable property in Soho. His conscience must have been eased a lot!"

Lily laughed cynically, while Jenny, confronted with her past, saw the truth for the first time.

"Anyway," Lily continued, "when nearly twenty years later Denholm and Bill were reunited, making their first movie together in Hollywood, Denholm felt it was too late to tell the truth. So having at least looked after you and Carol, he kept his mouth shut." She smiled, amused by Jenny's bewilderment. "And that's why I divorced Denholm two years after we were married. Because he really loved you and couldn't forget what he had done. In fact, it still haunts him." She slid her arm around Jenny and hugged her, then kissed her cheek. "He's not *that* bad, old Denholm!" she said. "So, can we go now?"

"Yes," Jenny said, touched and exultant. "Yes, of course, let's go back."

Leaving the graveyard, they wandered in silence down

the remainder of Holly Walk, past the tall Georgian houses in Church Row, then back to Hampstead Underground station, which as usual was busy.

"I'll take the tube," Lily said. "I hate wasting money on taxis. I like spending my money on better things, such as food, drink and clothes. Anyway," she added, preparing to take her leave, "whatever the rights or wrongs of the past, at least we've still got our health."

"Yes," Jenny replied, not wanting to disillusion her. "We can be grateful for that."

Lily grinned and kissed her cheek. "I'll be back next year, darlin'. In the meantime, if you'd like a good time, fly over and see us. OK?"

"Of course."

They hugged and kissed again, then Lily sauntered into the station, and Jenny, though aware that she would never see her friend again, smiled cheerfully as she waved her goodbye.

Then she turned away, looking up and down for a taxi, wondering what she should wear for her tea at the Ritz.

Chapter Forty-Three

At two o'clock in the afternoon, with Maureen's blessing, Bill took a cab from the Savoy to the Ritz, to meet Jenny for tea.

She was dressed in black again, simply elegant, with a matching wig, and her face, while no longer young, possessed a peaceful inner glow which age could not dim.

They kissed each other on the cheek, then linked arms and walked in – just as they had done forty years ago.

"Still so elegant," Jenny whispered.

"Some things never change."

"Not like you and I, who *have* changed."

"I'm not so sure of that, Jenny."

And indeed he wasn't. In many ways he felt the same as he had felt all those years ago; and now, when he studied Jenny, he felt that she, too, had remained unchanged and was simply hiding inside herself.

He also saw himself reflected in her eyes, which did not show his blemishes.

Jenny was a perfect lady, nibbling delicately, sipping

tea, and he watched her with growing affection as they talked about old times.

At the end of the tea, when they were discussing how they'd been separated by the war, Jenny said, "Just imagine, Bill! All those years thinking you were dead! When in fact it's *me* who'll soon be dead, leaving *you* with fond memories. Now isn't *that* funny?"

"Not funny at all." Bill was shocked back to reality. "How do you really feel about it, Jenny? You seem surprisingly calm."

"I wasn't always. At first I was terrified. But death is like everything else in life – it's a process of learning." She nodded to emphasise her point. "I'm not scared anymore."

Bill didn't know what to say, but Jenny, not as dumb as he felt, leaned closer to him.

"Can I tell you something even more personal?"

"Yes, Jenny, of course."

"You won't be bothered?"

"I won't."

Clearly relieved, Jenny took a deep breath and expelled it in speaking.

"For a long time after learning that I had cancer, I heard nothing but the sound of my own heartbeat. It was unnaturally loud and seemed to echo in my head, and it went on and on, day and night, like a metronome, until I could think of nothing else but what kept me alive. Then finally I saw, for the very first time, that my heart was no more than an old, worn-out clock, ticking away the seconds of my life, no matter how much I protested. That knowledge possessed me. It nearly drove me mad. Then, like a miracle, I saw you on my TV set – and apart from being stunned to learn you were still alive, I remembered the night we first made love, in my family's house in Cornwall."

Her eyes brimmed with tears. Bill choked up when he saw that. He opened his mouth to speak, could think of nothing to say, so just listened like a child in a schoolroom, learning what he might never use.

"Do you know what I most remember about our first night?" Jenny asked. "I remember the sound of my own heartbeat, magically amplified. A heart beating to tell me that love was life . . . and that you were that love."

Bill touched his wet cheeks with dry fingers and noticed their shaking.

"From that moment," Jenny continued, "when I recalled our first night, at least I found some light in my darkness, some joy in my pain . . . and when I heard my heart beating in the night, I no longer dreaded it. My heartbeat, which told me of the imminence of my death, also reminded me of the love I had known. It sanctified me, dear Bill!"

She stood up, preparing to leave, ignoring his wet eyes.

"No, Bill, I didn't write to you *just* because I needed that money. I also wrote because my heart told me to do so. The money was my proof, my sign of faith, but what I wanted was *you* . . . And you came. You gave me that proof. I loved and was loved and will go to my grave with that knowledge . . . Do you understand, Bill?"

He covered his eyes and listened to his beating heart, then sat back in his chair and removed his hand, to be drawn to her green gaze.

"Yes, Jenny. And thank you."

"Thank *you*, Bill. Now let's go."

They walked leisurely from the Ritz and stopped on the pavement outside, dazzled by the afternoon's pearly light, in the noise of the traffic.

Bill kissed her on the cheek. She pressed her hand to *his* cheek. Then she smiled and walked off, disappearing into the crowd, while he, filled with grief, but oddly uplifted as well, walked in the opposite direction, towards a more secure future.

Chapter Forty-Four

൜

Bill paid his final visit to Anthony Barker.

Looking revitalised, Anthony told him that the treatment he had received since being transferred to this hospital had improved him to the degree where he would only have minimal discomfort in the future, would otherwise be able to lead a normal life, and would certainly soon be able to return home and look after himself.

"I have to thank you for this," he said. "When you first arrived to see me, I was a mess, but now I feel like a new man. I think you saved my life, Bill."

"I doubt it. But I'm glad I was able to help. Put it down to my pitiful way of saying thanks for the past."

"All Denholm and I did in the past was get an inexperienced American boy drunk and keep him away from his writing."

"You were the first real friends I ever had – and that's worth a lot."

Anthony shrugged and smiled, raising his hands in a grateful gesture. It was a pleasure to see that he could do that, and Bill felt better for it.

"So, how have things been progressing with your precious home-movie?"

"A home-movie, indeed," Bill said ruefully. Then he gave Anthony the whole story, including his sense of outrage at Denholm's awful trick. "To actually tell Jenny I'd been killed! I still can't believe it! And I'll *never* forgive him."

"You should."

"Why?"

"Because Denholm *did* love Jenny – and what he did because of that was merely a *crime passionnel*, which the French understand and forgive so willingly. I'm sure he's been haunted by it, as Jenny told you in the Ritz, and certainly he made amends for his sins by secretly looking after her and Carol all of those years. As for him and Maureen, vile though it seems to you, it was the natural reaction of a man who was outraged by what his best friend had stolen from him when it really mattered – namely, that young Jenny of the war years, the one true love of Denholm's life. I know it wasn't honourable, but I repeat: it was perfectly natural. And Denholm has endured a lot of pain since then and made amends in his own way."

"Damn it, Anthony, he tore Jenny and me apart."

"Which led you to Maureen."

"That's English bullshit, Anthony! Pragmatism gone mad. Denholm lied to Jenny, betrayed me, and did it all for himself, not giving a damn about who he hurt until it was too late."

"Few of us recognise our mistakes until it's too late."

"I'll admit that. So what?"

"When you won Jenny's heart, you broke his – and it's

never been mended. Perhaps you're even now. Denholm's kept in touch with you and looked secretly after Jenny and did it all while living with his guilt for most of his life. Only a real friend could have shouldered such a burden – and Denholm *is* a real friend."

Hardly knowing what to say, Bill shook his head in defeat. "Christ, you English!" he managed. Then more moved than he cared to admit, he stretched out his hand. "Shake it," he said. "I've got to go now. And I know you can grip it."

Anthony gripped his hand without pain and vigorously shook it, his smile healthily mocking.

"I don't remember *you* having romantic problems in that hotel," Bill said.

"That's because I never had them," Anthony replied.

"Why?"

"I was gay. *I* secretly fancied Denholm! Not to mention you, dear-heart!"

Bill stared at him, stunned, then saw his wide, delighted grin. "Oh, boy, you goddamned English! You're too much! I love you, Anthony. Goodbye."

"Goodbye, Bill. Have a good old age."

"I'll have *memories*!" Bill said.

He turned away and walked out, stopping once for a farewell wave, then left the hospital and stepped into the fading light, feeling younger and happier.

That evening, as he and Maureen were about to get into a cab outside the Savoy, Denholm stepped out in front of them. He ran his fingers nervously through his hair and seemed distinctly uneasy.

"I've come to bid you farewell," he said. "And to

apologise for everything I've done in the past and the present."

After feeling an instinctive rush of hatred for his old friend, Bill remembered what Anthony had told him.

As Anthony had said, they were even.

"Please accept my apology," Denholm said. "I don't offer it lightly."

"We accept," Maureen said, her voice sounding constricted.

"Sure." Bill didn't know where to look. "We accept. Unfortunately, we have to be going now."

"Of course," Denholm said. "Naturally."

He was already turning away when Bill stopped him in his tracks. "Did you know about Jenny's cancer?"

Denholm turned back to face him. "Yes, Bill, I knew."

"And of course you knew about Carol and my grandchild, since you clearly looked after them."

"Yes, Bill, that's right."

"God," Bill said, ashamed, "no wonder you hated me! I must have seemed like a lucky, spoilt man, being protected by everyone."

"So it goes, old sport."

Bill sighed with relief. It all balanced out in the end. He gave Denholm his hand and Denholm shook it and stepped back, grinning ruefully. "Still friends?"

"Yes, Denholm."

Denholm glanced at Maureen, smiled forlornly and shrugged, then returned his bloodshot gaze to Bill. "I have the last twenty percent of the money, so I can start the wheels turning on the movie, if you still want to do it. Naturally, it's still conditional on – "

"Changes."

"Right, Bill, you've got it. A few little changes."

Bill thought deeply about it. Deeply, but not for long. He noticed Maureen's steady, loving gaze and knew what he would say.

"No, thanks, Denholm. To hell with it – it's not worth it. If I can't make the movie my way, I'd prefer not to make it. But thanks for the offer."

"My pleasure," Denholm said.

He embraced Bill and hugged him. Then Maureen embraced him. They clung to one another, rendered speechless, then broke apart.

"I'll see you next time – "

"Sure," Bill said. "It's a date. Goodbye, Denholm."

"Au revoir."

Bill and Maureen took their taxi and were driven away – through the bright lights and noise of a great city, no longer at war.

Sitting beside Maureen in the back of the taxi, Bill felt that he had travelled into his past and returned as a new man – stronger, set free.

"Well," he declared, "if I've learnt nothing else, I've at least found out that nothing stays the same and no one is perfect."

"We all learn a little something in the end," Maureen responded in a commonsense manner.

"Yeah. Right. We unlearn to learn again. We unravel the knots of our misconceptions to start seeing the truth."

"Damn it, Bill, you're starting to sound profound and you know I can't stand that!"

His happiness made him grin. "Can I say something, sweetheart?" Maureen nodded. "I know our relationship can never be as it was, but I'm hoping it's been strengthened, or at least deepened, by what we've learned from each other. Do you think that's possible?"

She stared steadily at him, a lovely cat in contemplation, then she broke into a tender smile and kissed the back of his hand.

"I hope so," she said.

Bill was feeling both chastened and uplifted when they reached the airport and made their way to the departure lounge. There his heart leapt for joy when, just before he went through Passport Control, he was confronted with Carol and David, the former holding his grandson, Mark, in her arms.

"We came to say goodbye," Carol explained. "And to tell you we're going to get married and you'll both be invited."

"We'll be there," Bill said.

Increasingly emotional, he introduced them to a touched, amused Maureen, then also showed off his grandson. Maureen treated them gently.

"You saw my mother?" Carol asked.

"We had tea at the Ritz."

"It went well?"

"It went very well. We were both better for it."

"I've always loved you damned Yanks," Carol said.

They embraced one another with the baby caught between them, then Bill and Maureen walked through Passport Control, beginning their journey home.

Shortly after, as Bill strapped himself into his seat in the airplane, he decided that his marriage had survived its greatest test and would endure, and perhaps even prosper, where it mattered the most – in the domain of the living heart.

When he took hold of Maureen's hand, she pulled it into her lap, and as the plane took off and dark fields gave way to starry sky, he sank back, breathing easily, at peace with himself, reconciled to his own imperfections and the world's treacherous currents.

"God damm it!" he murmured.

As the Concorde climbed gracefully into the stratosphere, reducing London to a mosaic of darkness and light, Jenny stood on the observation deck of the airport far below, frail and alone, silently watching the aeroplane disappearing into the dark sky.

She was weeping, but also smiling, her body trembling with life – renewed, at last prepared for death, her heart beating defiantly.

"God bless you," she murmured.

The End